CREATING CAPTIVITY

ORIGINS
BOOK 1

DISCLAIMER

This is a work of fiction. Names, characters, businesses, places, events and incidents are either the products of the author's imagination or used in a fictitious manner. Any resemblance to actual persons, living or dead, or actual events is purely coincidental.

All rights reserved:
No part of this book may be reproduced or transmitted in any form or by any means, electronic or mechanical, including photocopying, recording, or by any information storage and retrieval system, without prior permission in writing from the author.

Translation:
Don't steal the stories I worked so hard on, and occasionally cried over. Don't get upset at the absolutely made-up story lines: this is a romance, so of course it isn't realistic, duh! Don't be petty and hate on it because it isn't your kink. We've all got different tastes and there's no shame in that.

Warning: Author is dyslexic as hell.

The editing and beta reading team: Martha Collins, S. Feehery, and Lauren Meghoo

Profession Editing: Amanda Brown Edits, LLC

Feel free to contact me with questions, requests, or comments: author@rk-munin.com

Thank you to all my readers!

CONTENT WARNING

-There is a severe imbalance of power between the humans and Talins. The humans are drugged into unconsciousness by the Talins at one point. All the humans except the children are forced to wear collars.

-This story *does not* contain non-con or dub-con. All intimate relationships are consensual. This book includes several scenes of sexually explicit material.

-There are also several instances of characters remembering or discussing past loved ones who've died. No death on page.

-One scene deals with the corpse of someone who died before the book starts.

-Several chapters contain scenes of fighting and violence.

CHAPTER 1

__Advanced Squad Delta 223—Mission Q73 Report (Excerpt)__
Because they had no natural defenses and little inclination toward weapons, we were met by a lone female as the rest huddled in one room, clinging to each other. The single female was bold and immediately made it clear that she was no threat. Unfortunately, it quickly became apparent that communicating would be an issue as our translators weren't programmed with their language. This was hardly surprising considering we'd never encountered the species before. However, we were startled to discover that none of them have Intercranial Translators, making communication impossible.

Since we'd been assigned to remain on this mining colony until the Minding and Processing Assessment team arrives, I decided to study this new species in detail and add my findings to my reports as well as the Talin UniBase. Although this species is small and weak, I feel they might become significant in some way.

Advanced Squad Leader Bazium glanced over to his second in command and sounded a questioning rumble from his chestbox. Their ship's command room wasn't large but he was far enough away that he couldn't see what Norrium was studying.

Norrium looked up from his console and answered his commander's unvoiced question. "Whatever is inhabiting the mining colony isn't Orlok. The heat signatures are all wrong. There's also no sign of activity in any of the mines and minimal life support systems are on in the whole compound."

"Could it have been shut down by the Orloks and now there's some kind of animal infestation?" Bazium asked.

"Unlikely, the data I'm seeing denotes organized movement in a way that suggests sentience or at least some type of training," Norrium explained. He tapped his console and an image appeared on the large display that took up most of a wall. A few more taps and a pattern lit up. "You can see that they are all gathered in this room here. I think it was meant to be a large storage room, but if I'm reading the scans correctly, they have turned it into a den. Right here is their food preparation area, and as you can see that isn't where the galley is located. But the fact that they created a galley area tells me they are a thinking species."

Bazium puzzled over what he was seeing. "But why would they do that?"

Norrium sounded a confused rumble from his chestbox. "I don't know. It makes no sense at all. Perhaps they're a primitive species, only capable of doing mundane tasks without an Orlok overseer to guide them."

Hesarium got their attention with a soft rattle of his back plates. "I agree with Norrium. I've read that the Orlok like to use non-space-faring species for their remote locations. What we're seeing might be a low-intellect species that an Orlok mining company thought they could exploit."

"That would make sense," Tarrian said as he came over to stand next to Bazium. As the interstellar technology and strategy expert of their group, he was the best at deciphering what they were seeing on the display. "I don't see a single projectile or energy weapon signature on any scan, so we know they aren't some kind of mercenary group. And look, there is the date this facility was last contacted. It was just after the war with the Orloks started. My guess is that these poor creatures were transported as workers. When the war began, they were abandoned."

Sapurian, their medic, sounded a rumble of disgust. "That was almost an entire solar ago. Those mining outposts are normally visited three or four times a solar. If the workers are from a low-intelligence species, they must be close to starving to death."

Bazium looked to Norrium. "Do we have the supplies to support them for the duration of our stay? It could be thirty or forty rotations until the Mining and Processing Assessment Team arrives. I don't want to watch these creatures starve to death."

Norrium sounded a thoughtful rumble. "Assuming they can consume our food, we should be able to keep them alive. We overstocked for this mission because we were originally assigned to support Takian's team then got diverted here."

He'd forgotten about all the extra gear stored on the ship. "And we have spare medical supplies."

"How do we classify them?" Tarrian asked with an inquisitive rumble. "Should they be enemy noncombatants, prisoners of war, or tangible products?"

Bazium sounded a negative rattle. "We'll leave off labeling them until we've interacted and we can assess their intelligence level and political inclination. If they aren't violent, we'll see about helping them contact their homeworld."

Tarrian made an affirmative rumble. "Yes, Advanced Leader Bazium. I should have thought of that myself."

"I doubt they're violent," Hesarium commented. "The Orloks would have wanted a species they could easily manipulate and control, not one prone to aggression or obstinance."

No one even noticed the improper protocol of Hesarium speaking his opinion without permission. Far from being a typical unit burdened with strict protocols, his squad enjoyed a more relaxed and fluid dynamic. Bazium realized early that they'd all survive battles and incursions better if most formalities were left behind.

In some battles, he took orders because another was in a better position to lead the unit. He was sure that was why they were currently one of the highest decorated of all the advanced squads in the Talin military.

"We'll see." Suddenly feeling far more tired than the situation warranted, Bazium straightened up and regarded a display on the wall next to Hesarium. "How long until we dock?"

"Less than a mark," Norrium answered.

"Contact me when we're in position. Until then I'll be in my cabin studying the mining facility schematics."

As he left, Sapurian tried to catch his attention with a slight movement of his hand, but Bazium ignored his medic and was out the door before the male could call out. He knew what Sapurian wanted to talk about, and he had no interest in discussing his next medical check-in.

All of them were supposed to pass a medical evaluation every thirty rotations, but he'd managed to put Sapurian off for almost double that. And it looked like he'd managed another reprieve because Sapurian wouldn't be able to leave his position in command until they'd successfully docked.

Reaching the safety of his cabin, he let the hatch slide closed behind him before leaning back against it. His subterfuge with Sapurian wouldn't last much longer, especially after they secured this base, but he had a plan.

This was going to be his last operation. He'd oversee this mission and make sure the inhabitants were properly subdued. Once all operation parameters were met and he knew his squad was safe, he'd find a way to suffer a tragic accident.

The compound was an isolate; meaning the planet didn't have a breathable atmosphere for most beings forcing the miners to "isolate" from the environment. All he needed to do was find a rarely used airlock, mess with the control, and then seal himself in when no one was around. After he let the air out, his squad would find his body and assume there was a malfunction. Simple. Easy.

It was the kind of death that wouldn't dishonor him, his family, or his clan. And he got to have a quick, merciful death. That was preferable to the slow progression of the disease he was hiding from Sapurian.

There was so little research or data available on Fading that he didn't even know if it would show up on any of Sapurian's tests or scans. It was considered an illness of the weak-willed, and those who died from it were pitied. It also cast a dark cloud on their family genetics. He'd save his parents and sibling that shame if he could. Really, the death he planned would be better for everyone.

Sitting at the desk in his cabin, he unclipped his Ident Cube and called up the compound schematics before setting the Ident on his desk. The hologram gave him a detailed view, and he reached out with a single clawed finger to set the image moving in a slow rotation. He noted several rooms that might work to facilitate his demise.

It was strange, but planning his death put him more at peace with the Fading than he'd been since he realized why his appetite and waned and his sense of smell had diminished. He might not have had a choice about the Fading, but he could still control how he left this world. Instead of laying down and "fading" away into a coma and then death, he'd decide his fate. Not many were able to pick the manner of their death, but he planned to be one of the few.

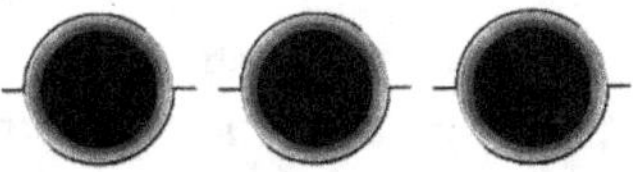

A mark later Bazium gathered with his crew, ready to enter the station. They didn't expect much resistance, but they were fully armored and armed anyway. He looked to his trusted compatriots, wishing one last time Lalorian was still with them. As much as he trusted Norrium, she'd been the best second he'd ever had. If she hadn't taken a deadly round in their last incursion, he was sure she would've made a fine Commander or even Over-Commander someday.

"No matter what happens," he told his warriors, pushing the missing Lalorian out of his mind, "This advanced leader could never ask for a better crew. Someday you will meet our ancestors and you can declare your worthiness with pride. They will not hesitate to welcome you into the Domicile of Souls." Then he made a loud war rattle that echoed in the chamber. "For the Talin Empire! For Talarian!"

They all sounded their war rattles, the combined noise drowning out their voices, but he knew what they were shouting.

"First our people. Then our clan. Next our families. For ourselves only last or not at all!"

And that was the succinct version of being Talin.

Kinship with his squad filled him while he quieted his rattle and triggered his armor. As the armor powered up, his warriors did the same. With a nod to Tarrian, the hatch slid open and they seamlessly maneuvered into the compound.

They'd already sent the Remotes through the compound, but the machines hadn't found anything to trigger warnings or aggression. That didn't mean there wasn't danger. Remotes could be fooled with the proper equipment. Because of this, it was always up to the armed Talins to truly secure an area.

Tarrian and Hesarium went first, their heavier armor creating an ion shield that would stop most energy weapons from reaching them. Although no conventional weapons of any kind had been detected, they all knew many mundane items could be turned into effective weapons, so they weren't taking any chances.

Even moving with care, it didn't take them long to reach the large main hallway connecting the three areas of the compound. What they saw there startled all of them into stillness.

A lone figure stood facing them with arms out and eyes focused on the floor. The individual was slight and appeared frail. If Bazium stood side by side with the stranger, he doubted the small figure's head would be as high as his chest armor. Long fur was growing out of the figure's head, reaching down to the middle of their body. No, he corrected himself, not fur but a mane, black and shiny. The figure was so bundled in clothes he couldn't see much exposed flesh, but what he saw showed no signs of fur.

Two things were abundantly clear right away. This little thing was trying to appear non-threatening, and it didn't belong to any species Bazium had seen or heard of.

He didn't release his warriors, so they remained in combat-ready positions, but he did cue his communicator. "Do any of you recognize this species?"

That question was met with a chorus of *no's*.

"I'm going to approach; all of you remain here," he ordered them.

"Advanced Leader, I don't think that's wise," Norrium spoke up.

"Your concern has been noted and dismissed," Bazium declared for benefit of the recorders embedded in each warrior's armor. If he ended up dead because of the creature, the recording meant none of his squad would be blamed.

As he moved closer, he realized his earlier assessment of the figure being small held true. They weren't simply small. They were tiny. He was reminded of a Talin youth on the verge of their first growth-shift into young adulthood.

Once he came to a stop only an arm's length away, the creature looked up. He was struck dumb for a moment by their eyes. He wasn't even sure he knew a name for the color. Brass, perhaps? But that didn't do justice to how striking they were.

When he saw a tremor shake the little thing's entire body, he found his voice. He needed to do his initial threat assessment, and then he could figure out how to put this creature at ease. He had the most overwhelming urge to comfort the petite thing. It must have taken a lot of courage to meet them in the hall instead of remaining hidden with the others. This individual was probably their leader.

"State your species, name, and duties," he demanded.

The long, black mane shifted around their shoulders as they tilted their head and regarded him for a moment. That mane looked so soft and luxurious he had to fight the urge to reach out and touch the shiny black mass. The color of their eyes reminded Bazium of the ornamental brass hanging in several room in his families home on Talarian. Were this creatures eyes luminous or was that trick of the light? Those bright eyes set in a delicate face made Bazium want to sound a soothing rumble.

Forcing himself to concentrate on the task at hand, he repeated his demand. "State your species, name, and duties."

When the silence continued Bazium considered that this species might not have a spoken language. Before he could try the silent tapping language of the Norka, the little figure finally spoke.

"Did any of you get that?" he asked his crew. "Or is my Innercranial Translator not working?"

"Your INT isn't faulty," Norrium confirmed. "That wasn't a registered language."

By the way the creature continued to regard him, he got the impression this was a mutual problem. He wasn't surprised there was going to be a language barrier. He'd hoped the Orloks had installed INTs in their workers. But Orloks were notorious for being cheap, and they must have considered it a waste of money to install the device on all the imported staff. To save a tiny bit of wealth, they must have picked only a few key individuals to receive the device. The ones with INTs were either dead or hiding while this one stood fearful but brave before them.

"Sapurian, we don't carry INTs. Correct?"

The reply came without hesitation, "No, sir. It never occurred to me to stock them. And I don't even have the equipment to do uploads and downloads." The medic sounded a rumble of incredulity. "Who doesn't have an INT?"

"This species apparently. Relax to ready," he ordered. "Tarrian, interface with the compound's system. See if they have a language on file at least. Also, find out what this species is and where they're from."

"Right away, Advanced Leader," Tarrian said and shut down his armor. Then he pulled his Ident Cube from under his chest piece and turned to the nearest display.

"They're so small," Hesarium commented.

Although Bazium hadn't given him permission, he didn't reprimand Hesarium as the squad's weapons specialist stepped up to stand next to Bazium. They all deactivated their armor now, and the little thing was looking up at their exposed heads, its mane swishing back and forth with the movement as their gaze went from face to face.

Reaching out, Hesarium tried to touch a hunk of mane. The diminutive creature flinched back and Hesarium jerked his hand away. He sounded a distressed rumble. "I didn't mean to be scary."

Acting on instinct, Bazium dropped to his knees and set his large weapon on the floor so his hands were empty. Thin arms wrapped around a slight torso as the figure watched him with wide eyes.

"Easy," Bazium said in a gentle voice. The creature might not understand the words, but perhaps the soft tone would help. "I'm not going to hurt you. We're going to find out where you come from and get you back there. I promise. You're safe now."

Mirroring his movements, Hesarium dropped to his knees as well. Both of them sounded a soothing rumble. The small creature seemed comforted by the sound and even took a step forward. Bazium sat back on his heels and kept up the soothing rumble. Soon the creature was standing with their shoes almost touching his knees.

"That's it," he urged. "You're so brave. I'm very proud."

The creature said something he was sure was a question.

"I'm sorry," he said. "We can't understand you any more than you can understand us. But I can see you have some intelligence. You might be helpless, but you have us now. You don't have to worry any longer."

"Look at the hands," Norrium said as he dropped to his knees on the other side of Bazium. "Small and clawless. I see soft skin with no quills or natural armor plating. They're defenseless."

"Even a tiny hand can operate a weapon," Hesarium pointed out dryly.

"I know, but if the species isn't evolutionarily programmed to fight, it would be hard for them to learn," Norrium countered.

"Maybe they have poison or venom," Sapurian suggested from behind Bazium.

"No poison or venom," Tarrian announced, making all of them turn their heads to look at him. His focus was on the display. "They're called humans and they come from a system with only one livable planet, Earth."

Before Bazium could ask any questions, Tarrian sounded a soft, sad rumble as he read. "Their planet is dead." He turned to face Bazium. "These humans might be the last of their kind."

CHAPTER 2

Advanced Squad Delta 223—Mission Q73 Report (Excerpt)
Outside of detailed information on human physiology, there was little in the compound's computer about this species except that their planet of origin recently became inhospitable to life. We see no evidence that they were a spacefaring species of note before the collapse of their homeworld. We've found no records of them colonizing any other planet or having any space stations. This means they're either of low intelligence or a newly developed species. As we've studied them, we've realized they have an intricate social order and interactions, which would disprove the theory of being newly developed.

Ari was astounded she wasn't dead yet. Of course the interaction with the invaders had only started, so there was plenty of time for them to rip her apart with those claws or blast her into itty-bitty bits with those weapons. She was going to take the win.

After Tomas had died of Leukemia earlier in the year, she'd been elected to the leadership position. Even as she mourned her good friend's passing, she'd been forced to focus on keeping everyone alive.

And now she was by herself, meeting some very threatening-looking individuals and hoping she wasn't the next one to be put in the past tense.

Looking at the new arrivals, she barely kept from shaking her head. Why did all the other species in the universe need to be bigger than humans? These guys were huge. Even kneeling in front of her, they looked anything but harmless. They were wearing armor on their upper bodies and all of them were heavily armed.

The matching armor and weapons clearly told her these guys were soldiers instead of mercenaries or looters hoping to make some quick money plundering the mining facility. That could be helpful because their superiors might be open to negotiations.

After they shut off the armor and the opaque ion shields disappeared, she was able to clearly see their bodies. Under the armor on their shoulders and upper torso that powered the ion shield, she could see they didn't wear shirts, gloves, or shoes. The only clothes they wore were pants that ended in a cuff under the knee.

They seemed to be covered in a natural armor plating without any visible body hair. They had a humanoid shape like many space faring species, two arms, two legs, and a head. She saw earholes with no ear shell and only the hint of a nose with slits for nostrils. Thin lips and no facial movement put them squarely in the hard-to-read category. Between their size, the long quill-like spines on their forearms, and the claws on their hands, Ari was beyond intimidated.

None of them had shown any teeth yet, so she was keeping hers firmly hidden. Although her interactions with other species wasn't broad, she had learned quickly that smiling was often taken as an aggressive act. It seemed humans were the only species who showed teeth to indicate friendliness or humor.

When one of them had reached for her hair, she'd instinctively flinched away. To her astonishment, none of them responded with aggression. When one of them had dropped to their knees, she realized that like her, they were trying to be nonthreatening.

This realization made her bold enough to step closer to the one she thought might be the leader. They tried to talk to her, but of course she didn't have an INT. Tomas had been the only one the Orloks had approved for the translation tech, so she had to muddle through as best she could.

"There are sixty-eight of us. Sixty-six adults, one child, and one baby," she said in Spanish first, even though she knew it was probably useless. When there was no answer she tried English. "None of us are armed or violent. We were hired to mine and that's what we want to do, mine. We want to work this compound if you'd only bring in more supplies. We need food. And we desperately need parts to fix the atmo generator."

Their only response was to keep up the purring they'd started earlier and talk quietly among themselves. The lack of understanding wasn't a surprise. It wasn't as if Earth languages were common enough in the universe to be part of an INTs core language program. She might as well go back to the combination of Mexican Spanish, Porto Rican Spanish, and American English that made up the mother tongue of New Rico.

The one interfacing with the display turned to say something, and the rest of them went silent for a moment. Then they all started up that purring again even louder, and the one at the display moved to stand behind the ones that were kneeling in front of her.

The one she believed was the leader slowly reached out a clawed hand. Adrenaline flooded her system and her breath caught, but she remained still as one of her hands was clutched gently in his massive claws. All five of them leaned in as her hand was turned over and examined. They murmured among themselves as each one of her fingers was individually scrutinized. They seemed especially interested in her pinky.

The actions were so slow and deliberate that her heartbeat slowed and her breathing evened out. It was obvious they had no harmful intentions yet. But communication was going to become an issue quickly, particularly if she couldn't make them understand what needed to be fixed right away.

It occurred to her the failing systems would be a good place to start. Show them around and let them see what was broken or barely working. Then she would lead them to everyone else and hope they responded as gently to her group as they had to her.

"Ari, are you still alive?" a harsh but familiar voice whispering in her ear made her jump. All five of the invaders reacted to her movement by going perfectly still.

She squeezed the clawed hand of the soldier holding hers and then relaxed her hand back in his grip. "You didn't scare me," she said to him in a soft voice. "My friend was talking in my ear."

Of course they didn't respond directly to her words. Instead, they said a few words to each other and resumed examining her, rubbing fingers on her clothing and touching her hair.

"I'm alive," she answered. When the one in the middle looked up at her, their eyes met and she pretended to be speaking to the soldier instead of one of her people. Her long hair was effectively hiding a small transmitter in her ear. It was tech they'd brought from Old Earth and compared with what other species had it was old, but it worked–mostly.

"What are they like?"

"There are five of them, all look military. You know, big guys with armor and weapons. So far they're being gentle and curious." She gave Mari a description of them, including the intimidating quills on their forearms and clawed hands. It was entertaining to hear all of Mari's reactions. Finally she let them know the bad news. "If they have INTs, they aren't programmed with any Earth languages. I tried all the ones I know and got nothing."

"What do you think they'll do to us?" She knew Mari was asking the same question all of them had.

"No idea yet, but I'm going to try and convince them to let us stay and work here for supplies," Ari replied. "*Cállate*, I need to concentrate. I'll talk out loud to tell you where we are. Make sure you guys are ready to meet them when I lead them to the dorm. Everyone needs to stay calm, no screaming. Got it?"

"We know. We know," Mari said with a huff. *"We gave Andres the last of the mild sedatives so he'll be either asleep or subdued. Lucia just finished nursing so she should be asleep for a while. That's the best we can do to keep the two kids quiet."*

"It should be enough," Ari assured her.

Mari sighed into her ear. *"I hope you're right. Be careful, Ari. We're counting on you to get us out of this alive."*

No pressure though, she thought wryly.

By now the three kneeling soldiers had finished exploring her upper body. They'd all touched the skin of her arm, ran their claws through her hair, and tugged at her clothing. The intruders commentary to each other never ceased.

Their interest and gentle actions made her daring enough to clasp the hands of the one in the middle and tug him to his feet.

"I think you must be the guy in charge," she said. "I'm going to call you Boss for now." She saw no change in facial expression, but the purring was interrupted briefly with another sound. They absolutely had a spoken language—that was obvious—but they must also utilize these sounds to convey thoughts or emotions.

She really hoped this sound was one of interest.

"I'd like to show you a few things if you'd come with me," she offered. Once standing, Boss towered over her but didn't take a step until she started leading him down the main hall. The rest were quick to stand and follow right behind them. They were all silent except for the purring so she kept up a running commentary. It helped her stay calm and kept her people informed on their movements.

"I'm going to show you our collection bay," she explained, deciding she'd start with what was valuable and then progress to what was broken. "We kept working until we filled it, and then we had to stop mining. It's all raw ore since we can't refine anything here. I assure you it's all high quality with very little slag."

To her disappointment they didn't react to the entirely too-full collections bay. No change in purring or excited body language. But then again, they were soldiers who might not understand the huge amount of wealth they were seeing.

But she was very sad they didn't have any strong reaction to the empty galley. The lack of food didn't seem to worry them so they must be well-stocked on their ship. She could only hope they could be persuaded to share.

The environmental systems room caused a strong response. They'd only been in the room a few seconds when one of them stopped purring and made a sound like many projectile rounds being fired very rapidly.

She'd been determined to remain calm, but that noise startled her so badly she cried out and jerked her hand away from Boss. No sooner had she yanked her hand away than she found herself picked up and cradled against a broad, powerful chest. Her eyes slammed shut and she went completely stiff and still, waiting for something bad.

But nothing happened.

Boss's chest started vibrating as the purr drowned out the low tones of the others. His body was as solid as it looked. She could feel his smooth but hard natural armor plating against the skin of her arm. Strangely, for all his strength he didn't crush her. And why was she smelling hazelnuts? It was such a familiar scent it triggered something soothing inside of her.

She risked opening her eyes to find her vision filled with the a dull-red colored natural armor plates taking up where a human pec would be. Looking up, she found it was Boss holding her. He said something in a tone that suggested he was trying to be comforting.

Between his voice, the purring, and the scent, she felt safe. She relaxed into his arms and looked at the other soldiers. The moment she looked away from Boss, they all started talking rapidly to each other.

"I know you said to be quiet, but are you still alive?" Mari whispered, her voice full of fear.

"*No hay bronca.* I was startled by a noise one of them made," she murmured to Mari. "But nothing happed, it was only a noise. I'm pretty sure I know which one is in charge so I'm calling him Boss. Remember those Ident Cubes all the Orloks had that were so new that some of them didn't know how to use them? Well one of these guys used an Ident Cube to interface with the compound's computer, so I'm going to call him Tech. One of them sticks close to Boss, so he must be second in command or something. I'll name him Riker."

A snort of laughter came through her comm and then Mari was telling everyone what she'd said. She heard laughter and almost chuckled as well.

"¿Riker, neta? Fine, nerd," Mari teased. *"But that's the only Star Trek reference you're allowed for today. Earlier you said there's five of them right? Give us the names you have for the rest of them."*

"Right," Ari agreed, fighting a smile. "One of them is carrying more weapons than the others so I'll name him Army. The last one has an old looking scar on his torso and is missing a few quills-like things on his lower arm, so I'm going to name him Lucky."

"Army? Lucky? Those sound like they're right out of a bad movie script. You suck at names," Mari informed her in a dry voice after telling everyone else what she'd said.

"Whatever," Ari said. "You try thinking about names while you're being held by a guy with spikes on his arms and claws."

"Held?" Mari called out. Her startled exclamation was loud enough in Ari's ear to make her wince.

"Yeah, he's holding me, like I'm a giant baby," Ari told her. When Boss looked down at her, she petted his shoulder trying to convey that she wasn't upset. "And he's doing this purring thing. He smells like hazelnut. It might be weird, but he smells really good."

Boss kept up the purring even as he started conversing with the others again.

She stopped talking for a moment to watch the soldiers interact. Mari was quick to prompt her. *"Ari? You still there?"*

Suddenly, she was tired. Exhausted. They'd all been living on half rations for a long time, and then with the atmo generator issues, she, Mari, and several others had been forced to babysit the system so they didn't all die of hypoxia. Life had been stressful back when they'd been getting regular supplies. Then the haulers had stopped coming, and everything had been slowly gone to hell.

After Tomas had passed, it had been her job to keep everyone organized and hopeful. Except she'd started losing hope too. Now she was faced with a new species who might have bought or stole the compound in an act of war or piracy. Worst yet, they had no common language.

Giving in to fatigue, she let her head rest against a hard chest. She noticed a strip of bare flesh at the base of Boss's neck where the natural armored plates met. Interesting that Boss was letting her rest her head so close to a vulnerable area. Either he didn't see her as a threat or thought he could trust her. It was probably the former because what could she possibly do?

Well, it looked like she didn't have to guide him to the next stop. He was heading there on his own. Drained, she closed her eyes. She was going to rest for a moment, and then she would introduce these soldiers to everyone else when they got to the communal room.

"I'm still here," she murmured to Mari as Boss carried her out the door followed closely by the others. "Get ready. We're heading your way."

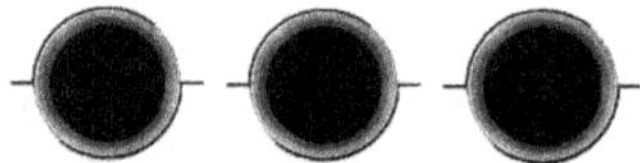

"We don't have a compatible system on our ship," Tarrian explained in a voice barely above a whisper. After becoming upset at the state of the compound's environmental systems, he'd accidentally scared the little creature by rattling in outrage. Now he was wary of even talking in a normal voice. "But we have the parts to fix this one for the short term. When the Mining and Processing Assessment Team get here, they'll be able to replace it. Their ships carry everything."

"I think you can speak in a normal tone," Bazium assured him. "Don't rattle. That seems to scare them."

"Yes, sir," Tarrian said in a normal tone.

He hadn't reprimanded his subordinate for frightening the delicate creature. He heard Tarrian's rumble of surprise and then embarrassment the moment the tiny thing had cried out and jumped away. But then something wholly wonderful happened. The creature remained still, and he picked the frighted being up. The weight was negligible and the softness overwhelming.

He had the strongest urge to bury his nose in that long, dark mane and pull in a deep breath.

No, that wasn't quite it. He had the compulsion to run his scent gland over the mane and scent mark the creature he held. It was an action so forbidden he could be stripped of his rank and cast out from both his family and clan.

The impulse was so strong he shuddered before gaining control of himself. The scent glands in his cheeks started aching, and he worked hard on ignoring them. He had a salve on the ship that would keep them from producing bonding oil. Long ago Talins scent-bond to partners by rubbing their oil on each other. With scent-bonding outlawed, even having noticeably producing scent glands was disgraceful. He was already suffering from Fading, so the last thing he wanted was to be discovered producing bonding oil. He longed for an honorable death not utter humiliation.

Bazium looked at the display Tarrian had been interfacing with. "When you say we can keep the system going short term, how long is that?"

"The atmo system shouldn't be an issue, but the rest of the systems are probably going to break down before the Mining and Processing Assessment Team arrive," Tarrian explained. "I don't have the parts or all the specialty skills to keep them going."

The loss of the mining compound wouldn't impact them because their ship could provide them with water, atmo, and warmth. But it would make the compound unlivable even for Talins. He needed to know how many more humans were living here and then decide how to save them before they all expired

"I'm going to call this one Brave for now," Bazium murmured as he examined the human in his arms.

"Is the little thing asleep?" Norrium asked, peering down at the creature in Bazium's arms. His question brought everyone's attention to the bundle he was holding. Head resting on his chest, eyes closed, and even breathing all indicated Brave was resting. Perhaps even content in his arms. He was awed by the little creature's trust.

"I believe you're correct, Norrium," Bazium answered. "The small being has succumbed to slumber."

Hesarium sounded a sad rumble. "If the rest of this place is in as bad a shape as what we've seen so far, all of them are no doubt underfed, overwhelmed, and fatigued. If they're low-intelligence they're probably used to a strong leadership telling them exactly what to do at all times. Being left to their own devices for so long probably stressed them to the point of exhaustion."

"Very true," Sapurian commented. "I'd suggest scanning them, but we don't have any data on them to read results with."

Tarrian made a soft rattle of excitement. "The compound's computer has detailed anatomy information we could utilize."

"With your permission, Advanced Leader, I'd like to interface with compound's system to download the information. I'll make sure to do a closed system test before uploading to the Med Bay."

"Granted," Bazium said without hesitation. If the rest of these humans were as tiny, adorable, and peaceful as this one, he didn't want a single one of them to suffer if he or his squad could help it.

Sapurian responded to Bazium's permission with a happy rumble as he pulled out his Ident Cube. Sapurian liked any excuse to use the tech that had just been adopted empire wide by the Apogee Assembly.

"I'll need to interact with the systems in Med Bay," Sapurian warned.

"When you're done rendezvous where we noted the remaining humans gathered when we scanned earlier. Our little one here hasn't taken us there yet, probably trying to protect the others. But we need to start assessing and treating immediately."

"Yes, sir," Sapurian said and hurried away.

Bazium looked at the remaining squad. "We're going to move slowly and keep up a soothing rumble. Even if they scream or run, we won't chase or react. We will do the same with them as we did with this one. Unless they attack, then attempt to subdue with minimal damage."

"We should be ready to kneel again," Norrium commented. "I think it made us appear less threatening."

"Good suggestion," Bazium responded. "If their fear turns to panic, we'll kneel and see if that alleviates the issue. If it looks like they'll hurt themselves from panicking, we'll exit the room with this one and administer a sedative to the rest. It's not ideal, but better than risking their lives from panic or self-damage."

The warriors sounded rumbles of agreement and they all eased into the room where the rest of the creatures gathered.

CHAPTER 3

Advanced Squad Delta 223—Mission Q73 Report (Excerpt)
When we first began interacting with this species, we didn't realize how truly delicate they were. Not only are their bodies small and frail, but we discovered they can only survive in a narrow band of temperatures and require sustenance several times within a single rotation. It's easy to damage them: too little food, too little water, insufficient sleep, or ambient temperatures outside an exact range.

We hypothesize this might be the reason they were all sharing a large communal nest with massive amounts of bedding. Due to their inability to thermoregulate, they must huddle together for warmth to guard against inadequacies in the station's biosystem monitors. I theorize they also require comfort from each other almost constantly to decrease emotional distress.

Ari rested as Boss carried her through the compound. Between the soldiers talking and the purring, they'd created a background noise she'd grown accustomed to. When everything went suddenly silent, she opened her eyes to find they'd already entered the communal sleeping area.

Had she fallen asleep, or did these soldiers walk extra fast?

Worried everything was about to go wrong quickly, she tried to sit up. Strong arms tightened and held her fast against a solid chest. For a brief second, she thought about fighting. That was when Boss started purring again. As if reading her mind, he slowly lowered her to the ground. All her fellow humans were watching with expressions ranging from surprise to terror.

"Uh, don't panic guys," Ari started. "They've been gentle with me so far. I don't think they're going to shoot us or anything."

No one spoke, but all eyes focused behind her. Before she could glance over her shoulder, a massive clawed hand was placed on her back and gently nudged her forward. She almost laughed as she took a few steps.

Santos was the closest to her and the first to speak. "Do they understand us?" he asked without taking his eyes off the soldiers. Although he was the tallest among them at six foot three, he was still a foot shorter than these warriors.

She shook her head. "I'm afraid not. But I showed them around and I think they understand what we do here and that things aren't looking good."

"You hide your teeth, right?" Mari asked, her light brown eyes bouncing back and forth between Ari and the soldiers standing behind her. Her specialty had originally been setting up comm relays, and her talent had transitioned well to maintaining the mining equipment. They probably would have been dead months ago if not for her.

"I did," she assured Mari. "And I didn't point or raise my voice."

"What happens now?" Daniella asked. Her tone was calm but her expression was worried. Behind her, Christos placed a comforting hand on her shoulder.

Ari shrugged and glanced at Mari. "I thought we should give them the compound base-coder so they could take control of everything. You know, kind of like offering them the keys to the place and hoping they fix it up."

Aubrey gasped and pushed past Mari and Santos. "But with the base-coder they could shut down the environmental room!" Her voice was pitched high and her eyes were already swimming with tears.

Ari pulled in a deep breath, fighting for patience. It wasn't Aubrey's fault that she was easily panicked. Back on Old Earth she'd managed to not only finish a Masters in Astrogeology but then went on to get a PhD in mining and ore processing on planets with little to no atmosphere. She was by far the most educated and experienced in their community and had been organizing and overseeing the mining before they'd been forced to stop.

Aubrey's anxiety meds had run out about a month ago. She'd been coping amazingly well, but an unmedicated Aubrey was an emotionally volatile creature. One of the things she'd started doing to deal with her anxiety was elaborately braiding her long, honey-comb colored hair. Today her hair was in a dozen braids coiled around her head. Personally, Ari thought she looked like she was wearing a basket on her head, but at least it had kept her from having a meltdown while Ari was off doing a meet-and-greet with five spikey newcomers.

"I wouldn't worry about them shutting the life support systems down. Almost everything in the environmental room keeps trying to die and take us with it," Ari pointed out gently.

They all watched as Aubrey fought to pull herself together. "Yes, you're right. We're on the verge of catastrophe already." Only a few tears fell from her dark brown eyes and she was quick to wipe them away. She looked up and past Ari only to flinch.

Ari swung her gaze around to see that all the soldiers were closer now. Boss was standing right behind her and Tech moved to stand next to Aubrey.

¡Ah caray! Considering their size, Ari assumed they'd make more noise when they moved!

Santos was quick to push Mari behind him and was reaching for Aubrey but Tech put himself between them.

"Ari!" Aubrey cried out, her eyes focused on the big, armored soldier in front of her.

"Stay calm, Aubrey," Mari called out as the soldiers rapidly talked to each other in low tones. "Don't make any sudden moves."

"I'm right here," Ari said. "I—"

Before she could reassure her friend further, Boss and Tech sank to their knees and then sat back on their heels. This put their heads lower than Ari and Aubrey.

Aubrey made a surprised sound and Ari relaxed a little. Maybe Aubrey would be able to hold herself together now that they weren't looming over the two women.

They were still talking to each other, but they'd added loud purring to the mix. Both were staring at Aubrey intently.

"The one closer to me is in charge," Ari told Aubrey. "I call him Boss. The one near you is Tech."

Aubrey turned her head to say something to Ari when Tech placed a hand on either side of her head. She gave a little *meep* of fear and went rigid. Tears started pouring down her face and Ari could see her body quaking with terror.

The soldier leaned in close, and Ari belatedly realized they were curious about Aubrey's tears. Most species didn't produce moisture from their eyes like humans did, and none of them did it as an emotional response.

That level of interest had to be a good thing. Right?

"I think they're curious about the crying," Ari whispered as she groped blindly for Aubrey's hand. When their fingers touched, Aubrey grabbed her hand in a grip so hard Ari thought she might lose feeling.

"Ari," Aubrey whimpered.

"Shhh," Ari soothed. "Let them look and then I'll get them the base-coder and they'll probably leave us alone."

As if the universe loved to prove her wrong, Tech finally let go of Aubrey's head only to pick her up the same way Boss had picked Ari up earlier. Aubrey curled up in a ball and started sobbing.

"I'm going to die," she moaned. "They're going to eat me. It's going to be slow and painful, and my life will have been for nothing."

Tech tried to turn and carry Aubrey off, but Ari was still holding her hand so she dug in her heels. Tech noticed the linked hands and said something to Boss. Ari understood Boss's intent the moment he reached for her and Aubrey's hands.

"No!" she yelled out sharply.

When all of the soldiers went still and silent, staring at her, she realized that might have been a miscalculation. Her panicked shout was loud enough to have bounced off the walls of the large room.

Crap, did she just get both of them killed?

Then the purring started up again and Boss scooped her back up without making her let go of Aubrey. The movement made the comm fall out of her ear, but no one noticed. As they marched out of the room Boss and Tech were careful to walk side by side so Ari and Aubrey could keep holding hands.

"This wasn't what I meant to happen," she grumbled under her breath. She could hear Aubrey sobbing. Between heavy sobs, she was listing off the elements that made up different compounds. Along with the braiding it was her second favorite self-calming technique.

Right now, Ari could use a little calm herself.

"Labradorite is made up of calcium, sodium, aluminum, silicon, and oxygen," Ari said, reciting the components of her favorite rock. What do you know, she was feeling a little better. Aubrey was on to something. "This feldspar mineral is calcium-enriched. It has—"

Her use of Aubrey's calming technique stopped working when she realized they were being carried through the dock's airlock and onto a ship. As she listened to the heavy ship's hatch close behind them, her mind went blank.

What now?

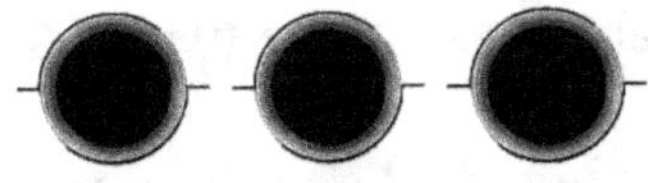

"The other human appeared concerned but not overly worried," Sapurian said, once again trying to ease Tarrian's fears that the little human in his arms was dying. Bazium had started calling that human Hurt in his head. Now they had Brave and Hurt.

Sapurian had met them at the airlock and was now hurrying with them through the ship to the Med Bay.

"She's leaking liquid from her eyes," Tarrian reminded him grimly. "What if it's essential fluid? Malicoves have clear blood. What if these humans are the same? Look, even more is leaking out. It's running down my chest plates."

Although he was trying hard to remain coolly detached like Sapurian, Bazium had to admit the sounds the human was making were alarming.

"No wonder the species is going extinct," Hesarium muttered as he followed close behind. "Bleeding out through your eyes because you're scared is a poor defense mechanism."

Hesarium's words might seem callous, but he'd stuck close and kept up a loud, soothing rumble along with Bazium and Tarrian. Norrium had sprinted ahead to get the Med Bay up and running for Sapurian.

"I'm sure I'll be able to fix whatever is wrong," Sapurian commented as they entered the ship's small medical bay. He went straight to one of the displays, and started bringing up menus. "Are they still gripping each other?"

"Yes," he and Tarrian replied in unison.

"See if you can set them both down on the same table," he ordered. "They're small, so they should both fit."

When they set the two humans on the table, the one making all the noise and leaking fluid flung herself into the arms of the other one. More than ever, Bazium was sure Brave was the leader of the humans.

Sapurian started up several of the diagnostic tools and turned to face the humans. Then he made a soft, thoughtful rumble. "I'm not sure I'll be able to scan the two of them while they're so close."

Tarrian started to sound a rattle of refusal but stopped himself the moment the wailing human jumped and looked over with wide eyes. "We might hurt them trying to separate the two," he argued.

"This could be a case of having to hurt a little to help a lot," Sapurian said as he stepped closer to the exam table. Both humans looked up at him. Bazium watched as Brave's eyes fixed on the scanner wand Sapurian was holding while Hurt's body shook. "They could keep holding hands and then I'd be able to…"

His words trailed off as Brave started moving. Speaking in their light, musical language that reminded Bazium of a nolik bird on Talarian, Brave worked loose of Hurt's hold. Whatever Brave said was working because Hurt stopped clutching so tightly. They ended up on either end of the exam table, separated but facing each other and holding hands.

Sapurian sounded a rumble of surprise and gestured at Brave. "Do you think this one understood me?"

Bazium felt a strange pride blossom in his chest. "Not your words, but your intentions, yes."

"Enough," Tarrian growled. "Scan the human and fix what's wrong!"

That spurred Sapurian into action. He was quick to run the scanner over the human, trying hard to touch only with the wand and keep his body as far away as possible. The display chimed, and he dropped the scanner onto the table and started reading the results.

Bazium itched to hold Bave against his chest again. He didn't need to, though, as she looked awake and steady, but the urge was strong. Something was so soothing about cradling her in his arms. He resisted the impulse. He was sure picking up his human would upset the delicate hold Tarrian's human had on remaining still for Sapurian.

His human. Tarrian's human. When did he start thinking of these humans as belonging to them?

"It's an autonomic emotional response to sadness, fear, or anxiety," Sapurian explained as he turned to face them with a rumble of amusement. "They have ducts in their eyes that shed a solution to clean debris from the cornea and keep the eye moist. They don't have the over-lens like we do. But that same duct will become overactive during times of high emotion. It's called crying."

"Crying?" Tarrian asked with a befuddled rumble. "She's leaking because she's sad?"

"Or fearful, or anxious, or any number of emotions. Apparently, some of them will even cry when they're very happy." Sapurian pointed to Brave. "That's why this one didn't seem too worried. It must be a common occurrence."

"We made her cry," Tarrian murmured, gazing at the sniffling human. "We scared the humans, and this one was so frightened she cried."

Sapurian sounded a rumble of agreement. "I'll study them more, but by all accounts, they're very delicate creatures." He pointed to the bulky outfits both humans wore. "They can't handle temperature change very well, so they have to add clothing. All those layers aren't about culture or modesty. It's survival for them. Oh, and these two are females. They have binary reproduction, just like us. They don't need three different sexes for reproduction like the Delorta or five like the Marpers. There's nothing in here about gender, so it's probably a fluid construct, like most species."

A strange feeling spread through Bazium when Sapurian told him Brave was female. He didn't want to dwell on it too much, but before he shoved it out of his mind, he acknowledged the feeling was joy.

Why he felt joy that Brave was a female didn't bear thinking about while surrounded by his crew.

"Can they hurt themselves from emotional distress?" Tarrian asked.

Sapurian sounded a startled rattle. "I don't know. I never thought—let me check." He turned back to consult the display thick with diagnostic data and information from the compound's computers.

"We should keep these two on the ship to better monitor them," Bazium thought out loud as Sapurian studied the information.

"I agree," Tarrian answered quickly. "It looked like the humans all had pallets on the floor with a blanket and pillow. The sight made me think of a nest. We should put together something like that and we can set the room temperature to be optimal for them."

Bazium wanted to take Brave to his quarters and make her a nest of her own. If she became worried or anxious, like Hurt, she could cling to him. He would comfort her and make the tears stop.

He could be her everything.

CHAPTER 4

Advanced Squad Delta 223—Mission Q73 Report (Excerpt)
Considering how neglected they were by the Orloks, I was
impressed at the level of information on the species in the
compound's computers. I became suspicious that Miox Minerals
meant to breed these humans and create a self-replacing,
subservient population. Several notable things were missing from
all the resupply rosters I found, and one of them was reproduction
suppressants. I can only assume the stressful environment and
later the lack of sustenance, meant the humans were unable to
reproduce at their normal, natural rate as reported in the
physiology information.

Ari had realized the moment they got to the ship's Med Bay why the two of them had been brought on board. The soldiers must have thought Aubrey was injured or ill. When she saw one of them holding a scanning wand, she'd known she was correct.

It filled Ari with hope that this species cared enough to help Aubrey. They could have easily separated the two women, but they took Ari along because Aubrey didn't want to let go of her hand.

Only a little while after Lucky had scanned Aubrey, they'd all relaxed a little. That must have been the moment when they realized Aubrey wasn't dying.

Lucky scanned both of them and then scanned Aubrey one more time. He made a rumbly sound in his chest that was higher pitched and faster than before as he read the data. After a while he selected a handful of medications from a cabinet. They all kept up a conversation and pointed to her, Aubrey, or the display behind Lucky. It felt strange to be the center of a conversation but not able to be part of it.

Aubrey had to be coaxed to swallow several vials, but Ari had downed the ones handed to her without protest. She figured they could have easily shot or strangled them much earlier than perpetrating an elaborate ruse to get them to swallow poison.

What they gave her had to be different from Aubrey's vials. Ari didn't feel artificially relaxed, but her head did seem a little clearer. The change in Aubrey was quick and noticeable. After only a few minutes she stopped crying, sat up, and studied her surroundings. The anxiety attack went from full force to gone.

Before Ari could even ask Aubrey about it, they were swept up and deposited in a fluffy pile and then presented with platters full of food. Neither woman even acknowledged the other as they attacked the food.

This was the biggest meal she'd seen in months. She knew she should feel guilty for eating so much while her friends were still starving, but she couldn't stop shoving the food in her mouth as fast as she could chew and swallow. Sitting on the pile with her and still sniffling a little from her anxiety attack, Aubrey was doing the same thing.

One of the things they'd been served was a black flat bread that tasted like a plain New York bagel. When she thought no one was looking, she tucked a few away in her jacket to take back to the others in case they didn't get served any food. Aubrey caught her doing it and followed suit.

Soon all the flat bread was hidden away and Ari's stomach was uncomfortably full. Dazed, she sat back and met Aubrey's gaze. The woman looked to be in a near food coma as well.

"What do you think they're going to do now?" Aubrey asked as Boss and Tech took the plates away and set them on the floor outside the small room.

"No idea," Ari admitted as she leaned back on some cushions behind her. She felt full and warm. She couldn't remember the last time she'd experienced both those sensations at the same time. Even if death was around the corner, she was going to enjoy this while she could.

Aubrey didn't lean back. She swept her gaze around the room, taking it in. "I think this might have been a storage room. Probably for items that needed to be kept at a precise temperature. Elaborate monitoring systems have been integrated with the normal wall display near the door."

Ari rolled her head so she could see what Aubrey was talking about. "Looks like," she agreed before looking back to her friend. "How are you feeling?"

It took Aubrey several minutes to respond. That was normal for her. She always liked to think about questions before answering.

"Good. It's like I can think again without all these panicky emotions filling my head. I feel even better now than I did when I was still taking my meds." She sighed and her shoulders slumped. "I hate that my brain's broken."

Ari sat up with a frown. "You're not broken. We all have challenges to deal with. Angel's kidneys keep acting up, and you wouldn't call him broken."

Aubrey's smile turned wry. "Having kidney stones is a bit different than having an emotional meltdown over everything."

"I disagree," Ari retorted. "Both are out of your control and neither devalues you as a human or friend. Using the term broken demeans how important you are to us."

Blinking furiously, Aubrey gave Ari a watery smile. "I miss Tomas, but I'm glad you took his spot."

"I wasn't given a choice," Ari teased. "You, Daniella, and Santos came up to me and said it was my turn to try and keep everyone alive."

Aubrey huffed out a soft laugh and started undoing her elaborate, braided coiffure. "I'll never forget the look on your face. It was half resigned and half terrified."

"You know," Ari said thoughtfully. "It looks like I did my job. I kept most of us alive and now it's out of my hands."

Aubrey paused long enough to shakes her head. "Oh no, you're not off the hook yet." She covertly gestured to Boss. "Most of the time that one is looking at you, even if all of them are talking. He's the one in charge. Right?"

Ari nodded. "Pretty sure he is. At least in this group."

"Then I elect you as our ambassador to these guys."

"Nice try, but I can't do much without being able to communicate. At least they seem to realize we're valuable labor and want to keep us alive." Aubrey went silent for a moment, making Ari suspicious. "What are you thinking, Aubrey?"

"The way they're treating us doesn't strike me as the way you treat laborers. At least not from our experiences back on Earth or with the Orloks."

"Maybe in their culture they treat laborers better, even ones from a different species," Ari suggested, wrinkling her brow as she considered Aubrey's theory.

"Remember how I told you my grandmother raised horses?" Aubrey asked.

Confused at the change of subject, Ari nodded. "Sure, I remember. She had to stop breeding them because all viable land had to be used to grow food for humans. What do horses have to do with this?"

"The way these guys are treating us reminds me of the way Grandma talked about treating her horses."

Worry made Ari's relaxed sleepiness vanish. "Are you trying to tell me you think they see us as slaves?"

Aubrey looked serious. "Weren't we already with Miox Minerals? They paid us in food and shelter. They left us absolutely no way to get out of here if we needed to. What would you call it when you're not paid for your labor and you can't leave?"

"It's called survival," she reminded Aubrey grimly. "We were all going to die within a few years if we stayed on Old Earth.

We're lucky Miox hired all of us, even those without experience or useful skills."

By now Aubrey had all the braids unwrapped from around her head and was starting to undo each individual braid. "Are we lucky, or were they? Between you, Mari, Santos, and me, they got expertise and education they would've had to pay a high price for anywhere else."

It was an old argument they'd had numerous times, but Ari wasn't feeling it. "It's all a moot point. What's done is done. Now we need to focus on getting these guys to let us stay, and we'll figure everything out from there."

Looking a little abashed, Aubrey shot Ari an apologetic look. "Right, sorry. I forgot your 'steps' speech."

"Step three only happens after you've taken steps one and two," Ari repeated the same thing she'd been saying since the beginning when she'd been helping Tomas organize everyone. "No point in worrying about step four until we get there."

"And you can't retake a step, so you better do it right the first time," Aubrey reminded her. Sometimes Ari hated the analogy she'd come up with on the fly while they'd been moving into the mining compound.

Ari nodded at Boss and Tech. "Let's take this next step slowly and carefully, yeah?"

Aubrey made a sound of agreement, then dropped her hands into lap. "My arms are too tired to finish," she admitted.

"Turn around," Ari ordered. "I'll undo the rest of them."

The familiar task was soothing for them both. After her normally straight hair was curled around her shoulders and down her back, Ari did her best to finger comb it out.

She wasn't surprised when the warrior took an interest in what she was doing. To a species without hair, Aubrey's braids probably looked fascinating as Ari methodically unraveled them. One of the warrior moved close to get a better look and Ari was thrilled to see Aubrey handled it without a hint of fear or panic.

Not only way she considering this a win, but a sign of good luck for the future.

"Norrium and Hesarium said all the food they took over was eaten quickly, and a few of the humans made themselves ill by eating too much too rapidly," Sapurian reported from the door.

Bazium turned his head to regard the medic. "Do you think we should go over there and scan them? Would the field scanner even work on their small bodies?"

"I'm not sure if the portable scanner would pick anything up, but I was going to suggest we bring them on board two at a time so I can assess and treat them. At the minimum I'm sure all of them need the same nutrient pack we gave these two."

"Should we begin right now?" Bazium asked reluctantly. He didn't want to leave his human. She looked too comfortable with her companion in the nest Norrium had hastily put together to pick her up and take her with him. Still, he couldn't shirk his duty to the other humans who might be suffering.

"Perhaps at the start of the next rotation," Sapurian suggested, coming further into the room to stand next to Tarrian. "Let them digest the food and see us as providers instead of invaders. That might help when we need them to remain calm and still."

Bazium had already worked out how long the food stores would last after watching Brave and Hurt eat. Even if they needed to eat several times a rotation, they consumed little in a sitting. There would be plenty of food to last for up to a Solar if necessary.

"Look at the way Brave is petting my human," Tarrian said, drawing his and Sapurian's attention to Hurt and Brave. "Do you think they'd like us to do that to them? Would it help soothe them?"

Absently, Bazium rubbed a hand over the plates on his head as he watched Brave run her fingers through Hurt's mane. "I think we might hurt them if we tried."

"They have a grooming tool," Sapurian said as he unclipped his Ident Cube and tapped it. Soon a holographic image popped up displaying what looked like a flat bit of wood with many notches sawed deep into it. Bazium had to study it for a little while before he figured out how it might be drawn through a human mane.

"I think I could make one of those out of a densel-instrumentation square," Tarrian commented as he studied the grooming tool. "What other types of things do they use?"

Sapurian tapped at his Cube, and then a few other items popped up. "I didn't find much information on their clothing except for the uniforms the Orlok mining company provided them." He brought up an image of the garment, pointing to it and then the females. "But as you can see by all the extra things they've wrapped themselves in, it didn't provide enough insulation."

"I believe they made this over-clothing from bedding material," Tarrian commented as he leaned over to study his human's additional clothing.

Hurt opened her eyes to see Tarrian was looming over her. She didn't flinch away, but both women stopped moving to watch Tarrian ease closer. When Tarrian turned his attention back to Sapurian's Ident Cube, Brave resumed grooming Hurt's hair.

"The Hulg don't handle any temperature lower than their desert homeworld so they use nano-infused fabric to create clothing that can keep them warm," Tarrian commented. "Perhaps we could acquire some and fashion robes for them."

"We don't need to," Bazium said as he pulled his own Ident Cube off his belt and started typing on it. "The Hulg make everything in a wrap-garment style so they don't have to bother with sizing their clothing. The wraps they make for their children would fit our humans."

Shutting down his Ident Cube and clipping back on his belt, Sapurian slid his eyes over to the humans. "But we aren't anywhere close to a Hulg outpost or colony."

Bazium held up his Ident to show the others the star map projection. "No, but we aren't far from a Veli traveling market. It wouldn't take much of an incentive for them to deviate here for a rotation."

"But isn't this sector still considered an active war zone?" Sapurian pointed out.

Tarrian sounded a rumble of amusement. "Veli are the unofficial neutral traders for every species. They won't hesitate to come here since there isn't any active fighting. But it will be expensive."

Bazium sounded a soft rattle that demonstrated his lack of concern. "What else am I going to spend my war bonus on?"

The moment those words left his mouth, he regretted it. His answer was far from what most Talins would say.

Instead of looking at his warriors, he focused on finding the contact coordinates for the closest Veli market ship and invited them to the mining compound with a minimum purchase guarantee. Once that was done and sent off through the ship's comm system, he looked up to find both Sapurian and Tarrian looking at items on their Ident.

"You're right," Tarrian mumbled absently as he scrolled through lists of products. "What else would we do with all our wealth? Using it on the humans is as worthwhile as anything else I could do with it."

Sapurian made a rumble of agreement without looking up. "I saw one cub hidden among the humans in their communal nest room. We need to see if we can get a wrap small enough that it would fit."

Far from his slip-up being noticed, it looked like his warriors were just as invested in the humans as he was. Without a doubt the humans were getting new clothes.

CHAPTER 5

Advanced Squad Delta 223—Mission Q73 Report (Excerpt)
Unlike Talin children, these humans have young that take many solars to learn to walk or talk. By the time a Talin child would be solving their first equations, these human cubs are still working on coordination and motor skills.

Despite their slow development, the human cubs are charming. They make a pleasing musical sound when they are entertained or happy. I will include a recording of the sound in my report; it's like nothing I've ever heard before.

"I think these guys might be Talins," Santos commented as he accepted the flat bread Ari had smuggled back to them. She felt a little silly handing him food after finding out everyone had been well-fed while she and Aubrey had been gone.

After a nap, she and Aubrey had been awakened, fed another meal, and then carried back to everyone else. After they were set down, Boss and Tech walked away, but Lucky stayed and was now kneeling near the door, trying to urge Andres closer.

Andres had his mother's black hair and dark skin, along with his father's light eyes, making him absolutely adorable. He was bold and curious, but life on the station had made him cautious. It would be some time before he got within arm's length of the stranger. His mother Liz would probably object to Andres getting so close the intimidating warrior, but she was fast asleep with baby Lucia slumbering next to her.

"You've been gone for about nine hours," Mari said with a shake of her head. "I still can't believe the way they picked you up and carried you away. They looked so fierce. I was sure I'd never see either of you again."

"Christos and a few others wanted to go after you," Santos added. "But Daniella talked them out of it."

"Good thing too," Ari responded with a grin. "We were too busy being pampered to have visitors."

Aubrey patted Mari's shoulder. "My crying upset them. They probably didn't understand that nothing was wrong. All they did was scan me and give us some vials to drink. I feel much better now."

"Let refocus on the important thing here. Santos, you said Talins?" Ari asked Santos. "What else do you know? Or is the species all we have?"

"I was up all night doing research," he explained. "You know how our tech doesn't mesh perfectly with the Orlok stuff, so it took me hours to comb through the UniBase because I couldn't simply look anything up."

"I know. I know," she said with a little sigh. Everyone knew how bad the system was because they'd all had to deal with it. Instead of making an integrated system for the humans to use, the Orloks had layered on a secondary system to interface with the mining compound's original system. It made everything complicated and difficult. Most days no one bothered to do anything extracurricular because it wasn't worth the headache.

Except Santos. It seemed Santos found it a challenge instead of a pain. But then again Santos was a bit twisted so it all made sense.

"You combed through the system and found…?" she pressed.

"Not much," Santos admitted. "I can tell you these ones are all males because they have those quills. Females only have bristles there, no quills."

Disappointment replaced hope. "That's it?"

Santos shrugged. "I also know they have a limited monarchy government and their civilization is organized a little like the ancient Roman Republic."

Ari gave him a flat look and said in a monotone voice, "Hail Caesar."

Santos snorted out a laugh. "Right, sorry. I forgot you weren't obsessed with ancient Earth history like I was."

"No one was as obsessed as you," Aubrey teased him. She and Mari had stopped talking to join Ari and Santos's conversation. "Go on. How are they like the Roman Empire?"

"Roman Republic, not the empire. Empire happened after Julius Caesar. Actually, it started with a consul named Sulla and—"

"Santos," Ari growled. "Focus, please."

Santos blushed a little. "Oh, right, sorry. Back when Rome was a republic everything was about expanding Rome: their power, their wealth, stuff like that. These Talins are the Roman Republic. Their military is all voluntary, no conscription or recruitment. It's a big deal to get to be allowed into the military."

"That would explain the discipline," Mari snarked. "I can't think of many species that wouldn't have gone through and looted the place before any higher-ranking personnel arrived."

Unlike the rest of them, Mari had found a coveted off-world job a full decade before the Final Cataclysm. But she'd been forced to accept the unpaid job with Miox Mineral to be with her brother, the last living member of her family. After Tomas died, she'd thrown herself into trying to help Ari keep everyone else alive.

Mari always meant well, but she had a tendency to become dictatorial. She could be downright viscous if things weren't done the way she thought they should be. Tomas had been good at keeping her in check, but she didn't give Ari that level of loyalty.

She was probably deferring to Ari right now because she didn't want to be the one dealing with the warriors. Eh, at least that meant Mari wasn't being a pain in the ass for the moment.

"Exactly," Santos said, beaming at Mari. "Disciplined is a good word for them."

"And caregivers," Ari interjected. "They seem to be taking care of us."

"They're definitely acting like caregivers," Mari agreed. "But that's both good and worrisome." Before she could go into more detail Andres squealed, drawing all their attention to the child.

He was standing in front of the Talin, laughing and trying to grab something from Lucky's hands. Ari's first instinct was to rush over and pull Andres away, but then she realized the Talin had his quills tucked tightly in and was careful to keep Andres's movements contained so he wouldn't get hurt.

The big fearsome Talin was playing with the preschooler.

As Andres grabbed for the bright teal Ident dangling over his head, the Talin quickly ran a small portable scanner over the little boy's body. He was making the same purring sound they'd all made almost the entire time she and Aubrey had been with them.

"I really hope we don't end up as cattle," Mari whispered to her.

Ari turned shocked eyes on the other woman. "What?" Thankfully, no one else had heard her. "What happened to them being caregivers?"

"What do you think farmers used to do with their animals before they ate them?" Mari said with a shrug. "They took great care of them. Fed them, kept them safe, and checked on their health." She pointedly glanced over to where the Talin was finishing up the scan of Andres and then returned her gaze to Ari.

She stared at Mari, wordlessly shaking her head. She couldn't think of a single response. Then she remembered what Aubrey had said. "Horses. Aubrey thinks we're being treated like pets, not cattle.

"Humans ate horses too," Mari answered. "In some places there was a fine line between working animals and dinner. Or maybe we will continue to be valuable workers. There's always hope. Right?"

"If I didn't know you better, I'd think you wanted to get eaten," Ari said, half-teasing and half-admonishing.

"I'm making sure you don't give this species human motivations," Mari groused. "We can't communicate with them yet, and until we can, we won't know anything."

"You're right," Ari admitted. "We need to be able to talk."

It stung, but she couldn't ignore Mari's point. A memory of being carried and the sound of the purring made her want to be held by Boss again. But for all she knew this was the way they treated domesticated meat animals. They simply didn't know enough and wouldn't be finding anything out until someone had an INT. If the Talins were inclined or capable of giving them an INT, it would have happened already.

If the Talins weren't going to give them INTs, she didn't have any choice but to do something gruesome.

They were going to need to get the INT out of Tomas's head.

When she met Mari's eyes, she saw the same conclusion there. "Daniella can do it," she said in a hushed voice, her expression resigned. "You have my permission." Then she got up and walked away.

Ari didn't want the INT of a dead man in her head, but really, she didn't have a choice. Time to find Daniella.

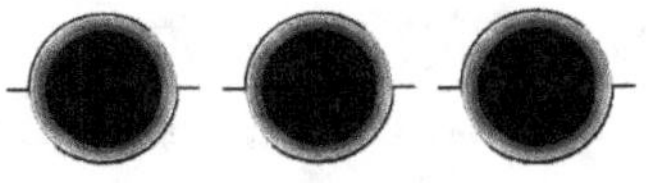

It ended up being much harder to leave the room than she expected. The first issue was Lucky wouldn't let any of them out the door. Ari tried being bold first. Grabbing Daniella's hand, she headed for the door. The Talin got in front of them and refused to budge.

During the entire interaction he'd kept purring, making Ari daring enough to try shoving at him a little. His purring was interrupted by a different rumbling sound from his chest that she was pretty sure denoted humor, but he didn't move.

There wasn't another way out of the room except trying to go through one of the access panels, but opening one of those up would be noisy and draw Lucky's attention.

Wait, that was it!

She found Santos and Mari and told them to gather a few people and make a big production of opening the access panel at the far end of the room. Then she and Daniella waited not far from the door.

Her plan worked.

The moment a handful of people started wrestling with the heavy access panel, Lucky rushed over, making a loud percussion sound that echoed through the room. The ones opening the panel froze as he sprinted toward them and Ari almost forgot to run for the door.

Talins were an intimidating sight when they were in motion at speed!

Grabbing Daniella's hand, she dragged her through the door. The hiss of the hatch opening and closing was covered by all the sounds Lucky was producing. She didn't slow when they hit the hall. They needed to be out of sight if the Talin peeked out the door.

The room the miners repurposed into a giant freezer wasn't far away, but they were both breathless by the time they got there.

"I haven't run like that for years," Daniella wheezed as they both caught their breath. The harsh lights in the room highlighted her high cheekbones, making them look even sharper than normal.

"Yeah, sorry about that," Ari said as she clutched her side and looked around the room. Five shrouded bodies were laid on the floor—family and friends they'd lost. Most of them died in the last few months. The only thing that was going to keep her from breaking down into a puddle of snot and tears was to stay focused.

Straightening up, Daniella's gaze fell on the closest body. "You don't have to be here while I cut out Tomas's INT," she offered gently. Trained as a physician's assistant back on Old Earth, Daniella had been at the side of everyone in this room trying to keep them alive despite the odds. If she could put aside her feelings to remain clinical, Ari would too.

"I'll help," Ari insisted. As if to prove herself, she ruthlessly knelt down and pulled back the thin sheet covering Tomas. The sight of his emaciated body made her bite her lip and blink back tears. They'd both had a passion for Old Earth telenovelas and had spent hours reminiscing about their favorite shows, episodes, characters, and plots. They'd been friends then lovers.

Dios mio, she missed him so much.

"Ari?"

She turned to find Daniella kneeling next to her. "Tell me what to do," she demanded.

Daniella must have seen the determination on her face because she nodded to a spot near the door. "There's an old rock kit in the corner over there. Grab it for me. The stone cutter should work for what I need."

Ari fetched the tool while Daniella moved Tomas's body away from the others. When she dropped to her knees next to Daniella, her eyes passed over Tomas's pale face. Emotion choked her throat, threatening to overwhelm her. Hastily, she looked away and wordlessly handed Daniella the tool.

Once she had the stone cutter in hand, Daniella made quick work of cutting open Tomas's skull and locating the INT while Ari held his head still and stared at a fixed point on the far wall.

The coin, the main part of the INT, was small. It was only the size of Ari's thumbnail. But the organic tendrils the INT grew inside the brain had to be carefully severed close to the coin or it couldn't be used again. If Daniella pulled one out of the brain instead of cutting it, it wouldn't be able to grow new tendrils in Ari.

It took Daniella close to an hour to sever each tendril from the coin without tugging on the coin itself. By the time she was done, both women were shivering from the cold despite how many layers they were wearing. Sitting back, Daniella gave Ari a triumphant smile.

"Done!" Daniella covered Tomas up again. Ari felt all kinds of relief once she didn't have to concentrate on keeping her eyes from wandering down.

Thank you, Tomas, she said silently to his corpse. *Thank you for this last gift.*

She could almost hear Tomas teasing her. *Having my dick in you a couple of times wasn't enough? Now you want my INT? At least something from inside of me gets to be inside of you one more time.*

He always had a strange sense of humor. But he would have always ended anything he said to her with, *I love you, cara mia.*

Daniella got her attention as she showed Ari the bloody coin resting in the palm of her hand. "Here it is! From what I read on INTs, there's no reason why it won't work once we stick it in your head."

Ari eyed the coin without enthusiasm. "Great."

Daniella chuckled as she stood up and walked to the door. "Don't worry, we're going to clean it off first. And I need to sterilize your head. Everything I need is back in the communal room."

Ari stopped her. "Should we do it here? If we go back I'm worried one of the Talins might take it away from us. At the bare minimum they might separate us from everyone else to figure out what we were doing."

Daniella frowned. Then shook her head sending her long, deep brown hair held up in a high ponytail swinging around her shoulders. "I hadn't thought of that. But I'm not doing anything without a sterilization kit. And I need to warm up a little first. My hands are going numb."

Wrapping her arms around herself, Ari ran through her mental map of the compound. "What about the lab? We have that big unit to treat the rock samples so we aren't bringing in some kind of biocontamination. We never needed to use it after the first few months, not after Sofia finished her biological threat assessment."

"That would work," Daniella agreed. "It's going to suck for you, but it'll work."

"What else is new?" Ari said and they headed out the hatch.

The run to the rock lab helped warm them both up but made Ari feel a little lightheaded. She might have gotten a few good meals, but it wasn't enough to make up for the last year. Dread was also making her feel a little woozy.

She remembered when Tomas had gotten his INT installed. It had been done in a Med Bay with all kinds of special medication and treatments, so Tomas didn't feel a thing until days after the procedure was over. Then he'd been given special drugs to keep the INT from hurting as the tendrils grew through his brain.

He said it hadn't hurt at all and the most he could feel was a little localized soreness.

But Ari was going to get to do this without any anesthesia or analgesics. Then she reminded herself that Liz had given birth to Lucia without any painkillers and no Med Bay. Having an INT shoved in her brain couldn't possibly be as painful as giving birth.

While Ari worked on not freaking out, Daniella sterilized the coin. Then she fiddled with the sample sterilizer until she got it to work without the safety barrier down.

"Time to stick your head in here," she said, tapping the floor of the machine. "It won't take long, ten seconds max, but you're going to need to hold your breath. And you need to stay perfectly still."

Without comment Ari laid her cheek on the cold metal. Daniella fiddled with her hair until the skin behind her left ear was bared to the machine.

Ari tried to keep her heart from beating out of her chest. "This isn't going to fry my brain. Is it?"

"Nope," Daniella said cheerfully as she tapped the machine's display. "But it's going to hurt. Close your eyes and hold your breath!"

Ari gripped the edge of the table and bit the inside of her cheek as the skin behind her ear lit on fire!

Don't breathe, she reminded herself. If you scream, you breathe!

This was one of the most painful experiences of Ari's life. She was sure Daniella was burning a hole through her skull.

"Done," Daniella announced.

Ari pulled her head out from inside the machine so fast she lost her balance and stumbled back into a nearby table, scattering old rock samples and equipment all over the floor. Daniella grabbed and arm to steady her. Ari tried to rub the spot behind her ear but Daniella was quick to bat her hand away.

"Don't touch it," Daniella ordered.

"Can I never do that again?" Ari asked. trying to ignore the dull burning sensation.

"Sure," Daniella agreed. "Next time we have to dig an INT out of someone, it'll be you. That means someone else will get to be sterilized."

The thought of being dead and no longer in pain or fear didn't have the effect on Ari that Daniella was going for.

Instead of looking horrified, Ari nodded. "Great, then someone else gets to be in charge. Now, let's shove this thing in my head before I lose my nerve."

CHAPTER 6

Advanced Squad Delta 223—Mission Q73 Report (Excerpt)
This passage was redacted from the submitted report: *Two of the humans were able to slip out of the room despite one of my men guarding the door. We didn't even realize they'd managed to escape and evade until I visited to check on the human I call Brave and found her missing. We don't know how long they were gone, but I soon found them in a hall walking back toward the room. I believe they were returning to the others after carrying out some secret mission that made Brave ill. This episode leads me to believe they are more intelligent than we first surmised. Later we'd make a discovery that revealed both their intelligence and determination.*

Bazium felt worry hit him the moment he scanned the room and didn't see Brave's face among all the humans. Fear made him search the area without regard to the other humans. He ignored the way they scrambled out of his way and the cries of surprise as he tore through the room, upending bedding and pallets looking for Brave.

"Advanced Leader?" Sapurian tugged at his arm. "You're scaring them, sir. What's wrong?"

"Where's Brave?" he demanded, pulling his arm out of Sapurian's grip to toss a last bed against the wall. Sounding an aggressive rattle, he turned on his medic. "You've been stationed here since I left. Where is she?"

"Brave?" Sapurian repeated with a surprised rattle, turning his head to take in the room.

All the humans were on their feet and gathered as far away from the two of them as they could get. The cub was gripped by one of the females in the back of the room while several others stood in front. It struck Bazium that they were getting ready to defend themselves. His loss of control might have undone all the trust he and his men had been slowly developing with the humans.

"You're right," Sapurian said, bringing Bazium back to the reason he'd acted badly. "Two humans are missing. How could they have possibly gotten by me?"

"We can figure that out later," Bazium said, striding out of the room. "Stay here and monitor the rest."

He heard Sapurian's rumble of assent as the hatch slid shut behind him. Stopping in the hall, he unclipped his Ident from his belt and pinged Hesarium and Tarrian; they were both in the compound working on fixing the environmental systems.

"Two humans are missing," he told them the moment their Idents connected with his. "Brave and one other. Hesarium, search the processing areas, Tarrian search the transition shafts, equipment storage and repair rooms."

Both of them rumbled assent through the Ident link, but Tarrian stayed connected even after Hesarium severed his link.

"Advanced Leader, is my Hurt one of the humans missing?" he asked.

"No, Hurt is still in the room with the others, although I might have frightened her when I was looking for Brave."

Tarrian sounded a rumble of relief. "Frightened is better than missing," Tarrian breathed before shutting down his link.

Later Bazium would help his crew calm and earn the trust of the humans again, but right now he needed to find Brave. Fighting chemicals flooded his system, exactly like he was about to go into battle. His senses became more acute and his coordination became effortless. Before long he'd covered almost all the ground of his assigned area and was entering a last corridor.

That's when he spotted them.

Brave was leaning heavily on another female as the two walked toward him. Her long black mane was tied in a loose knot on her head so he could clearly see her face. Her entire focus was on the floor in front of her, as if carefully planning out each step.

Fear that she'd somehow hurt herself made him rattle loudly as he ran down the hall. The noise made both of them stop and stare at him with wide eyes. They took a hesitant step back as he got close, but that was all they were able to do. The moment he was within arm's reach, he snatched Brave away from the other female and held her tightly to his chest. She was shaking slightly but he also noted her skin was glistening, which would indicate she was warm enough that her body was attempting to cool itself.

Why would she be showing indicators of both being cold and hot? It was highly worrisome. But as much as he wanted to rush his human to the ship and call for Sapurian, he had to deal with the second human.

It took a little maneuvering, but he managed to curl his arm under Brave's rear and hold her to his torso so he could reach for his Ident with his free hand. He keyed everyone's Ident.

"I've found them. Something's wrong with Brave. Norrium, take Sapurian's place. Sapurian, meet me in the Med Bay on the ship. Tarrian, come to my location and collect the other human."

Affirmative sounds came from his crew and soon he heard Tarrian running down the corridor. The moment he was in sight, he called out to Bazium. "I have eyes on the human, Advanced Leader."

Assured that the second human wouldn't find any trouble with Tarrian there, Bazium hugged his human to his chest and sprinted to the ship.

"Hold on, little one," he whispered to her as he ran. She'd gone limp in his arms, but he could feel her breathing, strong and steady. "I'm going to help you. And then I'm never letting you out of my sight again."

Bazium was rarely struck dumb, but Sapurian had managed to do it.

The human lay on the exam table between them, curled up in a tight ball and shivering. Bazium had let go of her only long enough for Sapurian to scan her, and then he'd started petting her head as he'd seen her do for Hurt.

He kept the motion up even as he stared at Sapurian and sounded a rattle of incredulity. "They did what?"

Sapurian sounded a frustrated rattle. "They put an INT in her. It's growing tendrils now. But they did it without any of the proper medications or preparation. She's going to be disorientated and in a great deal of discomfort for the next three days."

"Will there be permanent damage?" Bazium asked.

"I don't believe so. This INT was programmed for a human brain. It will grow correctly, but far faster than it should. I can't give the INT retardants now that it's started as that would hurt her. This process should take ten or fifteen rotations, but hers will be done in only one or two. When INT tendrils grow too quickly, they disrupt brain functions. Nothing as bad as heart or lungs, but her brain will send her body false signals until the tendrils are done."

"Is this shivering part of that?" Bazium asked.

Sapurian sounded a soothing rumble. "No, I think the shivering might be a combination of pain responses and a lowered core temperature. Before you ask, I don't know if the tendrils are causing the lowered core temperature or if she went somewhere in the compound cold enough to cause this."

"It wouldn't take much," Bazium commented. "Thank the ancestors, a Veli market ship got back to me. They'll be here soon and we'll be able to buy better clothing for them."

"That'll be a relief. Tarrian fixed some of the environmental systems so we can increase the load on the heating elements, but not enough to bring the compound up to a level where the humans would be most comfortable."

"I'm impressed at what he's managed, considering the state of things," Bazium said as he gathered Brave into his arms. She murmured something in her soft, musical voice but didn't open her eyes. "I'm going to take Brave to my cabin to care for her over the next few rotations. While I'm doing this, I want you and Norrium to work out where we could put the humans on the ship."

Sapurian sounded a rumble of agreement. "Having them on the ship will make it easier to monitor them and we'll have better control of their environmental conditions. But we'll have to split them up. We don't have any single room big enough to house all of them safely."

"That's why I want you and Norrium to work together. We'll need to be careful when we separate them so the two of you should observe and note which humans should be placed together."

"We'll start work on it right away," Sapurian agreed with an eager rattle.

Bazium was about to say something else when Brave moved her head on his shoulder. She nuzzled her face against the small bit of exposed skin there. The sensation was deliciously intense. He'd never had a simple touch make him feel like a current of electricity had shot through him. But it wasn't painful: it was both arousing and soothing at the same time. He didn't even know he could experience those sensations together.

He held perfectly still so she wouldn't move her head. Even her warm breath wafting across his neck felt wonderful.

She made it hard for him to focus on Sapurian.

"I'll leave it to you and Norrium to organize the move. I need to get Brave settled into a nest in my room."

"Of course, Advanced Leader. I'll put together medication vials for her and some nutrient rich hydration packs. I'll deliver them and then seek Norrium out."

"Good," Bazium commented as he walked out of Med Bay, careful to keep his movements slow and steady. When Brave had briefly opened her eyes earlier, he could tell she was dizzy despite her position on a solid exam table. But she hadn't made a sound of distress. She'd simply closed her eyes and stopped trying to move.

It was uncommon for Talins to become ill, but when he'd been a young child raised among many in the cresh, he remembered suffering horrible growing pains. He lay in bed, panting from pain but afraid to tell any of the staff for fear of being seen as weak and sent off to a cresh that specialized in "strengthening" young Talins.

The idea of his little human suffering in silence like he had as a youth made him feel off balance and helpless. Similar to when he was a child.

"I'll do my best to ease your symptoms," he whispered to her as they entered his cabin. "Cry and make sounds when you hurt. I'll do all I can to fix it. Don't be quiet, Brave. Don't ever be quiet with me."

He knew she couldn't understand him, but he felt better for declaring his intent.

Easing her onto his bunk, he watched her curl back up into a tight ball. He was sure Sapurian would arrive soon with medication vials that would alleviate the worst of the symptoms, but there was no way to make the tendrils less intrusive.

Although his bed wasn't small compared to the size of Brave, he didn't enjoy seeing her there. The thin bed mat, single sheet, and a small pillow were all wrong for a human nest. Hurrying temperature controlled storage room, he gathered all the pillows and bedding they'd used to build the nest for both Brave and Hurt when they'd first been brought on the ship. His arms were overfull for the journey back to his cabin.

Most Talins didn't use pillows, and some didn't bother with sheets or blankets either, but the ship had been stocked with plenty of both. That might appear counterintuitive to anyone who didn't know about the Domicile of Souls where all their ancestors waited to welcome the worthy.

Bedding was a common item to gift the ancestors, so they were often included in a dead soldier's memorial box. That was why all war ships always had far more bedding than necessary. No Talin wanted to meet his ancestors without a proper gift of bedding, seed, or a piece of iron ore. Many years ago one Talin had struck on the brilliant idea of putting a small packet of seeds and a tiny piece of iron in the center of every pillow. Now almost every Talin slept with one of those pillows so if they died in the night, they took with them the three most important offerings to their ancestors in the afterlife.

Bazium wasn't sure an afterlife or ancestors were waiting for him, but at least it meant his ship had soft, fluffy pillows in abundance.

First, he lifted both Brave and the mat under her and settled them on the floor of his cabin. Then he piled pillows around her. Her outer garments were filthy, and he didn't like the idea of her sleeping in them. Before he tucked the sheets around her, he decided to strip off some of her clothing.

When he eased the outer three layers off, she whimpered. The helpless sound broke something inside him.

"I only want to see to your comfort, Brave," he assured her as he started up a soothing rumble. "I have thick sheets to cover you with. I've already told the room's environmental controls to significantly raise the temperature. You'll be warm soon. I promise."

His voice must have eased some of her distress because she didn't make a further sound as he pulled off her heavy outer garment, the thinner second layer, and finally the one-piece uniform issued by the Orlok mining company. Under all of that she wore two items, a pair of thin, skin-tight pants and a long-sleeved top. Those two items were relatively clean, so he left those on her and bundled the rest of the clothing into the wall unit that would wash and sterilize them.

He tucked several of the thicker blankets around her, relieved to see her relax a little and snuggle down into them. The corners of her little mouth turned up and he thought that might be a sign of contentedness.

"That's it, Brave," he whispered to her as he lay next to her, watching the mounds of bedding move slightly as she breathed. "You don't need to do anything but heal. I'll take care of everything else.

CHAPTER 7

Advanced Squad Delta 223—Mission Q73 Report (Excerpt)
The human I call Brave reacted badly to the rapidly growing INT. I'll include my medical technician's evaluations on the INTs' too-rapid growth, but I think part of the issue might be that all the humans here were physically depleted, so she was already weakened before the INT was poorly inserted. It was a foolish thing to do but it will allow us to communicate once isn't finished growing. This species might not be highly intelligent, but they are courageous.

On another note about fitness, we've found where they stored their dead and which body they retrieved the INT from. My medic Sapurian observed that most of the humans have a darker color skin, eyes, and mane than those in the room they used for the dead. He had a hypothesis that the lighter the coloring the poorer their constitution might be, similar to the way Hamlershin born with more blue in their fins have more recessive genetics and are prone to more health issues.

Of course we have no way to test this, but it is an interesting concept. All but one of the remaining humans still alive have light brown to dark brown coloring. We'll monitor that one human closely to make sure she remains healthy despite her lighter coloring.

Ari wanted to scream but was too scared to make a single sound.

Nothing was right. Not a single damn thing.

The sound of a maintenance droids working in the hall made her shiver. The slight hiss of door hatches opening and closing made pain spike in her side like she'd been running. When she opened her eyes she swore she could taste the gray color of the walls around her. Spoiler alert—gray tasted terrible.

Thankfully, unlike the sound of maintenance droids and the color gray, Boss's touch felt gentle and soothing. When he settled her into a nest of pillows, she felt nothing but relief. She had a moment of panic when she felt her clothing being stripped off. The cool air of the cabin was horrible, making it feel like her skin was burning. But she was quickly covered in soft, thick fluffiness that she was sure was what happy daydreams would feel like if they had substance.

The worst part was that her brain itched. She wished she could open her skull and scratch it. Sleep didn't always help. She had strange dreams where she was licking the sky while falling or growing tentacles out of her head and using them to feed herself from a tree. It left her feeling disorientated and freaked out.

One good thing to come out of all of this, besides the fact that she'd eventually be able to communicate with the Talins, was she didn't feel cold. She wasn't sure if it was the INT messing with her senses or if she really was warm. In the end she decided it didn't matter. She was going to enjoy the sensation of being toasty warm for the first time in a year.

Then there was her Talin, Boss.

She knew she wasn't imagining him or his purring. Oh God, that purring. *Madre de Dios* save her from all the impure thoughts she was having about a nonhuman!

Not only did the purring stop the itch in her brain, but it also made all her nerve endings tingle, especially the ones between her legs. She'd liked the sound before the INT had mucked up her senses, but now it made her feel downright naughty.

If movement didn't make her dizzy, she'd be humping the pillow she was snuggled around.

A gentle clawed hand curled under her head, lifting her. She opened her eyes, letting the world swim around her until she could focus on Boss hovering over her with a vial of medication.

"That stuff tastes like static," she muttered before obediently opening her lips and letting him pour the contents into her mouth. She tried to keep her eyes open as the taste of the medication fizzled in her brain. She knew the tendrils were causing havoc, but it was still disconcerting to feel like she'd swallowed a bunch of electrons and now all of them were pinging around in her skull.

Without lowering her head, he set the empty vial down and then picked up something else. It was a bit of food he pressed to her lips. She kept them firmly shut. She wasn't going to try that again. The bite of black flat bread he'd fed her earlier had tasted like ash and made her violently ill. She could see this was something different, but she wasn't going to risk it.

The medication might make her feel like there was a party of charged particles dancing in her brain, but at least it stayed down and she was going to be content with that.

He continued to hold the food to her mouth and said something. When her lips remained sealed, the purring was interrupted briefly to make another sound. Probably one of impatience.

Closing her eyes, she turned her face to the side, and he pulled the food away. Still, he didn't lower her head. A cool cleansing cloth gently wiping her face. If her brain was working correctly the action might have made her tear up. It was a simple thing but caused memories of being cared for as a child flood her brain.

In truth, he was probably only doing it because she was dirty. Bathing was difficult because they couldn't heat the water very often or risk overburdening the systems that were barely running to begin with. Heating a pot of water and using a cleansing cloth was the best all of them could do. Hair was easier because you could remain dressed while someone else washed it for you. All of that meant she had been grungy before now. Being sick had only made her feel filthy, and not in a fun way.

"Sorry if I stink," she murmured to Boss once he'd finished cleaning off her face and laid her head back down. "You can leave the meds and I can take care of myself. You don't have to play nurse."

Of course he didn't respond except to purr as he tucked in the blankets around her. It made her feel like a cherished child and a smile curled her lips. She managed to catch herself before she showed any teeth, but it was a near thing.

"I really hope you guys don't turn out to be assholes who are going to eat us," she said to him, confident the language barrier would keep him from being offended. It was liberating to be able to say anything she wanted. Feeling the need to unburden, she started talking as he sat next to her, purring and stroking her hair. He was incredibly gentle with those big, clawed fingers.

"I mean, you're probably only being nice because you need our labor to get this mine up and running again. We were pretty good at it before the supplies stopped coming. But right here and now I'm going to pretend you like me. You know, as in I'm a girl who likes boys and you're a boy who likes girls. Although, if you like boys you should talk to Santos. He likes boys and girls equally. And from the gossip I've heard, he's really good in bed."

Santos's exploits back on Old Earth had been legendary, but once the Final Cataclysm had started, no one had time for fun. It was all about survival.

"We all lived in New Rico," she told him. "All the humans here. We're kind of a giant extended family. After Puerto Rico was swallowed by the Atlantic, our great-grandparents moved to Florida. But most of Florida ended up underwater with a few places becoming islands. All our great-grandparents were on one of those islands and called it New Rico. That's why we all speak Spanglish to each other. We kind of developed our own language. Anyway, by the time I was born only a few hundred people were on New Rico. We left too. Aubrey, Santos, Daniella, and Mari had great jobs and I was at school."

She made a soft, scoffing sound. She'd been so naïve back then. She was sure she'd get her master's in geology, specializing in astro-mining, and find a great job off-world. She planned to earn a ton of money and buy her family a domicile somewhere safe and comfortable. As if there was time to even finish her master's degree, let alone find a well-paying job and save up the money.

The world ended long before she could accomplish any of those goals.

"I was only one thesis defense away from finishing. Then the school shut down. We all came back to the island to help when the air went bad; we all had to shelter indoors all the time. I had the skills to set it up air filtration, but my family had died before I even made it back to the island. I poured myself into helping the hundred of us still alive. We used an old auditorium to live in and set up filtration systems. Aubrey and Mari contacted all the off-world employers they could asking about work. They didn't get any interest."

Tears tried to gathered in her eyes as she remembered that time. Everything just kept getting worse. There was little to eat and even with the filtration, the air was killing them.

"We weren't getting much news by then and it felt like someone was dying every day. We all saw the end coming so when Miox Minerals started offering humans jobs, we all jumped at the chance. Really Mari and Aubrey got all of us off that island. They did a great job of negotiating with the Orloks. I think Aubrey feels guilty sometimes that they didn't get us a better deal, but we lived and a lot of other people died—so there's that. By the time the Orlok's ship picked us up only seventy-one of us were left. Liz was pregnant at the time and had to give birth to Andres on the ship. But it turned out that was lucky because they had a decent Med Bay."

She pictured the rambunctious four-year-old in her head. "Sometimes I'm sad when I realize Andres will grow up never experiencing Old Earth. But I remind myself that being deprived is better than dead, and I don't feel bad anymore."

She was silent for a little while, thinking about all the people they'd lost both on Old Earth and here at the compound. She really couldn't handle losing any more people.

"If you're going to eat us, please eat me first. Okay? That's all I ask."

She thought she could hear Tomas laughing and teasing her. Although neither of them was religious, he'd called her a good little Catholic martyr a few times over rotgut vodka. He'd even threatened to petition the church to canonize her. They'd often banter like that, making up their saint names and what they'd be the patron saints of.

Saint Arianna Garcia Lee, patron saint of astro rockhounds and the clumsy.

Saint Tomas Morales De Leon, patron saint of homebrewed vodka, steadfast leadership, and INTs.

Dios mio, she missed him. "This is all your fault," she whispered to the absent Tomas. For a short time, they'd been lovers, but it hadn't been romantic. Their coupling had been more about two friends finding a moment to escape the stress of surviving. Then he was gone and everything had fallen to her.

The image of Tomas slid from her mind as Boss's purring took over her nervous system with delightful tingles.

"I'm not a leader," she told the Talin, feeling her brain starting to go into a stupor again. His purring was making her feel warm all over so she started to pull off the covers. Large hands helped and soon her heated skin was met with cool, refreshing air.

"You can be the leader now," she offered without opening her eyes. The words felt funny in her ears, giving her the sensation of cool water droplets raining down on her neck.

She was so ready for the stupid INT to be finished growing in her brain.

Time had become untraceable for her. She could have been snuggled in this bed for hours or days. She couldn't tell. She let her mind float off because everything was out of her hands now.

It was probably the most comforting thought she'd had in a long time.

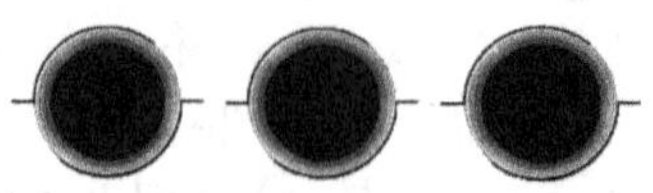

When she came back to herself again, she was confused. She knew where she was, so waking up on the Talins' ship wasn't surprising. But finding herself naked was a bit of a shocker.

"*¡Ah chingao!*" she cried out and tried to sit up.

Her brain did not like that sudden movement, and she crashed back on her soft pillow bed with a moan. Curling up on her side, she covered her mouth and worked on not vomiting. Eventually her stomach settled. That's when she noticed Boss was sitting on the pillows with her. She was curled up on her side facing him. He wasn't touching her but was purring and talking. Before the INT his words were nothing but nonsense; now she was catching a few words here and there.

"…still…help…afraid…"

The INT must be grown enough to start doing some translating, but nothing fluid enough to truly communicate. The few words being translated didn't lessen her confusion upon finding herself naked but it did reduce her outrage.

"…fluid…all…try…"

Very slowly he nudged her shoulder until she rolled on her back with a whispered protest. "Fine, I'm moving."

After she was where he wanted her, he re-tucked the blanket until she felt like she'd been swaddled. Careful not to tangling his claws in her hair, he worked his hand under until he was cradling her head then lifted slightly.

The cold edge of a metal canister was pressed to her lips. Refreshing liquid dribbled into her mouth and she greedily tilted her head to get more. He took the canister away before she was satisfied but the tone of his voice was soothing as he spoke rapidly to her.

"…future…more…"

He probably didn't want her taking in too much and risk her vomiting it all over him. She couldn't blame him.

Experimentally, she lifted her lids. Fluffy pillows took up most of her field of vision. Keeping her head still, she rolled her eyes. He was sitting next to her with a plate of something resting on his lap. Meeting her gaze he put something to his lips and mimicked biting. His sharp, white teeth were startling to see displayed so suddenly after only seeing hints of them while he talked. Then he moved his finger to her mouth and pressed gently.

He wanted her to eat something.

She opened her lips only enough to take a nibble and then shut them firmly. Whatever it was made sparks flare in her feet. Intellectually, she knew the tendrils were getting all her senses confused and crisscrossed, but she did not need to experience that again.

She really hoped food tasted like food soon. Feeling a taste with her feet, or as a sensation somewhere else, wasn't fun at all.

When he moved his hand away and laid her head back down, she murmured, "Maybe later."

Thankfully, he didn't press her to eat again. She heard him set the platter down elsewhere. He shifted position until he was north of her head. She couldn't see him now without moving so she contented herself with listening as he settled himself on the pillows north of her head.

Then she felt a slight tug on her hair. The sensation didn't register as anything else, so the tendrils must be done messing with that section of gray matter.

But what was he doing?

As with almost everything else, the scissor and clippers had broken long ago. A few people had tried to cut hair with knives or other tools. It was a giant pain in the ass, so most of them, men and women both, had given up and let their hair grow. Long beards had also become common. Tomas had referred to it as refugee haute couture.

Now Boss was doing something to her waist length hair. Was he cutting it off? Looking for lice?

She lay there catching bits of movements out of the corner of her eye but not able to get a full picture. Then he shifted slightly, and she saw what he was doing.

He had a comb. It wasn't familiar, and she was sure it didn't belong to the miners. It looked like it had been roughly fashioned from some kind of insulation square. The tines were thick, and he was being supremely gentle as he worked it through her black tresses. That's when she realized her hair didn't look greasy any longer. Also, she couldn't be sure because of her messed up brain, but she might be clean all over.

Was that why she was naked? Had he bathed her while she was unconscious?

Had she vomited all over herself? *Dios mio*, the thought made her flush with embarrassment.

Not only had this soldier been caring for her, but he also cleaned her up and was even working out the knots in her hair. She wanted to ask so many questions but didn't have the voice for anything other than a barely audible, "Thank you."

His purring changed pitch slightly and he said something that didn't translate, but she thought he might have understood what she said. Relaxing into her fluffy bed, she let the Talin groom her. She'd save her worrying for when her brain started functioning properly.

CHAPTER 8

***Advanced Squad Delta 223—Mission Q73 Report (Excerpt)**
When we decided to bring all the humans onboard the ship, it was
difficult to figure out what their family structure was. They were
constantly hugging, holding, and touching each other. There was
even some argument among my crew over which female the cub
belonged to because so many of the adults cared for him.
Eventually, we realized the cub belonged to the same female with a
recently birthed cub. Due to having two cubs, Norrium insisted we
put her in one of the more spacious rooms with only two other
females. Norrium seemed to have picked well because the females
were quick to settle in together.*

*We made sure to house as many as we could on the same floor, but
are not going to give them access to the rest of the ship. We set
aside one large room that many of them can use to gather in if they
feel the need to be together. I'm pleased to report they all seem
satisfied with their assignments.*

***This passage was redacted from the submitted report**: I've
decided to keep Brave in my room. She's been living here since the
INT was implanted and seems content with the nest I've built her.
She's even sought out my warmth and embraced me several times.*

*As I've stated previously, humans touch each other as a sign of affection and bonding. The fact that Brave touches me as she might touch another human is a clear indication she's including me in her sphere of affection. It's a unique feeling when a human voluntarily touches you. Their diminutive hands are soft, dexterous, and quick to perform a petting motion as if it's instinctual with them. While she sleeps, Brave will seek me out and pet me with her hands or wrap her arms and legs around me. I'm careful not to hurt her, but several times I've thought she was even aroused and interested in being mounted. I'll admit I've been tempted.**

Ari awoke to find herself snuggling Boss. He was in the nest of bedding with her, his head propped up by a bunch of very smooshed pillows. How heavy was that head?

She was half sprawled across him with most of her upper body on his chest and one of her legs draped over his thigh. Her face had been nuzzling into the crook of his neck. As she lifted her head, she realized she'd been sleeping with her nose pressed to that slip of exposed skin between his neck and shoulder plates.

What was it about that bit of skin she liked so much?

He had one arm curled around her while using the other one to manipulate his Ident cube. When she moved, he looked at her and started purring. Her sex was pressed against his side and both the sound and the faint vibrations of the purring affected her brain and her clit with a vicious punch of lust.

The tendrils had made the purring feel good before, but now they'd shifted. It didn't feel good. It felt fantastic. The scent of hazelnuts filled her nose and somehow the tendrils connected that smell to her sexuality as well. She'd never been turned on by smells before, but suddenly she couldn't get enough.

Lifting herself up on shaky arms, she moved closer to the source of the smell—his face. He went perfectly still and she closed her eyes as she put her nose to his cheek.

There it was!

She let out a moan and licked his cheek. She expected him to taste like the hazelnuts she smelled, and he did, but only a little bit. The rest of his flavor was hard to describe—masculine and sensual.

He was still purring, but a low growl rumbled out of his chest as he spoke. "…rut…compatible…aware?"

The word *rut* registered in her head as another word for sex. Combined with the words *compatible* and *aware* it meant he was probably worried he'd hurt her and maybe concerned about consent.

Awww, that was sweet. But if he kept purring like he was; there was no question, she was both ready and willing.

Unless his dick had a barb.

Reaching down she blindly groped his crotch. Her fingers encountered smooth, hard flesh and it took her a moment to realize Talins must keep their genitals in a flesh pouch. As she explored, she found the opening and slid her hand in. She finger encountered a hardening cock that felt very close to human. The head was more bulbous, and ridges lined both sides and the top. To her relief she didn't find a barb or anything that might do damage.

All she felt was a thick handful of man-meat she wanted to play with.

The purring changed in pitch and tone, causing her tendril-wrapped brain to shoot intense zings of pleasure down her spine. She gasped, and only when the big Talin looming over her jerked did she realize she must have tightened her grip on him.

"*Lo siento*," she apologized and started exploring again with more care. He grew harder under her touch until the flesh pouch was too tight for her hand. Reluctantly, she tugged her hand free and looked down the line of his body. The head of his plumping cock was emerging.

Would he taste like hazelnuts there too? She needed to know.

Wiggling down she heard a strange percussion sound but that didn't last long, and then the purring changed pitch and got louder. He didn't move to stop her, so she took that as tacit agreement.

She licked over the bulbous head, causing Boss to jerk and say something in a deep needy voice. She was happy to report that like his face, he dick tasted like hazelnuts and sexiness.

Eager for more, she licked and nibbled the head, feeling it grow even fatter from her attention. Soon the flesh pouch had retracted more, and revealed a gorgeous cock. She licked at it, enjoying the way it tasted as well as the way Boss gasped.

He moved a little under her, and she worried that she'd hurt him. Raising up, she caught sight of his erection and a heavy seed sack springing free of the pouch. Oh, she wanted to play with those!

Carefully, she cupped the seed sack in one hand. Unlike the rest of him, this skin was soft and easy to knead with her fingers. The weight of it felt good in her palm, even if it was too big for her to grasp as a whole.

Hmmm, would this taste more like hazelnut or less? Inquiring minds wanted to know.

Before she could lean over and taste him there, the world shifted and she was suddenly on her back with Boss looming over her.

"Hey, I wasn't done," she protested.

The increased tempo and change of pitch to his purring as he moved to kneel between her legs made her eyes roll back in her head. The sounds caused pleasurable waves of heat to move through her body. Her breasts felt heavy, and her nipples tightened even as her clit started throbbing with need.

"…you…touch…show?

Because the purring felt so good it took her a minute to understand what he was trying to tell her.

"You wanna make me feel good?" she whispered with a moan. "Fuck yes!"

Unabashed, she parted her legs and reached down. Pulling her labia apart she showed him her sex. She'd closed her eyes to keep from getting dizzy but sensed him moving closer to her. His warm breath wafted across her throbbing core, making all kinds of sensation riot through her system. Then he went still.

"On second thought," she said as she moved to finger herself. "I don't have time for show and tell. I need satisfaction now."

He didn't move as she used her right hand on her clit and her left hand on the entrance to her pussy. *Dios mio* that felt fantastic! She really wished she had a third and fourth arm so she could massage her aching breasts at the same time.

Something warm and viscous dripped on her thigh and the smell of hazelnuts saturated the air. to her shock that was enough to push her over the edge into orgasm. Crying out, she arched her back as pleasure sizzled through her. She remained rigid for a few seconds, trying to draw it out for as long as she could, and then collapsed bonelessly among the pillows.

Boss's purring had gotten even more intense, and before the aftershocks of the first orgasm had waned, she felt another building. She'd had a healthy libido before everything went to shit during the Final Cataclysm, but this level of sexual intensity was new. It was both outrageous and wonderful.

INT tendrils were the best and worst things ever!

Whimpering a little because that first orgasm had only taken the edge off, she moved to put her hands on her throbbing bits. When she encountered hard Talin flesh, she opened her eyes to find Boss had put his face only an inch from her weeping, needy sex. The sides of his face glistened as if thick, clear oil had been poured over his cheeks.

"...here?" he grunted and then licked a tongue over her clit.

"Here!" she echoed, copying the one word she understood from that short sentence as her hips moved on their own accord. "Here more!" she demanded.

He laved his tongue all the way from her pucker to her clit making her gasp. His tongue wasn't completely smooth like a human's, it had slight bumps on it. Nothing rough or harsh, but enough texture to make everything he was doing feel so much better. She couldn't remain still as he licked at her. Boss must have wanted her to stop because he grasped her hips to hold her steady.

Then he dined on her.

"You guys get full marks for quick learning and attention to detail," she gasped out as he switched between licking to sucking.

He even speared his long tongue deep inside of her and made hungry sounds as if she was a delicacy he couldn't get enough of.

With her hands now free, she cupped her breasts to squeeze and knead them, occasionally rolling her nipples between her fingers. The thick liquid on his face rubbed onto the skin of her thighs and belly as his face moved against her. Where the liquid touched, she felt warm, as if it had self-heating properties. She couldn't be sure if that was true or if it was the tendrils, but it didn't matter because it felt so damn good.

Reaching down, she rubbed her fingers in the oily substance. Once both hands were coated, she went back to massaging her breasts and nipples. The oil heightened the sensations of ecstasy and pushed her over the edge.

"Oh fuck!" she cried out. Another orgasm pulsed through her, sending spasms of pleasure throughout her body. Boss didn't stop licking and sucking on her. Even after she went limp, he kept at it until she placed a hand on the top of his smooth head.

Lifting off her body, he noticed the oil on her breasts. Leaning over he took an experimental lick across her nipple. She couldn't help it as she gasped and arched, her hands coming up to grasp the back of his head and urge him to continue.

What was going on with her? After two orgasms she should be sated. Hell, she should be unconscious. But no, after one little lick of that textured tongue over her breasts she was ready for more. If she wasn't so busy flying high, she might be concerned.

He drew one of her nipples into his mouth. The hint of sharp teeth against her skin heightened the way he was pulling and sucking on her flesh. His mouth did more than tug at her nipple, it stimulated her all the way down to her clit, making her moan. She cried out when one of his hands covered her other breast and the claws lightly scraped across her skin.

Her cry must have startled him because he tried to draw away but she held his head and hand in place until she was sure he wouldn't stop. His erection was brushing against the inside of her leg as he moved and suddenly, more than anything, she wanted that beast inside of her.

She managed to wrap her legs around his waist, trying to maneuver his cock into place without using her hands. He didn't seem to notice what she was doing at first, but then he went perfectly still. She stopped moving as he reared up and easily pulled out of her grip, but she kept her legs locked around his waist.

He stared down at her, breath heaving in and out of his lungs. Her slick combined with his oil covering his face. It worried her that he wasn't making a sound, not even a purr. Why had he stopped and gone silent? Had she pushed too far and crossed some boundary? Was he angry and her?

Tears pricked her eyes. She'd been so close again. Everything had felt perfect and wonderful, and now it felt like her pleasure was a house of cards that had collapsed around her. Wishing she could simply disappear, she waited and watched him.

With slow, careful movements, he took her hand and guided it to his cock. The moment her fingers wrapped around it, he let go.

"Sure?" His one word question filled her with relief. He was making sure she wanted this part of him too.

"Sure!" she assured him, running her hand up and down his shaft.

He made a loud, but mercifully brief percussion sound before the fast, low-pitched purring took over again.

"Sure," he echoed and lowered himself down.

"About fucking time," she sighed out and arched up to meet him.

CHAPTER 9

Advanced Squad Delta 223—Mission Q73 Report (Excerpt)
Humans will go through ruts where they feel a powerful urge to copulate, at least the females will. Brave entered into rut as she was recovering from having her INT implanted. Not only did her scent change but she was also wanton with her advances and demands. Unlike Talins, humans are quick to demand what they want from a partner.

__This passage was redacted from the submitted report__: I helped Brave through her rut. She was nearly insatiable for a time. The human capacity for sexual pleasure is immense. Be warned: they can cause us to become highly aroused as well, and it's difficult to maintain control. *

  Bazium knew he shouldn't. It was one thing to pleasure Brave as she suffered through her rut, but having intercourse with her went a step beyond. If he found pleasure, he couldn't pretend he was doing this for her own good. Before now he'd convinced himself this was only about making Brave comfortable. Even after his mating shaft and seed sack fully emerged, he could deny his own desire.

His body was displaying an instinctive response, nothing more. He might find everything about Brave's body sexual and exciting, but he was convinced he could hold himself back. Remain aloof and clinical as he helped her orgasm with his mouth and hands.

Nothing in the literature the Orloks had on humans had indicated they went through periods of heightened sexual need, but Bazium had evidence to the contrary under him.

Evidence that smelled luscious, tasted succulent, and felt more wondrous than anything he'd experienced before.

With his mating shaft poised at her hot, soft entrance, he paused, hunting for the control he'd lost from one second to the next.

He shouldn't do this. He should go into the cleansing room and wait until his mating shaft retreated back into his flesh pouch. Then he could wrap a sankin around himself to keep it from emerging again. It would be uncomfortable, bordering on painful, but it would keep him from crossing an invisible but significant boundary with Brave.

But she wants this. Why am I hesitating?

"If I do this, I'm no longer helping you," he whispered into the air, answering his question out loud. "I'm coupling with you. I run the risk of my disgrace becoming public. And I can't even ask you to keep it a secret because we can't truly converse yet."

"…to…up? Sure!" as she talked, she tightened her legs around his waist.

Her words made no sense but her tone and actions were clear. Start moving or she'd move so she could enjoy herself some other way. Her demands made all his tortured thoughts and worries vanish. He'd deal with the consequences in the future. Right now was for the two of them.

Right now was for pleasure.

"Yes, Brave," he groaned out as his rumble of arousal started up again. "You can have all of me."

Gripping her hips to keep her still, he started easing inside of her. Hot, tight flesh engulfed his mating shaft, causing him to hiss out a breath. He was half worried he would hurt her from their size difference and half worried he wouldn't be able to stop even if she cried out in pain.

As the head of his mating shaft disappeared, Brave threw back her head and moaned. Her hands fell to the bedding, gripping the blankets with white knuckles. Fascinated, he watched her breasts rise and fall with her panting.

The scent glands in his cheeks were already filling again. Brave's body was almost completely covered in his bonding oil. Shouldn't his scent glands be empty by now?

Even as that thought went through his head more oil trickled down his cheek. A drop of it hit Brave's belly, but she didn't even notice. She was too busy trying to pull him deeper inside of her with her legs around his waist.

He didn't move until she opened her eyes and looked at him, her brows furrowed in an expression he'd learned meant frustration or worry.

"I need you to look at me," he demanded, a fierce possessiveness driving him. "Watch me, little Brave. Don't close those amber eyes again, my sweet human."

As he spoke, he slowly pushed himself inside of her while observing every nuance of her expressions and vocalizations.

Her breath caught and he stopped moving. She said something and urged him on with her legs, clearly indicating she wanted more.

This time he didn't stop until he was fully inside of her, gripped tightly by her hot sheath. She felt so good he couldn't even pull breath into his lungs for a moment. He'd never felt such sweet torture.

"You're so perfect, my human. My Brave," he whispered. "I hope you want me even after your rut is over."

The thought that she might never touch him again after she was finished with her rut didn't bear thinking about. For a Talin who'd never felt much affection for anyone but his crew, he'd grown fond of this human rapidly and without restraint.

It was as frightening as it was glorious.

He started moving, pulling himself out and then slowly working himself back into her. Bonding oil dripped down onto her sex and his mating shaft. She gasped at the added sensation. Gathering some of the bonding oil onto his fingers, he rubbed it over the little nub that seemed to be the heart of her pleasure.

She moved restlessly under him while repeating the same word over and over again. Her hands reached up to grip his shoulders to pull him down on top of her. His little human must want his weight on her, but he didn't want to do that. He was so much bigger he'd crush her. Instead, he leaned forward and fit his mouth over her breast again while thrusting home in one smooth motion.

She screamed and her velvety walls pulsed around him. He recognized the cry from the other times she'd climaxed. Her body shook and he became perfectly still, unwilling to ruin her pleasure. It was a fight to maintain control, but for his Brave, he'd do it.

When her body finally relaxed and wasn't milking his mating shaft any longer, he began thrusting.

"…you…again?"

"Can you reach climax one more time for me, little Brave?" he asked.

As he spoke to her, he worked his hands under her back and lifted her onto his lap. Her feet came to rest on the bedding around them as her legs fell to either side of his thighs. He kept her supported with one arm under her backside and another around her back. Pressed chest to chest now, she languidly wrapped her arms around his neck. Her mouth went to the slip of exposed skin at the base of his neck and licked.

"Oh, dear ancestors, do that again!" he begged and craned his neck to the side in an effort to give her better access. Understanding what he wanted, she made a huffing sound he knew was one of amusement and did it again. Then she started to suck and nibble on him too.

He had to focus to keep from tightening his arms too much around her delicate body. But he could no longer restrain the needs of his mating shaft. Rising up on his knees, he held her body against his chest as he moved his hips under her. Her moan encouraged him until he was thrusting quickly, the sound of heavy breathing and flesh slapping flesh filling the room.

"…I…now!" she cried out then attacked his neck with gentle ferocity.

He couldn't hold back any longer. His rhythm stuttered as pleasure flooded his system. Nothing he'd done with other Talins ever equaled what he was experiencing now. He wanted to roar with the intensity of it all, but his voice was caught in his chest. His chestbox was frozen and his backplates went immobile while fully extended out of his back. For a breathless moment his entire body was motionless. Everything was so intense it bordered on pain.

In that moment he felt closer to her than he'd ever felt to another living being. A sense of perfect perfection washed over him as the pleasure caused his entire body to shudder.

Then she cried out again, her body convulsing in his arms. Her hot sex gripped him tightly, drawing out his climax as she found her own peak again. He could feel his seed filling her to the point were it was squeezing out from around his mating shaft.

He held her tightly as they slowly came down from the high. She went lax in his arms, snuggled her face against him, and mumbled something as she patted his shoulder. She must finally been stated because she went limp, her head resting on his shoulder.

He was reluctant to move while he was still firm and inside of her. When his mating shaft finally began to soften and retract back into the flesh pouch, he reluctantly separated their bodies. Settling his human into the nest, he debated fetching a cleansing cloth to wipe her down. Her body was covered in his bonding oil, but she didn't seem bothered by it. The sight of his seed visible between her thighs filled him with a sense of pride and possessiveness. He wanted her to wear his fluids on her skin. It was as if he'd marked her as his.

It was primitive and satisfying—both emotions wholly inappropriate for a modern Talin.

She mumbled something and tugged at him without opening her eyes. Guided by her tugs he lay down, and she was quick to drape herself over him. Within a few submarks of making herself comfortable, she was asleep.

Bazium was reluctant to close his eyes. His body was ready for rest, but he didn't want to lose this sense of peace. After fighting off fatigue for as long as he was able, he succumbed to sleep as well, comforted by the knowledge that his little human would be there when he woke up.

CHAPTER 10

The sound of one of the human cubs out in the hall woke Bazium. He was lying on his back, and Brave was curled up against him. One of her small human hands was resting on his chest and twitching a little as she slept. He wasn't surprised she was sleeping through the noises in the hall. They'd rutted three times during the last rotation, and he'd lost count of the times she'd climaxed during each rutting session. The last time she'd fallen asleep he could tell it had been a deeper slumber than before.

A sharp cry made him move from his comfortable position. Brave made a soft protesting sound but didn't fully wake as he moved pillows into the spot he'd vacated. She grabbed onto the pillows and settled back down. Once he was sure she was comfortable, he pulled on his pants and hurried out the door.

In the hall he found Norrium chasing the human cub. For a moment Bazium worried something had gone wrong but then noticed Norrium was rumbling out a mischievous sound.

That's when he realized they were playing.

The cub was sprinting full tilt toward Bazium while looking back at Norrium. The young human wasn't even aware he was standing there. Meeting his gaze, Norrium slowed his pace even more.

"Pick him up and toss him to me," his second in command instructed.

Bazium expected a scream of fear from the cub when he lifted him high in the air, but instead the human made a sound they'd learned was one of joy. With care, he heaved the tiny human into the air. Norrium could have grabbed the cub early in his flight, but he waited until the little body had started descending before snatching him out of the air and setting him on the ground.

Bazium expected the cub to start running again the moment Norrium set him down. Instead, the cub lifted his arms at Norrium and hopped a few times, all the while making his high-pitched sounds of happiness.

"This means he wants me to carry him," Norrium explained as he lifted the cub back up into his arms. "This one loves to play. By the way all the humans react to him, I assume most cubs are like this."

"Where is the dam or sire?" Bazium asked as he critically examined the cub. He looked healthy and seemed completely relaxed despite being surrounded by Talins with no other human nearby.

"I don't think he has a sire," Norrium said. "Because his dam is the one with the newborn cub, I've noticed many of the other humans take turns playing with this older cub. I believe humans might practice communal child rearing. Or the others are trying to fill in for a missing sire. Either way, when the cub started engaging with me, I acted as the other humans had. This is the first time I've taken him away from the other humans to play, but no one seemed worried."

As Norrium talked, the cub was holding his face with his tiny, clawless hands and speaking in an earnest tone. Human cubs were even more adorable than the full-grown adults. What was the cub trying to tell Norrium with such a solemn manner?

Soon Brave's INT would finish growing and would start successfully processing language. Once they picked up the equipment, they'd be able to download the humans' language into their systems and everyone would be able to communicate. He intended to buy all the humans INTs also. More ability to understand each other could only help everyone.

He hoped the humans had the ability to understand complex political and economic issues. He thought about the communication from command that he'd gotten while caring for Brave during the worst of her illness. He had sent them a preliminary report but not the full mission report; he wouldn't be writing that until they were traveling back to Talarian. The response to his preliminary report had been both positive and troublesome, filling him with conflicting emotions and urges.

He needed to consult his crew about it before making any decisions.

The cub's bright laughter as Norrium pretended to bite one of his hands drew Bazium out of his thoughts.

"Are all the humans on board now?"

"Yes," Norrium said as he shifted the cub around again. "We filled up deck three, and used five rooms on deck four. But those two decks have connecting stairs, so it's easy for the humans to move between decks."

"That was a good plan as those areas can easily be sectioned off without restricting the human's access to each other," Bazium said with a rumble of approval.

"I already took the liberty of reinstalling the blast doors for that area," Norrium explained. "We've been keeping it closed during the humans' rest cycle or when none of us are available to watch over them."

"Well done," Bazium replied. "Did the humans resist coming on board?"

Norrium sounded a displeased rattle but stopped the moment the cub startled in his arms. With a loud teasing rumble, Norrium tossed the cub into the air and caught him again. The hallway filled with the cub's laughter.

"Most of them were easy to herd here, but a few didn't want to go. Tarrian's human, Hurt, and two others were quick to talk to them and seemed to be instrumental in coaxing them on board."

"I wouldn't have expected that from Hurt after witnessing what she's like when she gets upset," Bazium commented.

"Whatever medicine Sapurian is giving her made a difference," Norrium explained. "She's very different now. She and the two others that Hesarium had dubbed Tall and Helpful have been indispensable."

"Tall?" Bazium questioned with an amused rumble.

"Well, he's tall for a human," Norrium said, echoing Bazium's amusement. The cub in his arms said something that sounded impatient. Unclipping his Ident, Norrium said something to the device and a holo of a golax migration appeared. Then Norrium handed the Ident to the cub. The cub murmured something as he became transfixed by the image.

"He likes to watch vids of animal migrations," Norrium explained. "If I need a break from playing, I often put on one of these holos to entertain him."

"It works well," Bazium noted and then went back to their earlier conversation. "I'm impressed there weren't more issues. I didn't think they'd be so calm."

"We had one female grab the door to their communal room in the compound and refuse to let go. They're so fragile we were afraid we'd hurt her if we pulled too hard. Hurt, Tall, and Helpful all talked to the female and she did eventually let go. Helpful and Tall walked with her all the way to the room we assigned her."

"And their health?" Bazium questioned.

Norrium made a rumble of assurance. "Sapurian has been scanning and treating about three or four of them each day."

"That's excellent progress. And they've been fine with Sapurian separating and scanning them?"

"They seem to understand what we're doing. Some were even eager to let Sapurian scan them. Hurt, Helpful or Tall were quick to accompany anyone who seemed reluctant. It's worked well. I'm sure those three understand what we're trying to do. How is Brave doing?"

"Recovering well," Bazium said and tried not to think of the pleasure they'd shared. A good Talin didn't engage in sex often, not because it was considered dirty but because intercourse was perceived of as a waste of time. Once married, Talin parents gave their genetic material to a cresh, and the Talin children were grown in artificial wombs. Talins didn't birth or raise their own children. That didn't benefit the empire, clan, or family. Wanting those things was considered selfish.

Generations ago a Talin monarch had started the trend and within his lifetime, it had been codified into law.

"Can she understand you yet?" Norrium asked as the vid of the migration finished and the cub pressed the Ident back at him. Norrium clipped the Ident to his belt with one hand and set the cub down with the other. The moment the cub's feet touched the ground he started climbing up Norrium's body. The male's nonchalance told Bazium this must be another game they'd developed.

"Not really," Bazium admitted. "A word or two at most. But I can tell she's starting to feel better."

"As soon as possible you need to take her to visit the other humans," Norrium encouraged as the cub used his belt to continue climbing. "I believe they might be worried. Tarrian has been keeping Hurt in his room during the rest period, and he caught her trying to sneak out several times. The other humans have repeatedly tried opening the blast doors when we aren't there. I'm convinced their actions are exploratory only, but it might settle them to see Brave."

"As soon as she wakes, I'll carry her to that section," Bazium confirmed. "I'm going to check to make sure she still slumbers. See if everyone else is free and we can meet in the control room. We all need to talk," Bazium told Norrium.

Keeping up the playful rumble, Norrium focused his gaze on Bazium. "Is this about the message that came in from command?"

Bazium sounded a rumble of assent. "It is. I'll tell everyone together as it will be easier that way, and we can discuss what to do.

"Of course," Norrium said and swung the cub up from where he was dangling off the back of his belt and onto his shoulder. The cub waved his arms and legs around while he made his musical happy sounds. They echoed through the hall even after Norrium had turned a corner with the cub.

He could easily become accustomed to that sound.

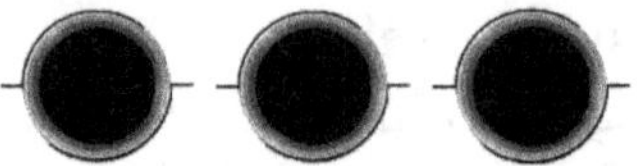

"The humans don't fall under any of the normal categories," Bazium said the moment everyone was in the command room. One of the displays in the wall was showing images from all the vid captures set up on decks three and four. With a quick scan of the display, any of them could make sure all the humans were fine.

The interesting thing was that his men were glancing at the display as much as he was. It was apparent all of them had quickly become entranced by the humans. Even Hesarium, the often-quarrelsome weapons expert, had grown more serene with the addition of the humans.

"They can't be considered prisoners because they are noncombatants," Norrium guessed.

"Correct, but there's more. They have no homeworld or cohesive government. It turns out they destroyed their own planet, so the External Affairs Council doesn't want them as laborers on any of our colonies."

"But they're good workers," Sapurian argued. "They kept this mining compound going even after everything started falling apart on them. I don't know what happened to their homeworld, but it could have been damage their ancestors did and later generations ended up suffering for it."

"We might never know," Bazium said. "But whatever the reason, the External Affairs Council has made a final ruling. They don't want the humans to work at any Talin installations. And we can't get clearance for them to come back to our homeworld because they don't have a government to negotiate residency with."

Talarian, the Talin homeworld, was notorious for not even allowing Talins who didn't have family compounds to live on planet. That made it rare to see a non-Talin there for more than a quick political or diplomatic visit.

"What about one of our colonies?" Norrium asked. "My family has a compound on Tovor Colony and that planet has a lot of room for population growth."

Now it was time for Bazium to give them the worst of the news. "Even if we could get the Colony Assembly to agree, the War Committee already sent out an information packet about the new species. They didn't include much, but the packet did lead the External Affairs Council to label humans as destructive."

"Destructive?" Norrium sounded a rattle of frustration. "That means no colony will allow them to live there."

"It gets worse," Bazium said with a regretful rumble. "At my request, command tried to see if any other civilizations wanted to take them, but the only places that responded were slave auction houses."

All of his men sounded angry rattles. Bazium couldn't blame them. He was frustrated too.

"Slaves?" Tarrian questioned with a loud, outraged rattle. "Slavery is abhorrent."

While all Talins might agree with Tarrian, they also didn't try to stop the slave trade. It was even legal to transport slaves in some areas of the Talin Empire as long as they weren't going to be there permanently.

"I don't know what to do," Bazium admitted to his crew. "We can't take them back to Talarian or any of our colonies, I don't want them to end up as slaves, but where else can we go with them?"

The normally taciturn Hesarium spoke up, surprising them all. "They aren't welcome in the Talin Empire as sentient, independent entities," he announced. "But what about livestock?"

They were silent for a brief moment before all of them spoke at once, even Bazium.

"But they aren't livestock."

"How would that work?"

"We'd still need to get permission."

Hesarium sounded a rattle of annoyance and they all went quiet so he could speak. "Remember the Living Items of War law?" he asked them. "If we declare the humans livestock, we can claim them for ourselves under that law."

Bazium rumbled out a thoughtful sound as Norrium pulled out his Ident and tapped. The Living Items of War law was passed many solars ago when Bazium was still in training. A squadron of soldiers had found themselves in charge of a deserted Sepera colony where livestock were left behind to roam around.

Wealth amassed during war was supposed to be collected and assessed by a member of the External Affairs Council and then allocated appropriately. Waiting for someone from the External Affairs Council to arrive meant there was no clear command about what to do with the animals. By the time a representative made it to the outpost all the livestock had died.

The Living Items of War law stated that if there was no native to care for them, individual squadrons could claim livestock and pets as personal wealth. This was a way to cut through the red tape so valuable beasts or exotic pets didn't die a wasteful death.

It had never occurred to Bazium to label the humans as livestock. They might be a low intelligence species, but they were far more than mere beasts of burden.

Tarrian must have thought the same thing.

"Hurt isn't some dumb animal," he argued.

"None of them are," Hesarium agreed evenly. "But if we want to save them, we might need to turn them into livestock."

"Not livestock," Norrium argued, looking up from his Ident where he'd been scanning the law documents. "Pets. We need to label them as pets. If they're livestock we have to show usefulness, but as pets all we need to do is provide documentation that they're free of parasites and can tolerate Talarian temperatures and atmosphere."

They all looked at each other, considering the implications. "We'd have to put collars on them," Bazium pointed out. "If they've been termed destructive, we have to show we have control of them before bringing them onto Talarian."

Hesarium sounded an unhappy rumble. "None of them will like that."

"Even worse, we need to do it soon," Norrium commented. "The window of registering them under the Living Items of War protocols will close in only two more rotations. We have to take image captures of each of them, create detailed medical reports, and put ID collars on them. Do we even have collars that would fit them?" Tarrian asked. Bazium could tell the tech expert wasn't happy with this solution, but like him, he wasn't willing to let any of the humans become slaves. Bazium suspected his men had become as attached to the humans as he had.

"The Veli ship will arrive soon. They'll have collars or will be able to make them," Bazium informed them.

"Is it a full market ship?" Norrium asked.

Bazium sounded a rumble of affirmation. "Full market ship with skilled staff and supplies. They'll have, or can make, anything we want."

"But do we want this?" Tarrian asked softly. "They are sentient beings, not beasts. Once we label them as pets, there's no going back."

"Do you think any of them will survive if we don't?" Hesarium countered. "If we make them pets, they're safe and taken care of. And we get to keep them. None of you can honestly say you want to be parted from the humans." He focused his gaze on Norrium. "I've seen you interacting with the cub. What happens when they get sold at a slave auction? The adult humans are fragile to begin with, but that cub? And the newborn cub? Neither of them will survive, and we all know it."

No one had a counter argument for Hesarium. It looked like they would be turning the humans into pets. He only hoped Brave wouldn't be mad at him for too long.

The thought of her refusing to touch him caused physical pain. When he explained why they'd done it she'd forgive him. She had to.

CHAPTER 11

Advanced Squad Delta 223—Mission Q73 Report (Excerpt)
The Veli ship was able to supply most things we needed to dress the humans in protective comfort. Many of them even came up to one or all of us and wrapped their arms around us and squeezed. Previously only injured humans or the cub had done this, but now we see it's a way to show affection even between adults. If an adult human clutches or clings to you, it's a strong indication they like you and perhaps even see you with the same affection they might have for another human.

Now I understand why Brave was trying to hold my arm or torso as she slept. She was attempting to cling to me for comfort. With this knowledge, the crew and I are quick to hold our arms out so the humans can decide to clutch or cling to us if they wish.

Ari woke up to find herself alone with a platter full of food. She managed a trip to the cleansing unit to relieve herself. Her brain still felt weird and she was prone to dizzy spells, but nothing so bad it was going to knock her on her ass.

After using the cleansing unit, she sat back down and realized she finally felt hungry. She was cautious at first, only nibbling a pieces of flat bread. But that stayed down so she dug in. The best part was that the food tasted like food! Not only that, she wasn't tasting color or feeling sounds. It seemed like her brain was finally returning to normal.

Then Boss walked back into the room.

The sound he made when he saw the half empty tray of food was vaguely sad. Before she could try to apologize for eating his food, he was wrapping her in a thick blanket and lifting her into his arms.

She'd tried to tell him to put her down and let her walk, but the language barrier was still a thing. As he walked, he spoke to her. So far, she was sure he was telling her to be still and calm, but that was all she could figure out.

To her surprise, he took her deeper into the ship, not toward the mining compound. When they went into an airlock, she got worried. Some species could survive in the vacuum of space for short periods of time, but humans weren't one of them.

"Uh, I'm not happy about this," she told him, staring at the door as he spoke to the display. He was purring and leaned his head over to rub his cheek against the top of her head. The scent of hazelnuts hit her nose and calmed her. He'd been caring for her, so he must know she wouldn't survive in space.

Then she heard familiar voices. Before they even appeared in the airlock with her, she was thrashing in Boss's arms. By the time Aubrey, Daniella, Mari, Santos, and many others were crowding through the airlock, Boss had reluctantly set her down.

"Ari!" Mari was the first to get to her, tears in her eyes.

"You're alive!" Santos exclaimed, rushing to wrap his long arms around her.

Soon people surrounded her; all of them talking, laughing, and hugging her. Boss didn't move away. He remained a solid, purring presence at her back and even helped her stay on her feet when Andres excitedly jumped on her.

Mari started asking questions once the initial excitement had died down. "Can you talk to them yet?"

Ari shook her head. "I get a word here or there, but not enough to have a proper conversation."

"You need to start negotiating with them as soon as you can," Mari reminded her with a frown. "Our future's at stake here."

"I'm sorry," Ari said with heavy sarcasm. "I've been so busy with my social schedule that I'd completely forgotten about our survival."

"How does your brain feel?" Daniella asked as she leaned over to look at the spot where she'd implanted the INT. "The insertion site looks like it's healed nicely."

"I still feel a little strange, but I'm not tasting sounds anymore," Ari answered, causing a few chuckles.

"It must almost be finished integrating. That's good. I was worried it wouldn't grow properly," Daniella admitted with an apologetic shrug.

"You and me, both," Ari said. "But it looks like it's going to work. Now, does anyone know why we're in this airlock?"

"They moved us onboard the ship a few days ago," Santos whispered. "You should have seen the meltdown Yasmine had."

It didn't happen often, but when Yasmine had an emotional meltdown, the results were often epic. There were even bets placed on when and how much damage she'd do.

"Who won the pool?" Ari asked, keeping her voice low.

Mari snorted. "Nina won, but partly because who could have predicted the compound would get invaded by a species we'd never seen before?"

"Hey, I had an infestation," Santos commented.

"You meant bugs or mold," Daniella countered with a grin.

"Infestation can cover bugs, mold, and military invasion," he argued.

They'd fallen into the familiar camaraderie and banter so quickly and easily that none of them noticed right away that the outside airlock doors were opening.

It wasn't until someone started screaming that Ari looked over to see what was going on. Even as she realized what was happening, there was a push of bodies as everyone tried to get back onto the ship, but several of the Talins stood in front of the closed inside doors. Boss was quick to sweep her back up in his arms so she didn't get pushed around.

The outside doors finished sliding open to reveal another ship's airlock, stopping the panic before it could really get started. As Ari watched, several Veli stepped into sight.

"Oh, well, okay then," Ari muttered. "A warning would've been nice."

On the heels of that thought was another that had her excitedly meeting the gaze of one of the Veli. She spoke in slow, clear Spanish. "*Hola,* some of your ships would come to Earth occasionally." Then she switched to slow, clear English. "Do any of you speak a human language?"

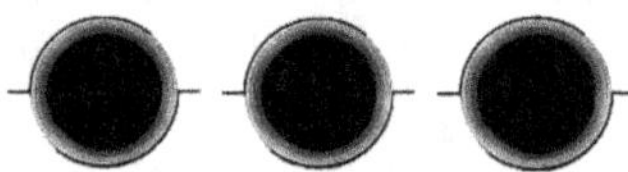

"Not even the Veli have our languages on file," Ari grumbled as Boss leaned over to pick her back up. "Not a single one. Some intergalactic merchants you guys are." She wasn't bitter; really she wasn't!

As Boss carried her into the main area of the Veli ship, she listened to the two of them talking. Her translator wasn't working any better with the Veli than with the Talin. Great, more guessing.

A question occurred to her: why were the Talins bringing all the humans on board a Veli ship?

Please don't be selling us. Please don't be selling us, she begged the universe. Veli weren't known as slave traders, but they buy and sell everything, so picking up some slaves here and there wouldn't be out of character for them.

As everyone gathered in the center of a large, well-lit room full of furniture, Ari watched the other Talins carefully urging the humans to sit on pads or chairs. That didn't seem congruent with being sold into slavery, so she kept her worries to herself.

Then the Veli started bringing in items. Two or three at a time the humans were given unisex wrap-around garments to try on. Some of them looked to be made of a light cotton-like fabric and others were thick and luxurious looking.

"You guys are getting us clothing?" she asked Boss.

He didn't answer her but kept purring and said something to one of the Veli. While that Veli dashed off, she could hear her friends all exclaiming about the quality and warmth of the clothing they were putting on.

"I would've liked some pants, but this is so soft and warm," Aubrey sighed as she snuggled down into something that looked like a long-sleeved coat that hung all the way to the floor.

Santo wrapped himself in one of the coats. "I can feel it self-heating. This is amazing!"

"I recognize it," Mari said as she eagerly pulled on a coat offered by one of the Veli. "This is faux fur that's been infused with nanos. This cloth is really expensive. I wanted to get a jacket made out of it but couldn't afford it. The thing would have cost the equivalent of half a year's pay."

"And we're all wearing them now?" Aubrey said, looking down at her coat with a frown. "Why would they give us something so expensive? Do you think they're going to take them away?"

"They'll have to fight me for it," Santos said with a grin, hugging himself. "This is the first time in forever that I've felt warm."

As they chatted, the Veli swept in and out, adjusting coats and cutting off the bottoms and ends of the sleeves with a little handheld device so they weren't too large for anyone. The machine did an excellent job of adding a decorative edge to the garment. When Aubrey noticed the edges could be customized, she took the device from one of the Veli, found an edge she liked, and handed it back. The Veli hesitated, but a few words from Tech and Aubrey got what she wanted.

The Veli and Talins kept up a constant dialogue. Occasionally, one of the Talins would point to an item or make a motion. It made Ari curious about what was going on besides getting them all clothing.

A Veli came in loaded down with dozens of boxes and unable to see their own feet. An old ratty coat made from a blanket had been carelessly discarded on the floor causing the Veli to stumble. All the boxes fell to the floor, spilling their contents everywhere.

"Oh!" Angel exclaimed as he picked up a pair of slippers. "I think the insides of these are made out of the same stuff as our coats!" Without hesitation he pulled off his worn boots and nasty socks to don a pair of the slippers. They looked a little big for Angel's foot, but he stared at them with a big grin on his face. "I was right, my feet are warming up!"

That caused everyone to do a mad dash for the shoes and start pulling them on. Soon the pile was diminished, but another Veli was quick to bring in more boxes so everyone got a pair that fit. Despite the fact they looked flimsy, the soles were made of something durable and strong.

They were probably the nicest pair of shoes Ari had ever owned.

Well, "provided" would be more accurate than "owned" because technically the Talins owned everything. It wasn't like she or any of the other humans could afford even a toe of one slipper.

"Is it just me, or does this feel a little like a uniform?" Mari asked. She was sitting on the floor next to Ari, her feet straight out in front of her to admire her new shoes.

"Now that you've said it," Ari murmured. "The whole matching clothing for all of us is uniform-like. But these will be way better than what Miox Minerals gave us."

Aubrey sat down next to them with a relieved smile. "If they're buying us uniforms, that must mean they're going to let us stay. Right?"

Ari shrugged. "Maybe. But if we get to stay on the mining compound, why move us aboard their ship?"

"Maybe to complete repairs on the compound," Aubrey suggested. "We'll know for sure soon. Your INT should learn Talin pretty fast now that it's almost done growing."

"Thank whatever deities might be close at hand," Ari said with feeling. "I'm really tired of not being able to talk to these guys."

"What else did you experience?" Aubrey asked. "Was it only colors that you could taste or did sound affect you also?"

Ari felt herself blushing as she remembered the way Boss' purring had made her go crazy. "Uh, nothing."

Mari narrowed her eyes. Leaning in close, she whispered, "Your face turned red! Spill. What happened?"

"I might have had sex with Boss," Ari answered only loudly enough for Aubrey and Mari to hear. She braced herself for their expressions to turn disgusted.

But their faces weren't horrified. They were fascinated.

"What's a Talin dick look like?" Mari asked in her typical blunt fashion, waggling her eyebrows.

"Mari!" Ari sputtered her blush turned supernova.

"I want to know too," Aubrey insisted and glanced over to where Tech was helping a Veli carry several boxes back through the airlock and into the Talins' ship. "Tech likes it when I sit on his lap, and sometimes I can feel, well, you know." Now Aubrey was blushing. "But he didn't do anything about it, and I wondered if I was even feeling his cock or if it might be some kind of tentacle or something. You know they're always telling us in astro training not to assume anything when it comes to other species."

"It's not a tentacle," Ari said, feeling a little better. "They have a very human-like dick, but it's in a flesh pouch and only comes out to play when it gets hard."

"Does it—" Aubrey started to ask something but Mari cut her off.

"Wait, he didn't force you. Did he?" Mari asked, anger making her voice low and harsh.

"No!" Ari was quick to assure her. While she didn't think Mari could kill any of the Talins, she really didn't want to challenge the woman's determination and ingenuity. "I really wanted it. The INT made his purring a super-powered aphrodisiac. Even before that I didn't mind being carried around. Then the INT temporarily crisscrossed my wiring and it was even better."

"I bet you're going to miss that part," Aubrey said with a grin. "Sounds like the crossed wiring had an awesome side benefit."

"It's still there, so maybe I'll get to keep it. But I'd rather not hear the color orange any more. It's jangly." That made the women chuckle. Mari's ire was extinguished as quickly as it had built.

Aubrey glanced over to her Talin walking back in. "You know, they've all been really gentle with us. I don't get the feeling of danger from any of them."

Mari nodded and pointed to where Riker was helping little Andres put on a miniature version of the wrap-coats all the adults were now wearing. The Veli must have just finished making it. Damn, that was adorable! He even had tiny little slippers too.

"He seems to have developed a fondness for Andres," Mari commented.

"Fondness doesn't even begin to cover it," Daniella told them as she joined the conversation by sitting between Ari and Aubrey. She looked at Ari. "What did you name that Talin again?"

"Uh, that one's Riker," Ari answered.

"Right, Riker. Second in command in Next Gen. Anyway, he really likes Andres," Daniella commented. "He played with him for hours last night. The kid was too wound up to sleep, and Liz and I were exhausted. I tried to keep Andres happy, but I kept falling asleep. Then Riker came in and started playing with him—high energy stuff like running around and tossing him up in the air. He kept glancing over at Liz to make sure she wasn't upset. I think he deliberately did all the playing within eyesight so she wouldn't get worried. He didn't leave the room until Liz literally pushed the two of them out so we could sleep."

"I caught a little of that before Tech and I headed to bed," Aubrey said. "Riker was so patient with Andres. Even when he started crying because the globe they were playing with stopped displaying colors."

"Hold up, before you and Tech went to bed?" Mari said, eyeing Aubrey. "Want to elaborate on that? You said you haven't had sex, but are you two sharing a bed?"

Ari glanced at Daniella, but the woman wasn't scandalized at all with the idea of humans and Talins pairing up. Of course she wasn't. Daniella had taken several classes on xenobiology, and she probably knew a lot of different species humans were compatible with. It wouldn't be a stretch to conclude Talins were one of them.

"Tech likes to cuddle," Aubrey answered primly, unaffected by Mari's inquiry. "But we haven't done anything but snuggle together yet. And now that I know it can be done, I might push the issue a little." She breathed out a frustrated sigh. "It's been a while, you know?"

They all made sounds of agreement. When Daniella paired up with Christos, that left Santos as the only unattached male in the group. Santos was bisexual and up for a horizontal adventure with anyone when they'd first arrived at the compound. It wasn't uncommon for couples to invite him into their bed for an evening of fun. But then stress of their situation got to him. His over the top sexuality had taken a backseat to the everyday emergencies the compound created. Maybe now he'd start accepting invitations again and they'd get their flamboyant Santos back.

Thinking about sex and pairing off made Ari sweep her gaze over to where Nina, Charlotta, and Sofia were sitting close together talking. The three women had been together before they all got jobs with Miox Minerals. Despite the hardships, the three stayed together and were stronger for it. Ari envied them.

"Those three are the luckiest of us all," she muttered. Mari and Aubrey turned to see who she was talking about.

"Our happy thruple," Mari said with a nod. "So sweet and perfect together it almost gives you diabetes. I mean, it's not natural that they never argue. All couples argue. You'd think disagreements would be even more common with thruples. But no, not a single one. Not even a misunderstanding!"

"Back when Isidor was alive, I think he and Liz argued enough for everyone," Ari said with a wince. When Isidor had stormed off and accidentally gotten himself stuck in a section of the mine without radiation protection, no one had really wept for him. If anything, Liz had looked relieved.

"Tell me more about sex with Talins," Aubrey demanded, pulling them away from the unpleasant topic.

"You're like a termogot on the hunt," Ari said with a laugh. "I'll tell you all about it, but keep in mind that my brain was all weird at the time. I might not remember everything accurately."

"If it was good, I don't mind you getting poetic," Aubrey said.

"Okay, I'll tell you what his male parts were like, but that's it," Ari agreed. "I'm not giving you a blow by blow."

"Don't you mean thrust by thrust?" Daniella asked with a suggestive eyebrow wiggle, making them all laugh.

Grinning, Ari told them what she could remember about Boss's impressive cock. But as soon as she could she switched the subject.

While they talked, the Veli went around to make sure everyone had a pair of slippers, one of the wrap-around coats, and several unisex wrap-around garments to wear under it. Along with the clothing, each person received a small bag of goodies that included a comb, a gentle skin and hair cleanser, tooth cleaning gel and a few other odds and ends they had run out of months ago.

After that, everyone was herded off the ship with her and Aubrey being carried by Boss and Tech.

From what she could hear around her as they left the ship, all the items gave everyone confidence that the Talins were going to let them stay and work on the compound. They were in high spirits and most were at least smiling if not laughing and joking.

It reminded her of when they first moved to the compound. None of them had much, and their future was full of dangerous and hard work, but they were alive. Sometimes that had to be enough.

Maybe with these Talins, they could hope for more than simply surviving. This might be the start of a new and better era for the humans of Miox Minerals Compound A785-D.

CHAPTER 12

Advanced Squad Delta 223—Mission Q73 Report (Excerpt)
The humans might not rattle or rumble to show their emotions like Talins, but they have ways of making it clear when something is wrong. I'm not referring to when liquid comes out of their eyes, yelling in anger, or screaming from terror. They have other, more subtle, ways to show emotions.

They have a mood that is difficult to describe, but their entire attitude dims, and they'll stop interacting. They make few sounds and talk little. The halls become oppressively quiet without their lyrical conversations or musical laughter. We open our arms to invite them to clutch or cling, but none are interested. The cub seems unaffected by the mood of the adults, but his dam and the females close to her will hold him back so he can't play with Norrium.

My crew is deeply troubled by the change in the humans, and I must admit, it's difficult to concentrate on anything else when they are like this. Brave will hopefully wake soon and soothe them enough to restore previous relations.

Bazium watched Brave sleep. She still hadn't woken up from the medication they'd slipped into all the human's food yesterday. Everyone had roused from their nests the previous rotation, but she still slumbered.

He hadn't wanted to, but drugging the humans seemed the easiest way to slip collars around everyone's necks without a fuss. He and his men had been hopeful the humans would wake and, after a little upset, accept the collars.

They'd been so wrong.

Pandemonium was the best way to describe the humans' reaction. He and his crew hadn't been prepared at all for how upset the humans would be. Some cried but most of them were angry. They wouldn't let any of the Talins touch them. The dam of the two cubs kept her young near her and would strike out when Norrium tried to get close.

Bazium was forced to lock down not only the ship, but the humans' rooms as well. They'd already caught Hurt sneaking out with several other females.

After that he'd had Tarrian set up trackers in the rooms and halls. He also turned on the collars so they'd send out an alarm if taken off. The Veli had offered him collars that would shock the wearer if they attempted to remove them, but he couldn't stomach hurting the humans that way. Even now, with how troublesome and fractious they were being, he didn't regret his decision.

Then the humans had gone from angry to withdrawn. They refused to acknowledge the Talins. They wouldn't even speak when one of them was present. Bazium hadn't realized how much human voices had made everything better until they were gone.

He sat in the middle of the nest he'd created for Brave, waiting anxiously for her to wake up. Sapurian had checked on her several times and assured Bazium that her sleep was natural. He explained that the medication was probably more effective on her because of the INT, but it wasn't anything to worry about.

Then Sapurian had hurried back to the humans' sector of the ship. All of his men were there, trying to get the humans to favor them again. Norrium hadn't left the room that held the dam and cubs since they awoke. His second in command probably wouldn't be exiting that cabin until the dam allowed her cub to play with him again.

He couldn't fault Norrium for his fascination with the cub. The human cub provided so much joy it made him curious what interacting with Talin children would be like. Would they be as free and easy with their affections, or were Talins born reserved?

He couldn't remember much of his own childhood except being deeply lonely. But he had Brave now, so he never needed to be lonely again.

"I know you're going to be angry," he whispered to her slumbering form. "But I'll make it up to you. I'll buy you better omnie wraps and get all kinds of soft things for your nest. You'll never be cold again. Or hungry! As soon as you can talk to me, I'll make sure to only feed you the food you tell me you like the best. As much as you want any time you want it."

Only after he said the last part did he realize something important. He was eating again.

One of the most common and early signs of Fading was the loss of appetite, but since he'd been caring for Brave, food had started tasting good again. He was sure his human had chased away the disease with her soft touch and melodic laughter.

"You saved my life," he told her.

She mumbled something and then rolled on her side and snuggled more firmly against him.

That's when he made up his mind.

"We're going to save all of you," he told her. "Not just those of you here, but anywhere we can find you. I'm not sure how, but we'll find other humans and bring them to Talarian. I'm going to make sure humans don't go extinct. I promise."

A unique sound from his Ident told him that a Talin ship was within hailing range and messaging him. Freeing both his arms, he waited until Brave had resettled before grabbing his Ident.

The message was from the Mining and Processing Assessment Team assigned to take over the compound. According to their estimate, they were going to be arriving early.

He sent an acknowledgement of officially receiving the message and then sent another message to his crew. They'd already been working together to bring the humans home, but navigating Talarian laws and politics could be difficult. Tarrian had assured them his uncle was well connected with the Apogee Assemble and would help their requests get to the right people. But still, they all worried.

The team's early arrival meant he and his crew needed to push for permissions from the Committee of Safety and Standards as well as the External Affairs Council regarding the humans. The biggest issue was going to be space. None of them had compounds on Talarian big enough to accommodate all of the humans. They could split them up, but that would be a last resort.

Norrium had said he had an idea and to give him a few rotations to see if it could work. It looked like his second-in-command needed to work faster as they were rapidly running out of time.

Next to him Brave stirred. Setting down his Ident, he watched her slowly wake up. The way humans gradually came to consciousness fascinated him. Brave would open her eyes but it would take her several moments before she was cognizant of where she was. Then she would focus on his face and smile.

Human smiles should have been threatening. They put all their front teeth on display, but instead the facial expression made them appear open and guileless. When she was fully awake, she was careful to keep her teeth hidden. He hated to see her fighting a natural instinct he found charming.

He looked forward to the day he could tell her it was okay to smile. Or clutch him. Or eat without permission. Or any of the many things he wanted to say, including how much he adored her.

"How are you feeling, Brave?" he asked as she smiled up at him. He knew his soothing rumble was far louder than it should be, but the way she looked up at him with unguarded affection was all-consuming. He envied the way the humans were so quick to trust and form emotional bonds. The only individuals he felt any kind of true affection or kinship toward were his crew; even then, he was cautious.

"Hello?" she answered, her expression growing more excited as she woke up. She said a few more words in her human language as she sat up.

"I'm sorry, little one, but I didn't understand anything after your informal greeting," he answered slowly.

She frowned and then shut her eyes to concentrate before trying again.

"…help…mining…" Out of the three sentences she spoke, only two words were in Talin. Her INT had probably finished growing but didn't have Talin programmed. This INT was already picking up words, but it would take time for it to learn from scratch.

"I'm sorry, but you're still not communicating with me." He recognized the noise she made as one of frustration. "Don't fret. I'm sure you'll be able to talk soon. Besides, you didn't need to have the INT in the first place, but I can tell you're used to being bold. I'll need to keep a close eye on you to keep you from getting into any more trouble."

As he spoke, he drew her into his lap and placed her arms around his shoulders to encourage her to cling to him as she did often in her sleep. But it all went wrong when she moved to rest her head on his shoulder. The collar shifted slightly, making her aware of its presence.

Sitting up she felt around her neck, tugging at the collar and making loud sounds of outrage.

"That is only so we can protect you," he said, although it was useless. Only one word did get through, though, and it didn't seem to do anything to soothe her.

"*Protect?*" she screamed as she moved away from him. He let her scramble off his lap and to her feet, putting as much distance between them as the room would allow. "…protect!"

He was sure she'd bracketed the Talin word for protection with human insults. He didn't know the words, but the expression on her face and gestures with her hands were self-explanatory.

It looked like his human was as mad as the rest of them. He'd hoped Brave would be different, but that was asking a lot when they still couldn't converse. Waiting patiently, he let her stalk back and forth; she talked in angry loud tones as she tugged at the collar with one hand and pointed at him with the other.

When she finally began to calm, he stood. He'd finished messaging Sapurian with his Ident so he clipped it back to his belt.

His only solution was to let her see all the other humans wearing collars. He didn't know if her disposition would improve or decline, but he was out of options.

He picked up one of the blankets from the nest. She eyed him warily, both her dainty hands balled into fists. She looked angry enough to hit him if he approached.

Throwing the blanket over her without warning, he quickly wrapped her up. Her struggles didn't slow his actions, and soon her entire body below the neck was secured by the tightly wound layer of comforter.

She stopped struggling and grumbled aggressively as he carried her out of the room.

Sapurian met him in Med Bay and did a quick scan. The machine wasn't happy with the layer of blanket, but Sapurian didn't ask him to unwrap her.

"It looks like the INT is almost done growing. A few spots in her brain might be changed permanently. But nothing should affect her balance or any other vital systems. When we can better communicate with her, we can reassess her treatment needs," Sapurian reviewed the scans while discussing her results.

Relief filled Bazium that at least she was healthy.

"I know she understands a few words," he told Sapurian.

"The learning pace will only get faster," Sapurian assured him. "I'm not an expert in INTs, but I've been researching them, and even as soon as next rotation she should have basic communication skills as long as we keep talking to her." Sapurian rumbled in regret. "It might be better if she kept trying to talk to us also, but she probably won't. She looks as perturbed as the rest of the humans."

Bazium sighed an agreement. "She is."

"They have to forgive us," Sapurian scratched between his chest plates while lamenting the situation. "I hate that they're so angry. I miss their clutches and listening to them talk."

Bazium sounded a sympathetic rumble as he held Brave to his chest. He took it as good sign that she didn't try to bite the small bit of exposed skin at his neck. "Have you finished cataloging all of them?"

"I have," Sapurian assured him. "And I filed everything with both the Committee for Standards and Safety as well as the External Affairs Council. I had to give all of them individual names along with their stock numbers."

"Names?" Bazium asked with an amused rumble.

Sapurian sounded a rattle of resignation. "I started naming them after their individual personality traits like you did with Brave and Tarrian did with Hurt."

"As long as mine is Brave, I'm fine with the other names you've chosen. We can start calling them by their proper names as soon as we know them."

"Exactly, Sir," Sapurian said with an excited rattle. "I had to send everything through a long-distance relay, so we probably won't receive an answer until we've already left the mining complex."

"I'm going to check with Norrium to see how his plans are developing," Bazium commented. "And all of us will need to meet and discuss the future."

"I'll walk with you," Sapurian offered. "Norrium is in the room housing the dam, cubs, Loud, and Helpful."

"Loud and Helpful?" Bazium asked.

"Helpful is the female who was walking back with Brave in the hall. The one that probably helped install the INT," Sapurian explained. "And Loud is the petite female that often talks with volume so the others have no choice but to listen to her."

The descriptions were perfect and Bazium was easily able to picture the humans in question. "Ah, those two."

"Shall I have Hesarium meet us there?" Sapurian asked. "Brave can visit with the other humans while we talk."

Bazium rumbled his agreement. Sapurian messaged Hesarium to meet at the secured humans' section. The blast doors were now kept closed and secured at all times, and the hatches to the individual cabins were shut and locked. None of them wanted to risk an angry human sabotaging the ship.

The whole crew hoped to start unlocking the cabins again soon.

CHAPTER 13

Advanced Squad Delta 223—Mission Q73 Report (Excerpt)
Bringing Brave to visit with the other humans didn't lessen their anger over the collars. Loud even became aggressive with Brave as if she was to blame. I hope I haven't ruined Brave's relationship with the other humans.

"What the fuck?" Mari said the moment Ari was standing on her own feet and no longer a blanket mummy. "Collars? Really? Are we fucking slaves now?"

Daniella took Ari's hand and led her to a bunch of cushions on the floor as she addressed Mari. "Give the girl a minute. She probably hasn't been awake long and just got carried in here like a giant burrito." As Ari perched on some of the cushions, Daniella's eyes stared unfocused at a far wall as she murmured, "Burrito. Oh man, I miss burritos."

"Can we concentrate on the here and now?" Aubrey addressed Daniella as she sat down next to Ari.

"Yeah, the here and now," Daniella agreed with a frown. "Like why we were drugged and then collared. I mean, the drugging makes sense. They didn't want us fighting the collar. But why did they need to collar us at all?"

"Fuck if I know," Ari answered with a yawn. She'd spent all her rage earlier while yelling at Boss and pacing. He hadn't intervened until he wrapped her in a blanket and took her to see Lucky. Boss set her down and removed the blanket just as Riker had arrived with Aubrey. Now all five Talins were near the door having an intense discussion.

"I wonder what they're talking about," Daniella said as she watched the Talins talking.

She nudged Daniella to get her attention from the Talin Telenovela. "When is this INT going to start working?"

"It should be starting now," Daniella told her. "Unfortunately, if they don't have the equipment to download languages, it's going to be a while before the INT learns enough Talin. You need to get him to talk to you, or stay close when they're talking to each other. It will integrate faster that way."

"I don't understand why their INTs haven't learned our language," Mari commented, making them all frown.

"That's true," Ari agreed. "Why the heck aren't they speaking to us in bad, heavily accented Spanglish?"

"That's an excellent question and the only answer I have is that their INTs might not be programmed for learning," Daniella answered with a shrug. "If you're going to download all your languages instead of needing to organically learn them, you can use the smaller INTs."

"Are you telling me you had to stick a super-sized INT in my head?" Ari asked.

"Probably," Daniella said. "That was the first INT I'd seen outside of educational materials."

"So their INTs can't learn and my INT is taking its sweet-ass time." Frustrated, Ari fell back against the cushions with a loud growl. "In the meantime, we could be at a slave market before I'm ready for conversational Talin."

"That's a cheerful thought," Aubrey said dryly. Ari was impressed at how well Aubrey was handling this new captivity. The medication the Talins were giving her was superior to anything available back on Earth.

"I think you're missing the point that we're slaves now," Daniella said, pulling Ari's attention away from Aubrey. "Even when you can talk with them, it's not like we could buy our freedom. There is no Earth government that we could put them in contact with to negotiate on our behalf. We have no power or money, so that means we have no options. We can't take those steps even with the language barrier gone."

"We have options," Mari argued petulantly.

Ari sat up and focused on Mari. "What options?"

Mari looked equal parts confident and angry. "We could escape and find another place to live. The Veli are always looking for cheap labor for their factories. If I can get access to a universal comm array, I might even be able to get my old job back."

Aubrey shook her head sadly. "Escape? In what ship? And even if we could take control of this vessel, how long would it be until other Talin ships came looking for us? Let's face it. Going by what we've seen so far, they must have an impressive military. We aren't going to be able to simply steal a ship and get away with it."

"Then we escape later on another ship," Mari insisted. "We keep trying until we're free."

"Or dead," Ari snapped. "Mari, I don't like this any more than you do, but if we attempted an uprising right now, we'd be doomed."

"We need to plan something," Mari burst out loudly. She got up on her knees to be taller than Ari. "We can't sit back and let them do this to us. We have to fight back!"

Mari was leaning over Ari now in a typical intimidation display from a woman who stood shorter than everyone except Andres. She would stand when they were all sitting or get on a nearby chair or step. Any tactic to make herself a little bigger.

Ari was used to this behavior from Mari; she didn't feel threatened or intimidated by it. Mari's action was enough to draw the Talins' attention, though. They stopped talking, and Boss started walking toward them, making the aggressive percussion sound she'd heard before.

"Crap," Ari muttered and scrambled to her feet. She ducked behind Aubrey and said the only Talin word she remembered. "Protect!"

That stopped the Talin in his tracks and he sounded a rumble she thought might be confusion. "...protect...but...now?"

The INT registered the sentence as a question, but she didn't have enough words to comprehend more than that. Suddenly a few other words came to her.

"No now. No," she enunciated as clearly as she could. It was hard for her to form some of the sounds, but it must have been enough to make Boss understand she wanted to be left alone. He grumbled a sad sound and she almost felt guilty.

Then she felt the collar shift as she moved. Nope, she didn't feel bad anymore.

"No now…later," Boss said and with obvious reluctance returned to his group of Talins.

With Boss's attention no longer focused on them, the miners all sat down again. The interlude had one benefit, it had calmed Mari down. She was quick to sit while casting a wary eye over at Boss.

Then Daniella said something that got all their attention. "You know what? I don't think we're slaves."

Mari tilted her head and rolled her eyes sarcastically. "Oh really? You think they put collars on their guests?"

"No," Daniella said, ignoring the woman's harsh tone. "But do you remember dogs before they either all died or were eaten?"

"Of course," Mari said. "I had a dog as a child."

Daniella raised an eyebrow, and Ari remembered what Aubrey said about horses.

"You're saying we're the dogs?" Ari asked Mari.

"No, yeah. I think Daniella's on to something. Look at the way they've treated us. Until the collar thing, it was almost like we were being pampered," Aubrey said and then focused on Ari. "Remember how I said it all reminded me of how my grandmother used to talk about her horses. They were more than livestock to her. They were beloved pets."

"But I've had sex with one of them," Ari argued.

"Maybe your Talin is into bestiality," Mari teased, but then sobered when no one laughed at her joke. "Sorry, it sounded funny in my head, but not funny when I said it."

"Super not funny," Daniella agreed with a frown. Mari dropped her eyes and mumbled another apology.

"I don't know," Ari said slowly to Daniella. "The uncomfortable truth is you're making sense." If Ari was being honest, she wasn't sure how she felt about what Daniella and Aubrey were implying.

"You think?" Aubrey asked.

Daniella spoke up again. "When food got scarce, I know some people went without their full rations because they were sharing with their dogs."

Ari jumped in with her own memory. "When I was eleven, the Garcia's dog died, and the whole neighborhood held a funeral. She was the last dog on the island, and everyone was sad when she passed."

Aubrey nodded in agreement. "They want to hold us, cuddle us, give us things, and feed us. What is that if not a pet?"

"But what about the sex thing?" Ari asked.

"I don't know," Aubrey admitted. "Maybe they're into puppy play?"

"You mean like BDSM stuff?" Ari asked. She'd had a partner that enjoyed being tied up during sex, but that was the extent of her kinky knowledge. "I'm not super experienced, but don't think that's it."

"They could have really relaxed sexual taboos," Daniella interjected. "The Micvee will have sex with anything. They even have a species of trees on their planet that they'll copulate with. They don't have any concept of things they're not allowed to have sex with."

"What about consent?" Aubrey asked.

"I think the Talins understand that," Ari was quick to say. "I'm the only one who's gotten down and dirty with these guys. Right?"

Aubrey blushed, but nodded along with Mari and Daniella.

"And I was pushing for it," Ari assured them. "My consent was obvious. So they must understand the concept."

"And even now, with the collars on, they aren't making us do anything," Aubrey pointed out. "We're still being treated the same. And Tech even respected my boundaries when I didn't want him to touch me after I woke up with the collar. He didn't force the issue at all."

"Do you think the collars could mean something different to them?" Ari asked. "Like a gift?" When everyone stared at her with raised eyebrows, she shrugged her shoulders. "It was just a thought."

"Drugging, remember?" Mari pointed out. "If the collar meant anything besides some kind of ownership, they wouldn't have gone to the trouble of drugging us. They knew we wouldn't like it. That tells you all you need to know."

"Crap, you're right," Ari acknowledged. "I guess the question du jour is are we pets or slaves?"

"All of this is going to be so much easier when you can talk to them," Mari grouched with a frustrated sigh.

"No shit," Ari replied in an imitation of Mari at her most sarcastic. The other women cackled with laughter as Mari smiled.

"You know," Daniella mused. "I just realized that no matter what we've done, no one's been punished. When Santos got his collar off and the room door open, he wasn't punished or isolated. They put the collar back on and returned him to the room. They didn't even deny him or anyone else food."

"I want to say something, and I don't want anyone to get angry about it." Aubrey shot a trepidations look at Mari.

"What is it, Aubrey?" Ari asked before sliding her gaze to Mari. "We won't get upset. Will we?"

Mari didn't answer but she did make an encouraging gesture at Aubrey.

"Right." Aubrey took a deep breath. Then she spoke quickly as if afraid she wouldn't be able to get the words out. "I think we need to acknowledge that we're better off right now than we have been in the last year. I mean, I'm not happy about the collar, but you have to admit it might be a small price to pay for safety and security. We're getting food and medical care. And we're not being forced to work fourteen hours a day."

Daniella put a hand on Aubrey's. "I'm glad you said that, I've been thinking along the same lines. They gave us really nice clothes and shoes. I bathed with real soap. There was even lotion in the bag of goodies we received. Real lotion! I haven't felt this nice in years."

"Being a pet might not be a bad thing," Aubrey said with a smile. "If they keep treating us like this, it's better than anything we ever had back on Earth."

"You trust too easily," Mari intoned with a frown. "All these nice things come at their good will and mercy. Bad things might be coming. They could be treating us well now so we look healthy for an auction house. I think we need to keep working on an escape plan."

"I don't think I want to leave," Aubrey said softly.

"I don't think you get to make that decision for all of us," Mari countered sharply.

Daniella was quick to jump to Aubrey's defense. "Neither do you, Mari."

Then all looked at Ari for guidance. Mostly she agreed with Aubrey; being with the Talins was nice. She wasn't sure how feasible an escape would be, but it would be good to have more information.

"Mari, I want you, Santos, and Angel to see if you can set eyes on any star maps, even better if you can see where this ship will be going when it leaves the compound. Keep a look out for stations with slave and livestock auctions."

"It's going to take some time," Mari warned her. "They don't like to leave us on our own and they have vid captures in the rooms and hallways now."

"I don't agree we should leave, but I don't want to hold back anyone, so I might be able to help," Aubrey volunteered. "Sometimes Tech leaves me in the room by myself to nap. I can pretend to sleep and see if I can access the star charts. Those should all be in Common language or with symbols in Common."

Ari nodded at Aubrey. "Don't put yourself in danger, but find out what you can."

Aubrey's shoulders went back a little and her chin lifted. "I'm on it," she said with an unusual amount of confidence. It made Ari grin.

They talked a little more before Boss walked to them. Stopping at the end of the pillows, he dropped to his knees and sounded a loud purr while opening his arms to her. It was clear he wanted to hug her.

I am a fucking dog, she thought sourly and then almost laughed as she realized both parts of that statement were true. She was a pet that fucked.

She looked at her friends. "I guess it's time to go. So far he hasn't left me alone. The moment I can communicate; I'll ask him to bring me back here and we'll get Santos in here too. Hopefully by then we can have a conversation with the Talins."

Stepping out from the pile of blankets, she stood in front of Boss. She didn't reach out to hug him, but she didn't fight when he scooped her up against his broad chest. He made a happy sound and then went back to purring.

She had to tug at her collar to remind herself not to react. That damn purring was still affecting her in weird ways, but she refused to have sex with someone who drugged her and slapped a collar around her neck.

She might have gone out on some shitty dates when she was younger, but a girl had to draw the line somewhere.

Sticking to her "no sleeping with the enemy" rule was so much harder than she anticipated. He didn't push her for sex or even touch her intimately, but he refused to abandon the pile of pillows and blankets on the floor. Even after she'd taken his hand and led him to his bunk, he'd simply urged her back into her bed and settled in with her. He didn't force her to lie touching him, but he refused to be anywhere else but with her.

She'd briefly considered getting into his bunk, but he'd probably follow her and there was a lot less room in the bunk. Surrendering, she covered herself in a blanket and faced away from Bosshole. The earlier anger and interaction with her friends had exhausted her brain; she fell asleep while he tapped on his Ident next to her.

When she woke up, she was cuddled against him. She would have loved to be outraged. Unfortunately, he was in the same place, and she was an octopus cuddler. She had wrapped her arms and legs around him.

It didn't help that he was purring, and she could smell hazelnuts. Those two things would have drawn her to him, even in her sleep.

She'd never been attracted to a smell before now. She didn't think it was simply because her tendril-wrapped brain had turned it into an aphrodisiac, like the purring. Even before the INT, she'd started associating the smell of hazelnuts with warmth and safety. Who wouldn't cuddle with a hazelnut blankie after a year of starvation?

She was so messed up.

Briefly she considered feigning asleep. But that would be the coward's way out. Besides she needed to engage him to merge her INT technology with his language. Opening her eyes, she looked up to find his gaze focused solely on her.

Setting his Ident aside, he started purring. "…sorry…will be happy…not a long journey…"

Looked like she was getting even more words now. As he talked, she did as Daniella had instructed and tried not to focus too intently while letting the words flow through her brain.

"Norrium… property…large enough…everyone together."

Wow, this was even better than she had hoped. Sitting up, she rubbed her eyes and then tried a few Talin words.

"Speak leisurely. Few words," she requested. "Norrium Talin?"

He jolted a little and made that sharp, percussion sound that caused her to flinch. He was quick to stop making the sound and pick up the purring again as words poured out of his mouth.

"Norrium…in command…connections…to…he…" He stopped when she rubbed her forehead with both hands. He must have realized what he was doing because he started talking again, but this time he went slower with fewer words.

"I'm in charge. My name is Bazium. Advanced…crew… Norrium, Sapurian, Tarrian, and Hesarium. Understand?"

"Wow," she whispered to herself. "I think I got all of that, or at least enough to understand." Then she worked with the Talin words she knew. Pointing to herself, she followed his speech pattern. "My name is Ari. I'm in charge."

"Ari," he repeated. "Soft name. Good name."

She slipped a finger under the collar. "Take off?"

He made a sad rumble. "No take off. Must stay. No hurt. Only nice. But must stay on."

She didn't expect her request to work, so his answer didn't surprise her. Then he started asking questions.

"Hurt any place?" he asked. "I can dissolve hurt." It took her a moment to realize he was asking if she was in pain and needed analgesics.

"No hurt," she responded.

"Hungry?"

"No hungry," she answered but then kept talking before he could ask another question. "Bazium, where take us? What *plan* for us?" Damn it, she didn't have the Talin word for plan in her head. The rest had been in Talin, though, so maybe he understood enough to answer her.

"All go to homeworld," he stated simply. "All come with us. Safe. Cared for. No more problems."

"There's one big ass problem," she muttered to herself before trying again in Talin. "No own. We free."

He didn't say anything for so long she thought she might have mixed up her Talin with human language by accident.

"Can't," he said finally. His next words made her realize he understood everything. "Freedom equals no home."

It was clear he knew Earth was a dead planet. Which reminded her how few resources they owned.

Welcome back to step one, she thought.

Flopping back on the bed, she rubbed her eyes with the heels of her hands. His purring got louder, making chills run down her spine. She let her arms drop and rolled her eyes to look at Bazium.

"This discussion isn't over," she warned him, knowing full well he wouldn't understand her. "We might be smaller and softer than you, but don't underestimate us. We're a tenacious species."

CHAPTER 14

Advanced Squad Delta 223—Mission Q73 Report (Excerpt)
*This passage was redacted from the submitted report: I'm glad
to announce the human I referred to as Brave has initiated
communications with me. She doesn't know many words yet, but
this represents progress. Sapurian assured me the INT would mesh
the languages quickly, but we must continue talking even though
she does not understand everything. I repeat things several times
with different words until her INT can translate. It's slow, but it
works. She's identified herself as Ari, but in my thoughts, she
remains Brave. One of the first things she requested was to remove
the collar. I did my best to explain it wasn't an option if all the
humans wanted to survive. She appeared upset. I'm unsure if it
was because I refused to take off the collars, or she knows how
tenuous the situation is for all the humans.*

"We might have a plan," Santos said in hushed tones as Ari
joined their group. About half the humans were gathered in the
largest room they'd been assigned, the max number that could fit
comfortably at one time. No one slept here. Instead, they used it as
a communal gathering place. She suspected that was the Talins'
intention.

The Talins were all standing near the front of the room, talking and occasionally pointing to someone. It was clear they were agitated, probably because Ari refused to translate for them. Tarrian had even made a loud and startling percussion sound Ari now knew was referred to as rattling.

When she'd asked Bazium about the noise in their cabin, he'd shown her his back. Down his spine were armored plates that had a limited range of motion. He clacked them together several times to demonstrate a few of the sounds he could make. He explained in few, simple words that the plates could denote anger, frustration, excitement or one of many other emotions.

Knowing the origin didn't make Tarrian's loud rattle of rage any less scary.

All he wanted to do was speak to Aubrey, but when asked, Aubrey bit her lip and shook her head no. Ari could tell Aubrey wanted to talk to Tarrian but still felt betrayed by being collared.

Tarrian must have thought Ari was refusing, not Aubrey. When she said no, he'd gotten loud fast. Bazium was quick to move between her and the enraged Talin. Tarrian had calmed down, but the humans chose to gather at the far side of the room to talk. The Talins had been engaged in an intense conversation ever since.

Santos's words were a great distraction from the myriad of emotions going through her both from Tarrian's anger and Bazium's quick defense.

"Plan?" Ari echoed.

Santos nodded at Aubrey. "Tell her."

"I was able to access their computers," Aubrey said. "I had to take an educated guess, but I think we're going from here to Unile Station. We could try to slip away there. The stats I could access in Common made it look like a massive station with lots of traffic."

Mari hissed out a breath. "It is big, but that place is a cesspool."

"Cesspool?" Daniella asked. "In what way?"

"When I was working for the Yormni conglomerate they would fuel there, but they didn't let employees visit the station. Unless you're the member of a powerful species like the Marper or the Talins, you're pretty much taking your life in your own hands when you board the station. Vicpor aren't big on security."

"It's the only stop this ship is going to make before it's in Talin-controlled space," Aubrey said. "I can't read Talin, but that much was obvious."

"*Mala pata*," Daniella muttered. "Rock meet hard place."

"No shit it's bad luck," Ari agreed. "Our one chance at escape is about as dangerous as it gets. I don't like it."

"Big risk means big reward," Mari said.

"But sometimes big risk means big loss," Liz argued as she cast a longing look over at Norrium. "Do we really need to run? I know the collars suck and I'm not all that excited to be a pet, but at least they've been treating us well. And Ari said Bazium indicated they want to keep us all together."

"Do you really want to give up?" Mari spat out. "My Tomas wouldn't have let this stand. He would have fought."

"He would have done whatever we needed the most," Ari argued. She didn't want to get into a fight, but Mari liked to remember Tomas as she believed him to be, not as he was. "He wasn't a dedicated fighter or pacifist. He was a leader who was always trying to do the best for everyone."

Mari's eyes lit up with anger. "There was no *trying*. He did his absolute best. He died for all of us!"

"Fuck, he wasn't Jesus," Santos muttered.

"He was a saint," Mari countered, rounding on Santos. Her expression was so irate that Santos took a step back and held up his hands.

"Mari, everyone loved Tomas," Santos said quickly. "But I know he'd be just as worried as Ari and Liz that escaping onto that station might put us in more danger."

Mari stepped away from Santos, but her expression was still intense. "I know in my heart that if Tomas were alive, he'd say run. Better to jump out of a burning building and have the few seconds of falling to come up with something than to wait to burn to death."

Ari barely held in a laugh. "You do realize that's a shit analogy."

Out of the corner of her eye she saw Daniella bite her lip to keep from smiling, and Santos covered up his grin by rubbing a hand over his mouth.

Mari rounded on Ari. "You might be content now that you're getting dicked regularly, but some of us still want more than to be a sex slave. Some of us have goals past being *a pinche puta!*"

Daniella and Aubrey gasped at Mari's vile words. Santos's eyes went wide and Liz's mouth fell open. For her part, Ari was working really hard on not losing her temper.

She lost the battle.

"First of all, calling me a whore as an insult implies some shitty things. We've both met individuals who decided to trade sex for things—money, food, or security. I didn't realize you believed sex-work was foul," Ari commented coldly. "If you do, you're not the person I thought you were."

Mari's face colored as she opened her mouth to talk, but Ari held up a finger and to her surprise, Mari closed her mouth.

"Secondly, I'd think you'd be the last person to chastise me about bed partners after you slept with Patrice's husband." Mari looked devastated at that reminder, but she'd pushed Ari past caring. "After Tomas died, there was a reason I was asked to take his place and not you. You and I both know it's mostly concerning that affair and the temper you just displayed."

Mari dropped her gaze to the floor and then looked back up at Ari, her expression no longer angry but still determined. "I think—"

Ari shook her head and interrupted her. "No, Mari. You're done. You've made your views very clear. I'm going to discuss it with everyone else. Then we'll decide. Your say in this is done."

"No!" Mari said adamantly, meeting Ari's eyes boldly. "I need to make sure people understand what's at stake."

In a rare show of anger, Santos glared at her. "*¿Neta?*" he spat out. "Do you think we don't understand what's going on? We're all wearing the same fucking collar, Mari!"

"I'll lay out all their options," Ari told her, silently applauding Santos's support. "But you don't get to intimidate anyone."

"I don't need to," Mari insisted. "They'll know what decision is right."

With that Mari stomped off. One of the Talins was quick to follow her, but he returned a short time later. Ari guessed Mari had returned to her assigned room.

"Well, that sucked," Liz murmured.

"That's Mari for you," Santos said with a tired shrug. "She gets caught up in the narration in her head and forgets that we aren't pieces she gets to move around a chess board. Tomas was the only one who could really keep her calm when she got like this."

Ari nodded. "It's a reason but not an excuse."

"She'll calm down and apologize later," Daniella said.

Air sighed. "I know."

She closed her eyes and rubbed her forehead, her head suddenly hurting. This wasn't the first time Mari had given her a headache, and it probably wouldn't be the last.

"Ari…in pain…help?"

She looked up to see Bazium standing over her as everyone else had silently moved back to give him space. They all watched with curiosity as he knelt in front of her and took her hands in his. It was a stark reminder of their size difference to see his giant, clawed hands envelop hers.

He started purring quietly and sat pack on his heels so she was looking down at him. He did this every time he addressed her now. She thought it was his way of trying to apologize for the collar or make her feel less vulnerable.

It made her want to forgive him despite the weight around her neck.

"…can…carry to med…" he said, his voice a little more worried now and the sound of his purring changed slightly.

"I'm fine," she said and then realized she spoke Spanglish. She relaxed her brain so the Talin words would come to her. "No bad. No difficulty in body."

Bazium paused and blinked before making the sound she associated with agreement. "No pain?" he reiterated. "No body pain?"

"No body pain," she agreed, relieved that they'd managed to communicate. "This would be a hell of a lot easier if you all used Common," she muttered.

"Species that aren't as powerful learn to read and write Common," Santos whispered to her. "If the species is powerful, or wants to be considered powerful, they refuse to learn it. I suggest not insulting the entire Talin empire at the moment by telling them to learn Common."

Bazium looked over to Santos, who stepped away again and dropped his eyes to the ground. Then the Talin shifted his attention back on her. "What say?"

This time she relented and translated, or at least tried. "Talin no Common read. Make difficult."

"You know Common?" Bazium asked, and she found his surprise insulting.

Fighting to keep her face blank, she answered. "All read Common. It's supportive."

He made one of his questioning sounds and she realized the last word didn't make sense. She tried again. "Common is valuable."

She could tell he finally understood, and then he spoke so fast she didn't catch much. "Common for…and…. Not for Talins!…better…superior! Humans… learn Talin and…."

If that didn't sound like a decree, she didn't know what did. Keeping her expression mild, she waited for him to finish so she could agree. Santos was right. They needed to keep the Talins mollified.

"Will learn," she said when he stopped talking to draw a breath. "All learn Talin."

He started purring again, loudly this time. "Good!…happy…"

Letting go of her hands, he gathered her in his arms and snuggled her to his chest. She felt the pressure of his cheek on the top of her head and the smell of hazelnuts filled the air. She opened her eyes to see Daniella and Santos watching her. They both had interested expressions on their faces, but in different ways.

Daniella's fascination looked clinical, as if she wanted to test the oil Bazium was rubbing into Ari's hair and ask both of them a lot of questions. Santos's eyes were filled with longing as he watched Ari and Bazium interact. It had been a rough few years for all of them, and it was nice to see she wasn't the only weak-willed human when it came to the Talins' over-the-top affections.

It was hard not to give in to the collars and let them take charge. This powerful species had all the resources and a willingness to provide a trouble-free life.

But the decision wasn't solely hers. They all had to agree, and if the consensus was to run she would have to go. No one could be left behind to bear the brunt of the Talins' anger when the rest were found missing.

"It's going to be hard to leave you," she whispered to him, knowing he wouldn't understand any of it. "But if I have to go, I promise to try and come back once I get everyone settled somewhere."

Then she pulled away from Bazium. He gave her a last purr then stood to rejoin his squad. It was hard, but she focused on her friends as they returned to her side.

"How do we want to talk to everyone about Unile Station?" Santos asked.

"Probably give them all the pros and cons," Ari said, feeling weary in her soul. "And answer any questions as best we can. The important thing is that everyone knows the unknown."

"What do you mean?" Aubrey asked.

"The Talins might keep us or sell us," Ari explained. "We might find a place to settle that will treat us well or we could end up dead because Unile Station is just that dangerous. We're surrouned by unknown factors and possible outcomes."

"So no easy answers then," Daniella said with a frown.

"Are there ever?" Ari asked with a raised eyebrow.

"Rarely," she responded with a half-smile. "It's going to take us a while to talk to everyone. Should we split up?"

"Don't leave me," Ari begged. "I need you guys to stay with me on this because I can tell you right now, it's going to be hard for me to be neutral."

Daniella, Aubrey, and Santos agreed, and the four of them set off to the first small group to begin discussing the future. They went from group to group and even ventured out to other cabins so everyone could be part of the discussion.

Over the course of the many conversations, arguments, and questions the Talins had fed everyone a meal and even tried to usher them back into their individual rooms.

Ari had been quick to intervene, explaining as best she could that everyone still needed to visit a little longer. Then Sapurian said something to Bazium about communal living, and they were allowed to stay together and keep talking.

Her voice was hoarse and her spirit beyond drained before they finished. Finally, Ari sat alone with Santos, Aubrey, and Daniella. Looking down at her hands clasped tightly in her lap, she blinked back tears.

It took almost five hours but they'd reached a consensus.

"That's it then," she whispered.

Aubrey laid a hand over hers. "I don't like it either." She glanced over to where Tarrian and Sapurian were speaking. "I'm like you. I'm emotionally vested in a Talin, so I understand how you feel."

Ari nodded wordlessly. She and Aubrey had recused themselves from the voting because they were too attached to the Talins. Daniella and Santos had also decided not to vote. All of them had done their best to present the facts, including the unknown dangers of Unile Station and the unpredictable conditions on the Talin homeworld.

There were so many questions no one could answer; a few people had gotten upset. Most decided running was a better option. There had been a few holdouts, like Liz, but eventually even she bowed to group pressure.

They were going to run.

It was going to take equal parts luck and planning for this to work. Maybe more luck than planning, if she were being honest.

She pulled her hands out from under Aubrey's and wiped away the single tear she hadn't been able to hold back.

"We need everyone to start being nice to the Talins," she said.

Mari appeared at the edge of her vision, scowling. "Why?"

She was so heartbroken she couldn't even muster any animosity toward the stubborn woman she usually considered a friend. "Because we need them to trust us. We need them to let us have the run of the ship, like they were doing before they put the collars on us."

"Does that mean I have to have sex with one of them?" she asked, her voice dripping in scorn.

Suddenly Liz was there, getting in Mari's face, with little Lucia clutched to her chest and her four-year-old clinging to her leg. "I agreed to this," she hissed at Mari. "Because I believe in Ari. She'll fight to her last breath to do what's best for all of us. I don't trust you. You would fight to your last breath to prove you're right."

Going by her wide-eyed expression, Mari was as shocked by the mild-mannered Liz's statement as the rest of them.

Mari shook her head violently. "I wouldn't—"

Liz interrupted, her voice low and vaguely threatening. "Norrium has been caring for Andres as if he were the father himself. When he holds little Lucia, he's so gentle you'd think she was made of spun sugar. The first day we were on board she wouldn't settle and I was exhausted. He rocked her and did that purring thing until she finally fell asleep. He was up half the night doing that. Half the night! Isadora said he wanted to be a father, but he wouldn't have done that for me. Do you hear what I'm telling you?"

Mari opened her mouth to speak, but Liz didn't give her a chance. "I'm saying Norrium is a better father to Andres and Lucia than their own biological father was." Angry tears were streaming down her face. As if sensing her mom's distress, baby Lucia began to fuss.

"A father who put a collar on you," Mari shot back.

Liz's answer was soft but filled with venom. "Isadora put a ring on my finger and then treated me like a slave. Norrium put a collar around my neck and treats me like a precious treasure."

"If he's so wonderful, why did you agree to leave?" Mari sneered.

"Because we're a community," Liz replied, the anger visibly draining out of her. "And I couldn't be the one to hold us all back."

Norrium must have noticed she was upset because suddenly he was there, lifting both Liz and the baby into his arms while purring loudly. Andres let go of his mother in favor of clutching at the Talin's leg, looking back and forth between the adults with an uneasy expression.

Norrium looked at Ari and spoke. "Pain?"

"Weary," Ari explained. "No wrong. No Pain."

"…liquid eyes…" Norrium argued as Liz snuggled herself and the baby against his solid bulk.

It took Ari a moment to figure out that Norrium was referring to Liz's tears. "Weary," she repeated. She racked her brain for the word bed or nest, but came up blank. "Needs rest spot."

Norrium stopped purring long enough to issue a sound of understanding and then went back to purring. "Tell her we…to use the rest spot," he said.

"He's going to put you to bed," Ari said to Liz.

"Good," she mumbled without turning her head or even opening her eyes.

Amused despite the heavy emotions sitting in her chest, Ari had to fight a grin when she looked to Norrium. "Rest spot good."

Assured of her consent, Norrium held Liz and the baby to his chest with one arm and reached down for Andres with the other. Easily swinging the now giggling four-year-old onto his shoulder, he strode out of the room with the little family.

"Out of all of us," Aubrey said thoughtfully. "I think Liz is giving up the most."

Even with her own heart breaking, Ari had to agree.

CHAPTER 15

Advanced Squad Delta 223—Mission Q73 Report (Excerpt)
Now that I can communicate with Ari, I've learned a bit more about human customs. As we already knew, they don't scent bond. They do "fall in love."

It was a difficult concept for Ari to explain because the term love can be used in many different ways, and Talins don't have an equivalent. They can love several people at once or no one. There is also a point where some can "fall out of love" and no longer want to be in an intimate relationship. One thing Ari went to great lengths to make me understand was that there was no wrong way to love among humans. I know Talins have some of the strictest taboos and laws when it comes to having partners and spouses, but it seems these humans have few or none. It's refreshing, if confusing.

But the important thing to note is that when "in love" humans feel a great deal of loyalty and affection for those whom they love. I strongly believe this love can extend to Talins also.

"Finish," Bazium urged as he held another bit of food to Ari's lips. They were sitting at the desk in his room with her on his lap, a platter of food in front of them. When they'd first started eating, she'd accept a bite of food herself for every one he ate. But then it had been one bite for every two he ate. Now she was refusing to even open her mouth.

He waited patiently, determined she would eat at least a few more mouthfuls. Then she managed to insert her hand between her mouth and the food he held.

Forcing back a rattle of impatience, he lowered his hand. "You need to eat more."

With his hand at a safe distance away, she lowered her hand to speak. "I'm full. If I eat any more, I'll be ill."

This time he couldn't stop his rattle of alarm. "Ill?"

She was quick to soothe him. Moving on his lap until she was sideways, she rested a hand on the slip of exposed skin at the base of his neck. It didn't completely relax him, but his worry calmed slightly.

"Not truly ill," she reiterated. "But I'll feel uncomfortable."

He marveled at how improved her Talin had become in the few short rotations since the tendrils were done growing. She still struggled with words at times, but she was fluent as long as she kept her sentences simple.

Sapurian, Norrium, Hesarium and Tarrian often requested she translate. It wasn't ideal but better than before the INT.

Norrium and Tarrian were particularly eager to get the humans they favored INTs as soon as possible. That was one of the reasons the Talins planned to stop after leaving the compound even though it was outside their mission parameters. Unile Station was an unpleasant place, but the station advertised high-end INTs for sale and enough medication to guarantee the INTs would grow properly with none of Ari's suffering.

Bazium felt the ancestors had blessed them twice over—first by making the INT successfully integrate in Ari's head and then leading the humans into forgiving the Talins for the collars.

Although Ari told him repeatedly she wasn't the reason the humans were mingling with his crew again, he knew better. He'd watched her talk to every single human. She'd even looked tired occasionally, but she'd kept going. He could tell some of the discussions had been fierce, and she'd returned to several groups repeatedly. Three of the other humans had stayed by her side the entire time, but they spoke only occasionally. She was doing most of the talking and interacting.

She must have convinced everyone his crew was doing what was best for the miners. Now the humans would be safe. Their life of neglect was over. He could understand their fear at an unknown future and anger over waking in a collar, but his sweet human had persuaded the reluctant ones.

"You should finish it," Ari insisted as she nestled against him.

He popped the morsel he was holding into his mouth. It was one of the blander food choices they had on board, but it was safe for human consumption, which was a small price to pay to share a meal with Ari. As with everything they did together, he enjoyed feeding her.

That lead him to thinking about all the other things he liked to do with her. Talking to her. Bathing her. Rutting with her. Snuggling with her. The way she touched him while they lay naked in the nest was addicting.

If he was trying to sell the officials of Talarian on humans making excellent pets, he couldn't let any of them find out that humans were sexually compatible with Talins. It was too bad really because it would be amazing to declare to everyone that he had found the cure for Fading in the arms of his little human.

Looking down at Ari's head, he regarded her hair, now saturated with his bonding oil. With a start he realized something else; he'd scent bonded with her.

It was bad enough he'd had intercourse with her. It was taboo to have sex with other species but not illegal. If he was discovered having sex with a human, he'd have difficulty getting a job or building a career in politics, but he wouldn't be fined or imprisoned.

Scent-bonding was another issue altogether.

He'd broken the bonding laws—that was enough to be outcast from the Talin empire. Worse, he'd done it with a non-Talin. It was believed that Talins couldn't scent bond outside their species. No scientist ever bothered studying it because it was held as a fundamental law of Talin biology. Like everyone else, he'd always believed that simple fact without question.

Until now.

More astounding, Fading was obviously linked to scent-bonding. He was no longer dying of the Fading, and he was scent-bonded to Ari. The two were facts irrevocably connected.

He wanted to tell Ari about his revelations, but before he could open his mouth, his Ident chimed. Wiping his fingers off on a cleansing cloth, he unclipped the Ident from his belt. Setting it on the table next to the platter, he tapped it and a message from Norrium popped up.

The Mining and Processing Assessment Team #291 is here. They are going to use the second docking spot. They requested we meet them at their airlock in half a mark.

Bazium was quick to send a reply. *Assure them we will be there to meet them. Warn them that we have the humans under control and on our ship. I'll bring Ari with me as an ambassador for her species.*

Tarrian wants to know if he should bring Hurt, I mean Aubrey.

There was no hesitation on Bazium's part. He'd come to realize Ari was close to several humans, and Aubrey was one of them.

Yes, have Tarrian bring Aubrey. Make sure she's fed and wearing the omnie coat. It will be below desirable temperatures on the station for the humans. You, Hesarium, and Sapurian will stay on the ship to look after the rest of the humans.

Orders acknowledged.

Bazium clipped the Ident back to his belt and then rubbed Ari's back. "The team taking over the mine has arrived," he explained to Ari. "I'd like you to meet them, but I need you to be on your best behavior."

Sitting up, Ari regarded him. "What does best behavior mean?"

"No anger or threat displays," Bazium said, picking easy topics instead of the ones he knew she'd likely not react well to.

"I know to keep my teeth hidden," Ari retorted as she crossed her arms over her chest mutinously. He'd come to learn that posture meant she was displeased about something.

"I also need you to be deferential," he said, making his soothing rumble as loudly as he could.

Ari was silent for a moment before she tilted her head a little and asked, "Deferential?"

Bazium tried to pick the mildest words. "They need to believe you follow me. As my men follow me."

She made a humming sound. "Or like a slave would follow an owner?"

There was no ignoring her bluntness. "Yes," he said simply. "Every Talin you meet needs to believe humans can be controlled by Talins or we won't be able to bring you back to Talarian. Meeting the team that will take over this compound will be good practice for when you have to meet government officials later."

He waited for her to respond, but she went silent and her face didn't betray her emotions. He didn't like this. He liked it when she forgot to keep her lips closed and he saw a flash of her flat, white teeth. It made him feel special because the humans only did that type of smile with each other.

But now she wasn't smiling or even tightening her facial features in what the humans referred to as a frown. When the silence went on too long, he began to worry.

"You can stay in my room if you're afraid," he offered. "You don't have to meet these Talins."

"I'm not afraid, not like you think," she answered. "I'll meet them and be charming and subservient. I'll help you pave the way for a future we might not get."

Before he could ask her what that meant, his Ident chimed. Tarrian was at the door with Aubrey and it was time to go.

CHAPTER 16

"What are these?"

Bazium saw Tarrian stiffen at Jolian's rude question. But true to his training, Tarrian remained silent and let Bazium interact with the leader of the Mining and Processing Assessment Team.

"They're called humans," Bazium explained. He had Ari in his arms, ready to turn away and shield her with his body if Jolian or any of his team became aggressive. "The Orloks imported them as labor. They were badly neglected by the time we arrived, but as you can see, they're quite tame and of a suitable intelligence."

"So these are the ones you're petitioning the External Affairs Council to bring back as pets?" Jolian asked, leaning in close to regard Ari. Bazium was about to draw away when Ari spoke.

"Hello," she said in her soft, musical human voice. "My name's Ari. It's my honor to meet you."

Jolian reared back with a rattle of surprise. "They can speak!"

"I can," Ari agreed. Bazium got the impression Jolian amused her. "And I can do other things."

"What other things can you do?" Jolian asked as he sounded an amused rumble.

"Would you like to see a *magic* trick?" Ari responded as she wiggled in Bazium's arms. Reluctantly he set her on her feet. Once standing she looked up at Jolian. "I'm sorry that word didn't translate. But if you lend me something small, I can show you what a *magic* trick is."

Jolian looked up at Bazium who sounded a permissive rumble. "I don't know what she's up to, but I'm sure it won't hurt to indulge her."

"Very well," Jolian said as he opened his pouch and rummaged around. Finally he pulled out a small donir, a triangular-shaped playing piece for a popular game of chance. Holding it out, he let Ari take it from his hand.

"Watch very closely," she said, her tone serious. "I'm going to make this disappear."

Jolian and his team's rumble of laughter abruptly cut off when Ari did make the donir vanish. One moment she was holding it between her fingers and then she was displaying both hands completely empty.

Without requesting permission Jolian grasped one of Ari's hands in his own. Bazium sounded a warning rattle, but Jolian didn't let go.

"I won't hurt the human," he promised as he leaned in close to examine her hand, separating each finger to carefully examine them. "I see no hidden flesh pockets or retraction spots. Her phalanges are tiny and delicate, but they have unquestionable dexterity as well. I'm suitably entertained."

Letting go of her hand, he reached into his pouch to produce another donir piece. "Do the same with this one," he demanded, thrusting it at her.

Without pause Ari took it from him and made it disappear. Bazium was as baffled as Jolian and the rest of them.

"Can you make them reappear also?" Jolian asked.

Instead of speaking Ari went on her toes to reach up and acted as if she was pulling something from Jolian's earhole. Then the first donir piece was back in her hand.

"You had it this whole time," she teased. "Let me see if the other one is there too."

Rumbling with amusement, Jolian leaned over so Ari could easily look into his earhole. "Hmmm, this one's empty now. Let me look in the other one." He let her move his head so she could "look" in his other earhole and pluck the second donir piece from there.

"That explains why he's so good at the game!" one of Jolian's team exclaimed. "His head is literally full of donir!"

The crew sounded loud rumbles of amusement at the joke, including Jolian.

"I told you my brain is always busy calculating chance," Jolian retorted.

Ari held her small hand out with the two donir pieces, but Jolian sounded a negative rattle as he rummaged through his pouch.

"Here," he said, dropping the remaining five donir pieces into her hand. "Now you have a full set to play with."

Bazium was sure Ari didn't even know what donir was, but she accepted the game pieces as if they were a prize.

"Thank you," she said, cupping the pieces in her delicate hand and examining them closely. "I'll study them."

"She's so precious," one of Jolian's team remarked as she stepped up to where Tarrian was still holding Aubrey. "Does this one do tricks too?"

Ari was quick to speak. "Aubrey doesn't have an INT, but I can ask her for you."

Jolian and his team watched with rapt attention as Ari and Aubrey spoke rapidly in their human language. He could tell the newcomers were entranced by the humans' voices.

"They sound so soft and melodic," Jolian commented.

"They remind me of nolik birds," a crew member said.

"Except they're even more adorable than noliks," another crew member gushed. A general rumble of agreement sounded from the rest of them.

"She says the best trick she has is that you can name any rock and she can tell you the atomic formula for it," Ari finally answered.

"Really?" the female standing closest to Aubrey asked, her voice full of doubt. "Any compound? From memory?"

Ari nodded. "Yes, as long as I can translate the rock, otherwise you might need to show her an image of it."

"The up and down movement of her head indicates affirmation," Bazium was quick to explain. He demonstrated the back-and-forth head movement humans used also. "When they do this it's an indication of a negative response to a question."

He saw Ari's face color a little, probably from mild embarrassment. He stepped closer to her and drew her back against this front, sounding a soothing rumble.

"You're doing very well, Ari," he assured her.

Jolian must have picked up that Ari was insecure. "Your master is correct, little human," he said with a soothing rumble of his own. "You're speaking clearly and acting with excellent decorum."

He felt Ari's body jerk slightly, probably from Jolian's use of the word master. But she didn't speak out against it. He wasn't happy that she had to be reminded she was owned now, but it couldn't be helped. She'd have to grow accustomed to the ruse or risk being rejected by the Talarian authorities.

"Your kind words mean a lot to me," Ari murmured and dropped the hand clutching the donir pieces to her side. He didn't like how tightly she was gripping the sharp playing pieces, so he gently took her hand.

"Will you allow me to hold onto your gift?" he asked in a soft tone. "I promise to keep them safe for you."

Jolian made a rumble of agreement. "That's a good idea. I wouldn't want her to lose a new toy so soon after receiving it."

Ari let Bazium take the donir pieces. He slipped them in his pouch as Ari raised her eyes to the female crew member standing next to Tarrian and Aubrey.

"Have you thought of a rock yet?" she pushed.

"Can she tell me what makes up a M-type asteroid?" the Talin asked.

Ari translated and Aubrey answered without hesitation. "She says that one is too easy. M-type asteroids are mostly composed of nickel and iron." Ari paused as Aubrey said something else; then she spoke again. "She said if you're not going to name a rock, she's going to tell you what her favorite is. It's called *benitoite*."

The word Ari used wasn't a Talin word, and she must have realized it hadn't translated. Looking back at Aubrey they spoke for a moment, and then Ari tried again.

"The name didn't translate, but it's a blue mineral made up of barium titanium cyclosilicate," Ari said, struggling a little with the complex Talin words. "And it has a hexagonal crystal system."

All of them, including Bazium, sounded rattles of surprise.

"You said that well," the female standing next to Aubrey commented. She unclipped the Ident from her belt and spoke a few words to it. A three-dimensional holo image popped up of a brilliant blue gemstone. Aubrey nodded, the edges of her lips curving up.

Bazium pointed to Aubrey's mouth. "When they do that, it's a sign of happiness or pleasure," he explained. "When they're really excited, they'll even show their teeth. I promise it isn't a threat display."

"How fascinating," Jolian commented. He regarded Ari. "Would you show me?"

Ari nodded and let her lips form what the humans called a smile. It displayed her flat, white teeth, making the team lean in closer to examine her. The moment they all crowded her, her lips closed and she pushed back against him.

Reacting quickly to her discomfort, he scooped her up and turned, using his body to hide her from the curious Talins.

"You're scaring her," he announced with a harsh rattle. All of them sounded rumbles of apology and took small steps back.

"If you set her back down, we'll keep our distance," Jolian was quick to offer, his team rumbling their assent to his statement. Looking down at Ari, he sounded a questioning rumble.

"I'm fine," she whispered. "They caught me off guard. That's all."

Setting her down, he stepped to her side instead of behind her, so he could easily put himself between her and the team if they tried to get too close again.

"Don't be afraid of us," Jolian said as he sounded a soothing rumble. "We wouldn't hurt you."

All the others murmured similar reassurances.

"We gave Ari a toy. We should give Aubrey something for being so clever," one of them said with a decisive rattle.

"Oh, I have something both of them would like," the female announced with an excited rattle. She turned to hurry back onto their ship, calling out that she'd "return swiftly."

Jolian sounded a rumble of amusement. "It seems your humans have charmed my team."

Bazium sounded a rumble of agreement. "They charmed me and my crew first, so it's no surprise."

Jolian eyed Ari as he spoke to Bazium. "They truly operated this place?"

"They did," Bazium agreed. "But they suffered casualties. You'll find them stored in a room set to a freezing temperature. We'll pack those bodies with us before we leave. I think the human tradition is to bury them in dirt with stone markers."

"Fascinating," Jolian noted with an interested rumble. "They don't have a Hall of Ancestors to intern bones in?"

"They don't have a homeworld any longer," Bazium explained. "They might have had something like the Hall of Ancestors at one time, but if they did, it's been long abandoned."

Jolian and the remaining crew reacted to this news with predictable pity. "Poor creatures," Jolian said, probably speaking for the rest of his crew. "No homeworld and probably no political power. It's good we stumbled across them or they would have come to a bad end."

"My crew thinks the same thing," Bazium said, ignoring Ari's sharp intake of breath. She might not like the collar, but she couldn't disagree that the humans here had been close to death when he and his men arrived.

"Would you like to leave some of them with us?" Jolian asked. "We have plenty of supplies, and we would take good care of them."

One of Jolian's team rumbled in agreement. "That's a good idea. It might be better for them to be allowed to stay in a familiar place. Rapid change might be disastrous for such delicate creatures."

Tarrian's rattle of displeasure was quickly quashed by a look from Bazium. Refocusing on Jolian, he sounded a soft negative rattle.

"We will be taking all the humans with us. It would be far more damaging for them if we tried to separate them. They form strong attachments to each other and can become distraught if parted. When we moved them from their communal living quarters on the compound to smaller accommodations on the ship, we had to separate them into groups. They didn't react well at first and it took some time for them to settle."

"That's good to know," Jolian commented with a thoughtful rumble. "If the Orloks used them for labor at this mine, there might be more of them at other mines or processing facilities we haven't discovered yet. We could end up finding some humans ourselves."

"The Orloks lack of a centralized UniBase is highly frustrating," one of Jolian's team muttered. "We keep discovering new mining and processing compounds that weren't on any list or documents. How did they run everything for so long with such sloppy information keeping?"

"That would be one of the reasons we were able to defeat them at war," Bazium pointed out with a rumble of satisfaction. "Their poor organization wasn't limited to their business practices. Their warriors and military were managed equally badly."

"How much more work do you need to do until they're registered as official pets allowed on Talarian?" one of Jolian's team members asked, taking a small step closer to Aubrey.

"Not much more. All our initial requests have been granted. We only have to complete one last step before they have full approval. A representative from the External Affairs Council has to meet and assess them," Bazium said.

"I can't imagine they won't be welcome," Jolian said with a gentle rumble. "They're so well-behaved and clever. Look how polite and entertaining these two are. May I ask," he gestured to Aubrey. "Why is that one being held?"

"She was very ill when we first arrived," Tarrian explained.

"Is she still sick?" Jolian asked with a worried rumble.

"No, she's recovered well," Bazium interjected. "But humans will clutch and cling to each other for comfort. Tarrian holds Aubrey because it soothes her."

"That's odd," Jolian murmured. "How did they get anything done during the day if they were clinging to each other all the time?"

Ari made a sound, drawing all their attention.

"Uh, sorry," she murmured. "That was a *laugh*." The word she used didn't translate and she wrinkled her nose in annoyance. "Um, that sound is our version of a rumble of humor. We make it when we're amused."

"Did I make you rumble, little human?" Jolian asked indulgently.

Ari nodded and smiled, flashing teeth at Jolian. The male sounded a rumble of elation. "Oh, you showed me your teeth. How delightful!" He dropped to a knee and held his arms out. "Would you like to clutch or cling to me?"

Ari's teeth disappeared as she looked up at Bazium. "I, uh, no?"

Bazium sounded a rattle of warning. "Humans take time to become familiar enough with a Talin to be comfortable clutching or clinging to them. When they decide to come to you, then you know they have developed a similar level of affection for you as they would for each other. It's not something that comes quickly or can be forced."

Jolian stood up with a disappointed rumble. "I hope you're keeping detailed notes about human behavior," he said.

"I have been," Bazium said. "And I'll be submitting my report to the UniBase so everyone can read it."

"Excellent," Jolian said. "If we look for humans of our own, your insight will be invaluable. We are the highest-ranked Mining and Processing Assessment Team, so we get to pick our assignments. After we've assessed and repaired this place and a permanent team takes over, we'll submit a request to explore other areas for undiscovered Orlok mining compounds."

Bazium looked down at Ari to gauge her reaction to Jolian's words, but he couldn't interpret her expression. She looked at Aubrey and spoke quickly. The two of them had a rapid conversation before she returned her gaze to Jolian.

"We're easily scared," she told him and pointed to Aubrey. "She can become so scared that it makes her sick. If you find any humans, they might be so scared they'll try to fight you off. You'll need to go very slowly and be gentle. Don't be offended or angry if they hide or resist."

Jolian accepted Ari's words gracefully. "I won't hurt any humans," he promised. "I can only hope they are as wonderful as you and Aubrey."

"No one is as great as us," Ari answered and then flashed her teeth again causing the miners to all sound loud rumbles of amusement.

Then the female was back with her arms full of several large, rectangular, hard cases. "I've brought goodies for the Aubrey human," she declared with an excited rattle.

Tarrian sounded a soft warning rattle when she got close, but Aubrey was wiggling in his arms at the sight of the boxes and speaking rapidly to Ari.

"She's requesting you let her stand," Ari told Tarrian. "She recognizes the packaging."

"I'll set her down," Tarrian conceded with obvious reluctance. "But she needs to agree to rest when we get back to the ship. All of you are still so easily fatigued."

Ari translated as Tarrian set Aubrey down. If Bazium hadn't been paying close attention he wouldn't have noticed irritation flash across Aubrey's face before she smiled up at Tarrian and patted his arm. He sounded a soothing rumble and rubbed his check across the top of her head.

It was obviously a subconscious gesture and made Aubrey breathe in deeply as Tarrian's bonding scent filled the air around her.

"He smells like *peppermint*," Ari murmured so quietly Bazium was the only one who could hear her.

Bazium leaned close to his human and repeated the foreign human word. "What is *pep-er-ment*?" That word felt strange on his tongue but at least it wasn't too hard to say.

"Peppermint is an herb back on Old Earth," she explained. "I think the smell comes from the oil in Tarrian's face." She ran her fingers over his left cheek, making it tingle. "Your oil has a strong smell too."

"And the smell pleases you?"

"Peppermint's not my favorite, but Aubrey says she loves it," Ari said casually.

Pain flashed through him at her words. "My scent isn't pleasing to you?"

Ari must have realized he was upset because she turned and wrapped her arms around his neck. It was easy for her because he was still bent over. "You smell like *hazelnut*," she told him. "Sapurian smells faintly like *sage* and Norrium smells a little like *saffron*. I can't pick out what Hesarium smells like at all, but I'm sure if I could smell him, he'd be another scent entirely. None of you guys smell alike, and to me, you smell the best. *Hazelnut* was my favorite back on Earth and I guess it's my favorite among you Talins."

Her reassuring words chased away his worry. He was quick to rub one of his cheeks on the top of her head, mirroring Tarrian.

That's when he realized Jolian's team were reacting with a combination of shocked and scandalized rattles.

"Have the two of you scent-bonded with the humans?" Jolian asked, his tone incredulous.

Tarrian went completely silent and quickly straightened away from Aubrey. His actions told Bazium that like him, Tarrian had developed a forbidden scent-bond with Aubrey.

Thinking quickly Bazium sounded a rattle of ridicule.

"How could we possibly scent-bond with humans?" he scoffed. "They have no scent glands. But we have found that the smell of our bonding oil helps them remain calm. It's part of their constant demand for reassurance. They can be needy creatures, but as you've noted, they make rewarding pets."

Rumbles of assent filled the hall, helping to cover Ari's soft gasp of outrage. Bazium rubbed her back, hoping she'd remain quiet. He could feel her stiff muscles there and was sure she'd voice all her displeasures at his little speech later when they were alone.

But he believed everything he said was partially true. The humans were weak and needy compared to Talins.

"I can see how our bonding scent would help them," Jolian murmured thoughtfully, running his clawed hand over the scent glands in his left cheek. Realizing what he was doing, he dropped his hand.

The sound of objects hitting the floor drew all their attention to where Aubrey was eagerly opening boxes and dumping the contents out. Once Tarrian had stopped rubbing his scent glands into her hair, she'd dropped to her knees to see what Jolian's team member had brought her.

Only after Bazium studied the growing pile for a moment did he realize the box was full of mineral samples, all packed in individual clear cases about the size of Ari's fist. As he watched, Aubrey opened one up and plucked out a brilliant red stone. Holding it up triumphantly, she said a word.

"Yes, you can have that," the female Talin said with a delighted rumble. "You can have all of them. I can always get more sample boxes if I need to recalibrate anything."

"That was a good idea. I wish I'd thought of it," another team member commented as he dropped to his knees next to Aubrey. He helped her open another case and presented her with the contents before discarding the empty case on the floor. Soon all the miners except for Jolian were kneeling around Aubrey, eager to hand her the most striking mineral sample they could find.

Ari tugged at Bazium's belt. He leaned over so she could whisper in his earhole. "Aubrey actually said the rock was a magnesium-aluminum spinel. It's one of her favorite minerals. She doesn't need to keep them, but it is fun for her to rummage through them," she explained.

"They were a gift. She has to keep them," Bazium told her as he watched the pile of rocks in front of Aubrey grow as the mess of empty cases built up around the group.

"Is this how Talin parents interact with their children?" Ari asked. He wasn't sure, but he thought her expression was bemusement.

"Absolutely not. Our upbringings are closely monitored and assessed by skilled care workers," Bazium commented.

Ari looked confused. "Wait, you're not raised by your parents?"

"Of course not, that would be inefficient," Bazium said dismissively.

"I have so many questions," Ari murmured. "But later, when we're alone."

"That's probably wise," Bazium agreed as another excited exclamation from Aubrey drew their attention. The little female was so happy with what she'd received, he worried Ari might now view her gift of donir pieces as inadequate.

"I could get you boxes of mineral samples also," he offered.

She shook her head. "I'd rather not have to carry all that around."

Bazium was quick to correct her. "You wouldn't have to. You're my human. I'd carry it for you. I'll carry all your things. You never need to worry about being overburdened again."

She tilted her head as she gazed up at him. "You make me feel a strange combination of cared for and dismissed. I don't even know how to describe all the emotions flowing through me right now."

"Are they mostly good or bad?" Bazium asked. Her tone was so mild that he couldn't believe she was truly upset with him.

"More good than bad," she told him. "For now, at least. We'll see how it goes later when we talk."

Her words sounded so ominous that it was Bazium's turn to be unsure of his emotional reaction. It was a strange experience, and he wasn't sure he liked it at all.

CHAPTER 17

Advanced Squad Delta 223—Mission Q73 Report (Excerpt)
Humans can become so engrossed in a task or item that everything else goes unnoticed. They'll be unlikely to react to movement, voices, or other sounds. Tarrian's human, Aubrey, is very much like that. The rest of the humans do it also but to a much lesser degree. Tarrian has told me Aubrey spent hours playing with the minerals the Mining and Processing Assessment Team gave her, and he was sure at one point she might have forgotten he was in the room. When it was time for her to rest, he tried to put them away and she got upset. Eventually he found a pouch for her to store them in, and she insisted on keeping the pouch on her person.

She was so emotionally vested in the rocks that Tarrian posed a theory that humans form attachments to items as well as other people. It's another example of how quickly humans can develop emotional attachments to even nonliving items.

Bazium expected Ari to be upset with him, but she was mild-mannered and curious when they got back to their cabin.

"Did Talin parents originally raise their children and that changed at some point in your past?" she asked the moment the door to his cabin slid shut. He hadn't even had time to set her down in the nest.

"Yes," he answered. He was reluctant to share Talin practices and laws with her, but he wasn't sure why.

When he didn't say anything more, she made that same sound she'd made with Jolian's team. "Don't tell me too much at once."

"I haven't told you anything," he answered, confused. This caused her to make the sound of humor again. "What did you call that sound? There isn't a Talin equivalent, so pronounce the word slowly for me."

"It's called a laugh. Or laughing. La-augh," she enunciated. "I laugh. He, she, they laugh. I'm laughing now. I laughed earlier. I will laugh."

"Laf," he responded. "La-a-augh." He liked the sound of the word. It was simple and pleasant, much like the human sound it represented. "And it means you're happy. Correct?"

"Usually, yeah," she agreed. "Same application as your rumble of humor, I think."

"You laughed at the miners," he started, wanting to know what she found amusing, but stopped when she shook her head.

"Oh no, you're not going to get away with distracting me. I want to know why you guys don't raise your own kids," she countered. "If you did it in your past, what changed?"

"It's complicated," he warned her.

"Then let's get comfortable and you can explain it all to me," she answered as she settled in the nest and patted the bedding next to her. He sat and then opened his arms. To his delight, she crawled into his lap and nestled up against him.

"I'm going to miss this," she murmured softly.

"You never need to go without," he assured her. "I can always make time to clutch or cling. You never need to suffer without it. I swear to you."

Nuzzling her nose against the slip of exposed skin at the base of his neck, she made a soft humming sound. Her warm breath wafted across the skin, making his mating shaft attempt to engorge and emerge from his flesh pouch.

It took a great deal of willpower to keep himself in check.

"About twenty-five hundred years ago we started to emerge as a spacefaring species," he explained.

"Oh, we are going way back," she said with a little huff that he thought might be a shadow of a laugh.

"Not that far back for Talin history, but I'll try to be concise," he said. "At the time we were not the powerful empire we are now. We had little in the way of defenses and were attacked at a regular interval. Although we were successful at defending our homeworld, the decision was made to expand our holdings to create a buffer between our homeworld and the rest of the universe."

"So you guys went out and started building space stations and colonizing viable planets?" she asked.

"Exactly. At first there were no issues because it took several decades before we were reaching far distances. But when it started taking forty or fifty rotations to get from the outskirts of the empire to the center, we began to encounter difficulties."

"Because you can't be away from your homeworld for too long?" she asked.

He sounded a soothing rumble. As he hoped, she made the soft sighing sound she often made in reaction to that rumble. When the sigh hit his ears, it settled something inside of him and made it easier to talk about things that no one spoke of.

"The distance from Talarian wasn't the issue. We couldn't be away from each other for too long," he said. "Talins used to scent-bond with each other."

She reached up and ran gentle fingers over the scent glands in his cheek. "Is that the smell that comes from here?"

"Yes, those are my scent glands, and what you're talking about is my bonding oil. When we scent-bond with each other it's a lifetime commitment. If we're separated for too long, we suffer from Collapsed-Scent disease. Most Talins simply call it Ending. It's a painful death. There's no cure and every Talin is different. You can't predict how long a couple can last being away from each other before it starts happening. The partners might even succumb to Ending at different rates with one growing sick within a handful of rotations and another lasting an entire solar. But no matter what, separation is a death sentence."

"How horrible!" she exclaimed and wrapped her arms around his neck to hug him.

"At first the empire tried to keep couples together. Eventually it was too difficult, and missions suffered from a deficit of skilled crews. That's when one of our monarchs decreed he wouldn't scent bond. Instead, he would pick a willing female and they would marry without scent-bonding. They would both donate genetic material to have a child grown in an artificial womb."

"Hold up," she said, letting go of his neck and sitting up. "I'm confused, what does an artificial womb have to do with scent-bonding?"

Sounding an apologetic rumble, he explained. "Talin females can't get pregnant unless they've scent-bonded to a male."

"Oh, now this all makes much more sense," she agreed. "And was probably a helpful evolutionary trait. Having a dedicated male to help raise offspring would make you a more successful species."

"It probably did until we were in space," he agreed. "At first using artificial wombs was only a trend. There were no laws. But taboos quickly formed as many realized how efficient this method of reproduction was. Along with the wombs, the creshes were developed and integrated. Now parents could have their child grown and raised in the same place as the married couple worked to further the glory of their clan, family, and the empire."

"I can see how that would be helpful, but it sounds so cold," Ari murmured.

"I promise the artificial wombs and cresh buildings are kept at an adequate temperature," he assured her.

She made a soft laughing sound. "Among humans the word cold is often used to denote something emotionally remote or unfeeling."

"Ah, yes, in that case they were very cold," Bazium agreed.

"Did everybody decide this was the way to do things?" she asked.

"Not all at once," Bazium explained. "Those who insisted on scent-bonding, having children, and raising their offspring themselves were seen as old-fashioned and backward. Eventually, it was codified into law. For the good of the Talin people and empire, we needed to give up unnecessary personal pleasures like scent-bonding. Marriages needed to be about alliances and growth, not raising children. Our offspring should be reared by people specially trained and educated to best prepare them for achievement."

"You sound like a promotional advertisement," she murmured as she nestled into him again. "Were you raised in one of these creshes?"

"Of course," he answered, eager to tell her about his worth. "In rare circumstances it's legal for children to be raised outside of a cresh, but they often start their careers at a disadvantage. But I wasn't one of them. I was an excellent student and progressed well in my cresh. By the time I joined my family, I was already accepted into the military."

"Is that rare?"

"Highly," Bazium said with a rattle of pride. "Most have to train with their family or clan for solars before the military will accept their application. Not only did I get to join early, but I was assigned to an elite squad as a weapons specialist. Others had to settle for their second or third choices in assignments. I achieved the rank of Advanced Leader within four solars, which is rare. When I retire I will have a full set of honors to display in my home."

"How much longer until you retire?" she asked.

"This is my last mission," he told her with a contented rumble. "This is the last mission for all of us. We've served together for ten solars, which is the normal military rotation unless injured or family requires us to return to Talarian."

"Then we were really lucky you and your squad found us and not someone else who might have been trigger happy," she said.

"No, little Ari, I'm the lucky one," he argued. "You have added joy and color to my life."

"Tell me about life as a Talin," she demanded.

"That is a large question," he said with a rumble of amusement.

She nodded her head against him. "Then I'll narrow it down, tell me about families and clans."

"Clans are made up of many families," he began. "Each clan has a head family and one member of that family is sent to the Clan Assembly for that area. Most clans specialize in something. For example, my clan produces exceptional warriors. My family…" as he talked she relaxed and after half a mark he was sure she'd fallen asleep.

Then she jerked suddenly and sat up, almost hitting his chin with the top of her head.

"I think I might love you," she whispered, her voice tight. He rumbled out a soothing sound and petted her back, a thrill of excitement going through him.

His human loved him? It was something he'd hoped for but had little belief would happen. Why would a tiny, delicate human want to love a giant, hard-skinned Talin who put a collar around her neck?

The scent glands in his cheeks ached and swelled with oil. Dropping his head down, he rubbed his cheek against the top of her head, saturating her hair and filling the air with the scent of his bonding oil.

"Hazelnuts," she murmured in a throaty voice. "I never thought the smell was sexy before now."

"You said you liked hazelnuts," he reminded her once he'd emptied one cheek and moved to the other.

"I do," she explained. "But hazelnuts are a food back on Earth, so it's a little weird to associate them with you."

"Does that mean I smell good enough to bite into?" he asked. He wasn't worried; because even if she tried to bite him, she wouldn't do much damage with those flat teeth. His question made her laugh.

"Yes, you smell good enough to eat," she huffed. "But not in the way you think."

Relishing the happiness he heard in her voice, he started up a rumble of arousal. Another Talin would correctly interpret his rumble but he didn't expect it to cause her to moan.

Then a faint scent of her excited sex hit his nose.

"Ari?"

Her voice was a little breathless. "I can't help it. We've been snuggling and sharing. *Dios mio,* I think my brain might be permanently rewired from the INT tendrils because that purring you're doing right now is such a damn turn-on! It tingles down my spine right to my clit!"

Although he didn't understand some of her words, his mating shaft responded to her statement. The thing swelled viciously, causing the flesh pouch to retract so fast his seed sack bounced out. He gasped and flinched from the sudden pain. It was over quickly and replaced with roaring lust.

Ari's small hands searched his body with frantic haste. "What happened? Are you hurt?"

Her exploring hands dropped below his belt and landed on his erection. His mating shaft was so rigid it was straining the front of his pants.

"Oh," she exclaimed, a soft smile curling her lips. "I guess I'm not the only one turned on."

"You don't have to do anything," he was quick to say. He never wanted her to feel forced. His rumbling might cause her excitement, but that didn't mean she wanted to rut with him right now.

Raising her eyes, she met his gaze. Her cheeks were flushed and her pupils dilated—both clear indicators of her state of arousal.

"I know. You've been nothing but a *gentleman*." She must have realized the last word wasn't in Talin because she made a frustrated sound. "*¡Ah chingao!* So many words don't translate. And my brain feels mushy right now."

Alarmed, he reached for his Ident. Ari caught his hand and drew it to her. "I don't need Sapurian," she insisted, accurately reading his intent. "There really isn't anything wrong with me."

He sounded a rumble of worry but then switched back to a soothing rumble when her brows wrinkled. In this context he knew that meant she was displeased. When the wrinkles smoothed back out, he was proven correct.

"Let's enjoy the here and now," she urged

Despite his worry, his erection hadn't flagged. He wanted her. He couldn't imagine a time when he wouldn't want her.

Like most of his crew, he wasn't a virgin. Although sex outside of marriage was frowned upon, indulging in trysts during training was ignored by command and even expected. He'd bedded several females and one male. It had all been satisfying but nothing like the intensity he experienced with Ari.

Ari made him understand why they'd outlawed scent-bonding so long ago. This little human filled him with the urge to find a remote place for the two of them and never leave. He wanted to ignore protocol, duty, and even the law—all for her.

CHAPTER 18

***Advanced Squad Delta 223—Mission Q73 Report (Excerpt)**
Humans are surprisingly easy to entertain. They enjoy watching
vids of all types or sitting around and conversing with each other.
They can't possibly be exchanging much information, so what do
they spend so much time talking about? I asked Ari and she said
they'll remember things together, talk of the future, or speak about
each other. Perhaps a result of communal living, they're
constantly talking to help reenforce their emotional bonds. It must
help to reduce tension and keep everyone aware of each other's
emotional states.*

*Because Ari is a leader, she frequently goes around talking to
everyone. It must be exhausting for my little human to coordinate
so many lives. Hopefully when we are on Talarian and everyone is
more assured of their safety and future, she won't need to expend
so much energy keeping everyone calm and happy.*

When she'd listened to him explain why scent-bonding was
now against the law, she'd felt bad for Talins in an abstract way.
Their conversation had made her realize why Jolian's team had

been so upset when they'd caught Bazium and Tarrian rubbing her and Aubrey with their scent glands.

But now, as she caressed his cock, she realized what it meant to have Bazium scent-bonded to her. He would die if they were parted too long.

It was a knife to her heart.

She'd be leaving when they got to the station. She didn't have a choice. She promised everyone. She even recused herself from the vote because she knew she didn't want to leave Bazium. But things had changed now. His life was on the line.

No, she couldn't let him die. The moment she got passage for all the humans; she was coming straight back. If she was quick, she might even be able to get back on the ship before Bazium realized she was gone.

It was a dangerous plan. She knew Bazium would never hurt her, but the other Talins would be enraged to find everyone gone. Tarrian might even become violent at the loss of Aubrey.

Tarrian!

Like her Bazium, he was scent-bonded to Aubrey. He'd die if she left. And Aubrey didn't know. Guilt filled her.

New plan; tell Aubrey.

If she wanted, she could come back with Ari after they saw everyone safely onto a transport. They'd have to be quick and sneaky because no one would want the two of them to leave. Mari especially would throw a fit if Aubrey wanted to stay behind because she was such a high-value employee. Having her would make finding jobs for all of them easier to negotiate.

But wait, what about Liz and Norrium? Had he scent-bonded with her also? Right, she added Liz and the kids to the list of humans she'd let in on the whole scent-bonding/death thing. It was going to be much more difficult to sneak Liz and the kids away from everyone, but Ari knew Liz would want to stay if there was even a chance Norrium had scent-bonded with her.

Ari was going to need to be quick on her feet to get them away from the group, but she was confident. If all else failed, she'd wait until the doors to their transport were about to shut and then rush the five of them out. It worked in the old fiction vids back on Earth, so it would work here. Right?

What did it mean if you had to make an escape plan for your escape plan? Nothing good, she was sure.

Just in case everything went to hell, she decided she had to confess her love to Bazium. It came as a surprise to exactly no one when her confession turned into sexy time. Let's be realistic, that's where she was almost always heading with Bazium when they were alone and he was purring.

Oh, those purrs!

"I need you to do something for me," Ari said.

"Anything," he agreed without hesitation.

"I need you to take me hard," she whispered as he lifted her off his lap and laid her on the nest. "Take me hard and fast. And whatever you do, don't stop purring."

"This rumble?" he clarified before he changed the rhythm and pitch a little. "Or this one?"

Her eyes nearly rolled back in her head. "The first one was good, but this second one is better."

"That first one is a rumble of soothing or contentedness. The second one is a rumble of arousal," he explained as he nuzzled his face against her neck.

He kept his cabin at such a nice warm temperature that she'd set her coat on his desk when they'd gotten back. It left her dressed only in a simple wrap with the two sets of ties at her hips. Pulling away from her he found the outside ties and pulled them apart. Then he tugged the inside ties on the opposite hip free. After that it was easy for him to part the wrap and expose her entirely.

Ari didn't expect him to pause to stare at her. As he gazed down at her naked flesh, she started to feel a little self-conscious.

"You're perfect, my Brave," he murmured.

"I'm not that brave," she responded. Secretly she loved what he'd named her before they could communicate. When she'd told him she'd dubbed him Boss, he'd rumbled out a laugh and said some days he wasn't sure that was true.

When he didn't move to touch her, she got impatient. "Less looking and more touching," she demanded.

His sexy purr was interrupted for a moment by a rumble of amusement. Then he went back to making the sound that sent all kinds of delightful shivers down her spine. She would never get enough of this purr. Already her clit was throbbing and her breasts felt heavy.

He was quick to pull of his belt and pants, revealing is hard cock. He carelessly tossed the items off to the side as he lowered himself back to his knees. He moved his head down to lick over one of her nipples sending sparks of pleasure through her. She arched up, silently begging for more.

"That feels so good!" she moaned. As he switched breasts, she felt something blunt, warm, and heavy fall onto her stomach. Groping blindly she found his thick cock, hot and throbbing with his smooth seed sack hanging heavily below.

"It don't want to hurt you," she murmured as she ran her hand up and down his length.

"You won't," he whispered between licks. "My mating shaft wants all your touches. It's as if I'm back to being an untried youth with little control over my own body."

"Trust me, there is nothing youthful or untried about you," she assured him. Oil was dripping on her chest from his face, so she reached up and covered her palm in the warm, viscous fluid. Reaching back down she covered his shaft in oil, loving the way his turgid flesh felt in her hand.

He groaned as she worked him with her hand. She even reached down and tugged gently on his seed sack. His hips rocked slightly, his purring intense and constant.

Dios mio, she needed to come!

"Baz, please," she begged. Letting go of his cock, she tried to get her legs around him. "I want you inside me."

Instead of letting her maneuver him, he grabbed her thighs. Pushing her legs apart he moved his body back a little so he could lower his face between her thighs. As much as she liked what he'd done with his mouth before, she'd really been looking forward to having his giant cock thrusting inside of her.

"No, I want—" she started but his growl cut her off.

Oh, that growl. Along with the continued purring it nearly made her come. She was the luckiest fucking girl in the universe. She could almost orgasm from sound and smell alone.

"You will let me taste you," he growled, his words causing all kinds of pleasurable spikes to her blood pressure. "You can climax many times. I want my fill of your pleasure before I find my own."

She didn't get a chance to say anything before he was attacking her clit with sexual ferocity.

Could a clit be licked off?

Did she care?

"There!" she cried out as his tongue, mouth, teeth, and purring hit the perfect combination.

Her entire body seized with her climax. Her vision grayed a little as pleasure controlled her body. She couldn't remain still. Despite her thrashing, Baz managed to keep from hurting her. And he kept touching in all the right ways to make the orgasm last.

He didn't stop until she went limp under him. Sitting back, he grabbed her by the hips and flipped her on her belly.

"Mine!" he roared and pushed her legs apart and under her. She pushed her ass in the air, eager to help. She was shaky and was able to stayed in position because Baz held her there.

Then he was fitting the bulbous tip of his cock into her. This was what she'd wanted before, but she was glad Baz hadn't listened to her. Even now, wet and primed from her first orgasm, he had to wedge himself in.

"Yours," she moaned out as he stuffed his heat into her. He was roaring, rattling, and purring now. The room echoed with all the sounds he was creating, and every single one of those sounds affected her in a different way.

The purring kept pleasure coursing through her with every movement of his thick cock forced into her body. The rattling felt like a mouth nipping down her back, riding the edge of pleasure and pain. And the roaring triggered some kind of primal need to feel him fill her with cum.

When he bottomed out inside of her, it felt like the size of him forced the air from her lungs. Had he gotten bigger since the last time they did this? She never thought of herself as a size queen, but she couldn't imagine going back to a regular sized cock after this. He was putting pressure in all the right places.

Then he started moving, slowly at first but picking up speed quickly. Along with the roaring, rattling, and purring, the sound of flesh slapping flesh filled the air. Every time he moved, he dragged his cock over sensitive flesh sending ripples of pleasure through her. Tension tilled her as his body thrust in and out of her.

Oil dripped down her spine and he let go of her hip with one hand and rubbed it all over her back. It warmed her skin and added yet another sensation to her already overwhelmed system.

Then he rested a thumb against her back hole. He didn't push in, only massaged her there with oil. It made her body tingle and clinch around his cock. When he pressed the pad of a finger a little harder against her pucker, she was lost. She exploded into a thousand little pieces as her second orgasm hit. She was vaguely aware of her screams as her body jerked and she lost all control of her limbs.

"You're mine!" he roared. "My human! My Brave! MINE!"

Baz's movements became faster and more frantic as her climax crashed through her body. His rattle and roar became so intense they vibrated deep in her chest, causing her climax to rekindle and keep going. It was so strong she was riding on the edge of pain when Baz thrust one more time and went perfectly still. She felt warmth flood her, setting off one last orgasm.

Or was it a renewal of the last one? Fuck if she knew.

She might be crying, but she wasn't sure. Her body felt super-heated, as if she'd just gotten out of a sauna. She might have lost feeling in her toes, and there was a good chance she'd forgotten how to breathe.

When Baz pulled out of her, she took in a long, startled lungful of air. So it wasn't that she'd forgotten how to breathe. It was just his dick had been taking up all the room!

Gently, he lowered her and rolled her onto her back. His sexy purr was replaced with one she knew meant he was worried.

"Did I hurt you?"

"No," she croaked. "In fact you better promise to do that to me again."

He rumbled with amusement as he settled next to her and gathered her into his arms. "As often as you wish," he promised.

"Then I'm voting for forever," she quipped, her voice a little ragged from all the screaming.

"Then it will be forever," he agreed in a soft voice. "Rest, my beautiful Brave. I will take care of all your wants and needs from now on."

CHAPTER 19

Advanced Squad Delta 223—Mission Q73 Report (Excerpt)
Through an unfortunate event we learned that once a human has bonded with a Talin, the scent of someone else's bonding oil can make the human ill to the point of being violently sick. Once exposed, the only way to help is to thoroughly cleanse away the other's bonding oil and use medication for their nausea and headache.

Ari lay in her nest with her body still thrumming from Bazium's love-making and her skin coated in his bonding oil. She loved it. Not only did the scent of hazelnuts make her feel content and happy, but the oil made her skin feel soft and luxurious. Bazium had left a little while ago to have a final meeting with Jolian and go over what he knew about the compound.

Assuming no unforeseen issues or sudden threats came up, they'd be leaving in two cycles to let Jolian and his team work on the compound.

No, not cycles, she reminded herself, *rotations.*

Talins didn't use cycles or days, they used the term rotation. Years were solars and individual rotations were made up of marks and strikes. She needed to get used to their terms and different time-keeping with marks that denoted the passage of time during daylight hours and strikes for nighttime. The easy part was remembering that each mark and strike was made up of one hundred submarks.

But then it could get into sectioned-submarks and it all got a little confusing but nothing as bad as the way the Orloks organized their time-keeping. No matter how much she'd studied, she'd never gotten all their terms and notations correct.

Sleepily she snuggled deeper into her pillow and let her mind drift. After Bazium got back, she'd ask him if there was any way she could talk to Aubrey and then Liz alone. Aubrey should be easy. She was staying with Tarrian in his cabin. But Liz was going to be a little harder to get alone without raising Mari's suspicions and potentially causing a big blowup.

The thought of Mari made Ari both frustrated and sad. She'd never met siblings as close as Mari and Tomas. Of the two, Mari had the strong personality but Tomas was inarguably the more emotionally stable sibling. She had the tendency to bully or be narrow-minded; while he was often more tolerant and permissive. They'd balanced each other out well with him being leader and her there to help push everyone to do tasks he assigned. Santos had jokingly referred to her as Tomas's enforcer.

Now she was an enforcer for a ghost.

Sighing, she tried to push thoughts of Mari out of her head. She would deal with everything later. Right now she was going to indulge in a nap. It'd been so long since she'd felt rested that simply getting to lounge in a bed seemed opulent.

The sound of someone in the hall and the door to the cabin sliding open didn't register as worrisome to her. Lazily she sat up, covered only by a sheet with a smile on her face. She expected to see Bazium, but instead two of Jolian's team members were rushing at her.

Ari reacted without thinking. Scrambling on all fours she went for the cleaning unit. The door didn't lock, but if she could get it closed, she might be able to bash the display and freeze the hatch shut.

She didn't make it.

A hand wrapped around her ankle and dragged her back before she was even halfway through the cleansing unit door. She knew Talins were quick but didn't realize how fast they could be.

She didn't even get a chance to draw in a breath before a hand was clamped over her nose and mouth. Frantically she clawed at the hand, but to no one's surprise, it didn't do any good.

"Tumial, she can't breathe!" one of them said as he grasped her wrists and bound them behind her back. Tumial moved his hand slightly, uncovering her nose. Even as she pulled air into her lungs, she tried to bite the hand over her mouth, but it was useless.

"By the ancestors, she's naked and covered in Bazium's bonding oil," Tumial said.

"He probably had to do that to keep her calm while he was gone," the other Talin answered. "He's already been gone for an entire mark and won't be back for at least three more marks. That must be long enough that he worried she'd grow anxious."

"This concerns me, Dutamier. If she needs that much attention, do you think we're going to be able to care for her correctly?" Tumial asked with a soft, worried rumble.

Dutamier sounded an unconcerned rumble. "There are three of us to care for her, and duties here are light. It will be easy for one of us to stay with her at all times. Remember, after Bazium and his men are gone, we'll simply tell Jolian we found her hiding. I'm sure he won't ask too many questions."

By now they had her arms and legs secured and a gag in her mouth. Tumial lifted her into his arms and followed Dutamier out of the cabin.

What kind of idiots were these guys? Did they think Bazium wouldn't notice she was missing? Her heart was beating hard and adrenaline was flooding her system, but she wasn't scared. She was pissed!

A third Talin in the hall was quick to examine her. "Oh, you got the Ari human!" he exclaimed. "She's very clever. Good choice."

"She was the easiest," Dutamier explained. "Opinal, did you rig an escape pod to look like it was triggered by someone inside?"

"Yes, it will perform a silent launch in a few submarks and fly directly at the nearby satellite," Opinal explained. "The resulting crash will leave very little behind. They will assume she is nothing but particulates."

Looked like they weren't as dumb as she first thought. Even knowing it wouldn't do any good, she started struggling.

Tumial made a soothing rumble. "Easy," he whispered to her, putting his mouth next to her ear. "We aren't going to put you in the pod. You're in no danger. The three of us are all going to take very good care of you."

"Just think," Opinal said as they all started walking. "You'll have three masters to look after you instead of having to share a master with other humans. We'll be an improvement for you."

¡Pinche pendejo! If she ever got loose, she was going to poison them all!

Sweating and breathing heavily, Ari gave up on wiggling out of Tumial's grip. Better to save her energy for later, but there was no banking her fury. She hadn't been this angry in a long time. It was good because the anger kept her fear at bay.

Before she knew it, they were entering the airlock for the Mining and Processing Assessment Team's ship. Then she heard Bazium talking to Jolian. He was only a hallway away!

She tried to scream through the gag again, but she wasn't any louder than a whisper. He was so close but she couldn't signal him in any way.

The men ducked into one of the rooms, the hatch hissing closed behind them and cutting Ari off from her last hope of rescue.

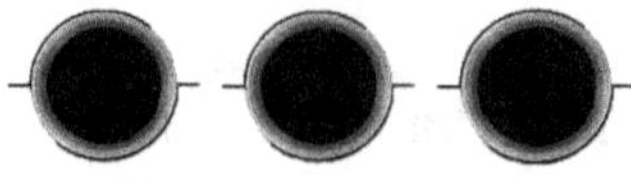

"It's my turn to hold her," Opinal announced with an impatient rattle as he stood over Dutamier. "Let me have her."

"Must you be so insistent?" Dutamier asked as he reluctantly handed her over to Opinal.

"I'm merely following the rules we agreed on," Opinal said as he cradled Ari to his chest and stepped over to an empty chair to sit. He was quick to arrange her sideways on his lap.

"You don't need to watch even the sectioned-submarks tick by," Dutamier grumbled as he pulled his Ident off his belt and brought up a schematic holo to study.

Opinal ignored Dutamier. Taking hold of Ari's wrists, he placed her arms on his shoulders. "Now you can cling to me," he urged her.

She wasn't sure how much time had passed, but it was enough that all three of them had her sit in their laps and "cling" to them. It wasn't the worst or most painful thing she'd ever experienced, but her arms were getting a little tired. At least she wasn't bound or gagged any longer. After they'd locked the cabin door, they'd freed her with a warning to behave.

"I'm thirsty," she whispered.

"I can fix that," Tumial was quick to say as he snatched a canister from the table and came to stand next to Opinal. "Hand her to me so I can help her drink."

"No, it's my turn to hold her, give me the canister," Opinal argued.

"I'm not handing it to you," Tumial said with an angry rattle. "I want to do this."

Ari listened to them bicker with a flicker of hope. This level of dysfunction could only help her. Bazium and the rest of the Advanced Squad wouldn't be leaving for another two rotations. The trick would be to get loose and get back to him before they departed.

She knew the compound better than any Talin. She'd seen all three studying charts, maps, and schematics, but none of that would help them when they got to all the stuff Ari and her people had been forced to jerry-rig.

If she could only get back on the compound with a little head start, she could make sure they didn't find her. Then it would be easy to make her way to the Advanced Squad's ship.

Getting free was her responsibility. There was little hope Bazium or his men would come looking for her after Opinal launched the escape pod to fake her death. She had to hand it to them, that was a clever plan. And it left her with only herself to rely on.

On top of everything else, these three were making her doubt her decision to stay with Bazium. Would other Talins attempt to steal her? If she even made it to Talarian, would she be under constant threat of kidnapping?

"So much for civilized," she muttered to herself. "You guys are more like kids with a new toy than members of a mighty empire."

"What did you say?" Opinal asked, ignoring Tumial's angry rattle.

"I'm really thirsty," she said meekly.

Tumial held the canister up. "Come here, little human. Then you can have all the water you need."

Suddenly Opinal picked her up and basically dropped her on the ground before launching himself at Tumial with a rattle loud enough to bounce off the walls. "Give me that canister!"

Forget the fact that there were plenty of other canisters of water and an entire food-syth system not too far away. Apparently Opinal had to have that one canister that Tumial was holding. The level of immaturity with these two was beyond ridiculous. Moving quickly, Ari ignored the pain in her hip and scrambled under a nearby bunk. Big bodies crashed around the room as the two warriors fought.

"What is going on in here?" Dutamier shouted as he rushed into the room.

Unlike Bazium's crew, Jolian's team had to share rooms. This one belonged to Dutamier and Tumial, but they had agreed to let Opinal join them. The room might be spacious for two Talins, but three made it a tight fit. When Dutamier joined the fight, there no place she was safe.

A body smashed into the bunk over her causing it to crack in the middle and sag dangerously. With her current spot no longer secure, Ari was quick to wiggle out from under it. All three males were still busy beating on each other, so she took advantage of the wide-open hatch. Part of a chair had fallen over the hatch tracks, making the display chime loudly and the hatch remain open.

None of them even noticed when she slipped out of the room. Heart beating wildly she dashed down the hall, her sole focus on finding the airlock back onto the mining compound. She was within sight of it when big arms wrapped around her and lifted her off her feet.

"Don't ever do that again," Dutamier said as he easily held her despite her struggles. "I know we scared you, but if you run away again, I'll be forced to punish you."

Ari almost laughed at that. Punish her? As if they'd been doing such a good job of taking care of her so far!

Feeling a little hysterical, she flailed around wildly. "I want to go back to Bazium!"

"Bazium isn't your owner any longer," Dutamier insisted calmly as he carried her back to their room. Her struggles were no more a problem for him than if she wasn't moving at all. "We're your owners now and you might as well grow accustomed to us."

If she opened her mouth, nothing but cuss words would have come out, so she remained silent and went still as she imagined all the ways she could hurt these guys. He better hope she never got her hands on a rock puncher or core-sampler because she was experienced with those tools, and she'd show these Talins no mercy.

Punish her? Ha! She'd drill a hole right through their thick skulls and see if they had any brains inside!

Seething, she didn't realize right away that Dutamier passed right by his shared cabin. The room he carried her into was small with only a single temporary bunk and no other furniture. Not even a small table or shelves.

"This is the isolation room," he explained as he sat on the bunk. "The team uses it when someone requires solitude. Our room is in shambles so you and I will sleep here this rest cycle to allow Tumial and Opinal time to clean up and repair or replace items."

He arranged her on his lap with a loud purr. "I know the fight must have been distressing, but I took care of it and those two won't act up again."

She highly doubted he would be able to control the other two when his answer to seeing the battle going on was to jump in with them. This team was far different than the highly disciplined squad led by Bazium.

And where was Jolian and the rest of the team while these three Talins had been destroying their cabin? They must have heard the ruckus, but none of them came to investigate? Were fights so common they didn't bother responding to them any longer?

Still thirsty, her hip throbbing, and no closer to escape, Ari thought things were looking pretty bad. Then Dutamier leaned over and rubbed a cheek across the top of her head. The smell of juniper filled the air, and mere seconds later a blinding pain exploded in her head.

Forget the water. Now all she wanted was to keep from throwing up!

CHAPTER 20

Advanced Squad Delta 223—Mission Q73 Report (Excerpt)
It's important to keep humans safe from other Talins. The urge to own one can be far stronger than a Talin's common sense or even their desire to be a good member of their family and clan. The allure of owning a human all their own can cause a Talin to act irresponsibly. We must be prepared to police our own people without mercy, even if they're friend, family, or clan.

The moment Bazium received an alert from his ship on his Ident, he rattled with worry and rushed out of the meeting with Jolian. He didn't even say anything, simply turned and started running. He was at the far end of the compound and forced to wait for several large, heavy safety doors to open due to Jolian testing the systems with him.

By the time he was striding back on his ship, all four of his men were gathered around the display next to the escape pod. Tarrian was rattling with irritation as he read something off one side of the display and tapped on data points on the other.

"What happened?" he demanded.

Norrium made a soft, concerned rumble. "Supposedly someone got into the pod, launched it, and hit a nearby satellite obliterating both the satellite and the pod."

"Supposedly?" Bazium asked gazing at the closed door that indicated the pod was gone.

"The pod did launch, but we did a head count and no one's missing," Norrium explained and then sounded a rumble of worry. "Except Ari."

Dread washed over Bazium. "Did you check to see if Ari was in my cabin?"

"We thought she was with you and Jolian," Norrium admitted.

Bazium didn't waste another moment talking. Within submarks he was at his cabin door and then he was staring at an empty cabin.

"Ari," he whispered as he stared at the room uncomprehendingly. He felt his men at his back but didn't turn to look at them.

Slipping past him, Hesarium checked the cleaning chamber. "She isn't in here. We should search the ship."

"I know she isn't with the other humans," Hesarium said. "I was careful to double check that area before I locked it down and went to the pod. But she could have wandered into many other parts of the ship."

"She might have been looking for Hurt, I mean Aubrey, and gotten lost," Tarrian suggested. "That pod is on the way to my cabin. She might have triggered it by accident and is now hiding. I could see any of the humans being scared of reprisal for losing a valuable item."

"What if she was in it?" Norrium asked. "You said it was triggered from inside, not outside."

Tarrian sound a rumble of disagreement. "That could be wrong. The data trackers on those pods are notorious for being easily corrupted."

Bazium could hear them talking around him, but it was as if he was far away.

Despair tried to drag him under but his warrior will wouldn't allow it. He was sure she hadn't been in that pod if for no other reason than he refused to believe she could be dead.

"Tarrian," he barked out. His crew stopped talking and snapped to attention. "Take your human and close yourself in with the rest of them while running diagnostics."

"Systems and hull integrity?" Tarrian asked.

"Systems only," Bazium clarified. "Double check for any faults or anything somewhere else that might have made the pod think someone was inside requesting launch."

With a rattle of determination, Tarrian headed for his cabin, no doubt to collect Aubrey and then lock them both in the human section while he did as Bazium ordered.

Next he turned to his second in command. "Norrium, go over every single thumb's width of this ship. Don't leave a single access hatch or storage spot unexplored."

"I'll shut down and lock up as I go so no one will be able to sneak back into a section I've already searched," Norrium assured him, and then he was gone.

"I want you two to start going over the compound," he said. "I'm going to find Jolian so his team can help us. We're going to find her."

His words were met with rumbles of agreement and rattles of determination. Turning on his heels, Bazium left the ship with Hesarium and Sapurian right behind him. Once in the compound, they veered off to begin sweeping the far end of the mining facility while Bazium searched out Jolian.

He found the team leader standing near an open cabin on his team's ship. He was speaking in angry tones to two Talins who appeared to have been in a scuffle. A few quills were broken and they had some scuffs on their keratin chest plates, but other than that, neither looked truly injured. Jolian's team might be the best, but Bazium knew from past experience that the programs run under the Expansion and Resettlement Authority weren't as well-disciplined as those who served under the War Committee.

"What's happened?" he asked with a worried rumble as he turned to face Bazium. "You rushed off and then I had to deal with a disturbance between these two."

"One of the humans—" Bazium began but then stopped when he caught the scent of something familiar. Mixed in with the smells of the other Talins was his own bonding oil. It was faint but unmistakable.

Leaning in close, he took a deep breath, causing Jolian to sound a confused rumble. "Advanced Leader Bazium, what are you doing?"

He didn't bother answering as he stepped past Jolian. One of the men standing there met his gaze unflinchingly, but the other refused to raise his eyes. It only took another breath before Bazium realized both these men had traces of his bonding oil on them.

That could have only happened in two ways—if he'd rubbed his scent glands on one of them or if they'd recently touched Ari. She'd been covered in his oil when he'd left earlier and the simple act of carrying her would have transferred some of the scent.

"Where is she?" he roared and launched himself at the one who wouldn't meet his eyes.

Rattles of surprise sounded from Jolian and the other team member as he drove the smaller Talin into the nearby wall.

"No!" the young male gasped as he tried to get away from Bazium. "I don't know what…what you're talking about!"

Hands went around his arms, trying to pull him away. "What do you think you're doing? Let go of Opinal and explain yourself!" Jolian demanded.

Ignoring Jolian, Bazium wrapped one clawed hand around Opinal's throat, making sure to sink the tips of his claws into the strip of exposed flesh at the base of his neck. Opinal went perfectly still the moment he felt the pointed end of Bazium's talon.

"Please, by the ancestors, don't kill me," he begged.

"Where is she?" Bazium asked again. He was so focused on Opinal he didn't notice when Jolian and the other Talin stopped trying to pull him away.

Opinal opened his mouth to say something but two bodies hurled into him, sending him to the floor. Sounding a war rattle that echoed through the hall, Bazium used his impressive strength to shove the two bodies off of him. Staggering to his feet, he caught sight of Opinal disappearing down the corridor shouting for help.

Both Jolian and the third Talin were still on the ground. He turned to grab the other Talin that also had the faint scent of his bonding oil only to have Jolian grab his leg and pull him back to the floor. The two were back on him, trying to use their superior numbers and weight to immobilize him.

It wasn't going to work.

First he pounded a fist into the side of Jolian's head. The Team Leader sounded a surprised rattle and flailed, dazed from the blow.

"Tumial, run!" Jolian ordered as he managed to grab one of Bazium's wrists by sheer luck. Bazium broke the hold with ease, but it gave Tumial a chance to stand and stagger away.

Bazium launched himself from a crouched position, managing to wrap his arms around Tumial's legs and take him back down to the ground. From there he dragged Tumial under him and locked one arm around Tumial's head, forcing the Talin to bend his neck forward and separate the plates on the back of his neck. With the vulnerable skin over his spine exposed, Bazium shoved several clawed fingers between the plates, stopping with only the tips of his talons digging into the skin there.

Tumial went perfectly still at the clear threat. If he moved, Bazium would sever his spine.

"No, please," he whimpered, sounding a rumble of fear. "It was Dutamier's idea."

"Where is she?" Bazium growled, shoving his fingers a little closer.

"Sp-spare room!" Tumial wailed. "She—"

Something hard hit Bazium across the back of his head. His armor plates took most of the blow but there was still enough impact to cause his arms to loosen around Tumial. The Talin under him was pulled away as he was forced to roll on his back to fend off the next blow.

Rattles of aggression came from several different places as Bazium deflected a blow with the hard-plated and quilled covered section of his right forearm. He felt several of the quills break from the impact but other than that, he was unharmed.

That wouldn't be the case if he couldn't fend off the next blow coming at his face.

Rolling sideways, he bowled his body into a set of legs, knocking his attacker off balance. Another opponent rushed forward, but he had enough time to lurch to his feet and recognize the female who'd given Aubrey all the mineral samples coming at him with an improvised stabbing weapon.

Reacting on instinct, he moved to the side at the same time he grabbed Jolian and shoved him forward. The female tried to pull back but didn't have time. Jolian took the blow to his abdomen, the tip of the weapon sinking a finger's width into him between two plates. Not deep enough to penetrate skin, but deep enough to get the weapon stuck.

Taking advantage of the trapped weapon, Bazium kicked out. His blow landed hard on the female's chest and sent her flying into the nearby corridor wall. Standing back up, she tried to shake off the blow and come at him again. As much as he wanted to admire her as the toughest fighter among Jolian's team, he needed to focus on finding Ari.

Before she could bring up her defenses, Bazium grabbed her head and smashed it into his knee. She went down with a muffled cry. He'd been careful to keep his blows from permanently injuring any of the team yet, but if they kept him from his goal, that might change.

Opinal was huddled against a wall next to Jolian, trying to pull the weapon out of his team leader. Grabbing Jolian by one of his legs, Bazium sent him flying into several more team members coming down the hall brandishing clubbing weapons.

He could only be thankful that these Talins hadn't taken advantage of the free warrior training and armaments offered by the War Committee to all the civilians working in war zones. If they'd had projectile or energy weapons, he'd be at least wounded if not dead by now.

Grabbing Opinal by the throat, he lifted the smaller Talin to his feet. "Where is she? Take me there!"

Without a word he pointed and Bazium dragged him in that direction. Objectively, Bazium knew he was hurt. Several of the blows he'd received were inhibiting his movements and coordination skills. Once he was no longer in his warring mindset, his body would be in pain. But all of the damage he'd received was easy to ignore with his goal so close at hand.

Opinal stopped him at a door with a gesture and whimper. Bazium shoved the Talin away from him as the hatch slid open. Inside was one of Jolian's team members sitting with Ari in his lap. This had to be the Dutamier that Opinal had mentioned.

Relief and worry warred inside of him. Ari was hunched over in Dutamier's lap, her skin pale and coated with a fine sheen of sweat. He could tell from her expression and body language she was in intense pain. She was alive, but he didn't know what was wrong with her. Her eyes were closed tightly and her hands were locked over her mouth as if to keep from crying out.

At the same time Dutamier sounded a rattle of shock, Ari opened her eyes and focused her gaze on him.

"It's about time you got here," she whispered through her fingers before her eyes shut and she went limp.

"I'll kill you!" Bazium roared as he stepped forward. Dutamier stood up and quickly set Ari on the small bunk behind him.

"I found her hiding in the compound," he said, turning back to meet Bazium boldly. "You must have missed her when you collected the humans. You left her behind, so she's mine to claim."

Bazium was about to launch himself at the thieving, lying Talin when Jolian and a dozen of his team tumbled into the small room. The tangle of bodies pushed Bazium forward and Dutamier took advantage. Striking out he caught Bazium in his already abused head, making him see stars and sending him to his knees.

He caught sight of Ari behind Dutamier, her unconscious body lying in an unnatural position. Anger and fear flooded his system, making him forget all about his pain.

Rattling with rage, Bazium gathered his legs under him and rammed his shoulder into Dutamier's body. He managed to twist them both so they hit the wall near the bunk instead of crashing on top of Ari. Without hesitation Bazium started raining blows on the Talin, pummeling Dutamier's body with all the skills and power he possessed.

Only when Dutamier cried out and went limp did Bazium stop and let the male's body fall to the floor. When he tried to move to Ari on the bunk, his legs folded under him. The room swam and he barely kept himself up on his knees.

Many arms reached out, grabbing and dragging him away from Ari. He was distantly aware of Jolian giving orders about separating all of them while he figured out what was going on. He sounded a challenging rattle and started fighting the hands, but there were too many bodies and the quarters were too tight to move. They managed to pile on top of him, forcing him face first to the floor.

"Get a full set of restraints!" Jolian called out. His voice was close to Bazium's earhole, making him think the Team Leader was the one kneeling on his neck. He was still able to breathe, but barely. If he wasn't able to move soon, he would pass out, and it would be easy for them to lock his arms and legs together.

Then he heard Norrium's familiar war rattle and the distinct sound of a body hitting a wall accompanied by a sharp cry of pain. That was followed by Sapurian and Hesarium's rattles filling the air, and soon no more bodies were on top of him.

"Advanced Leader?" Norrium asked as he helped Bazium to his feet.

"Ari," he croaked out, his lungs and throat on fire.

"What's happened?" Norrium asked with a horrified rattle before issuing orders. "Sapurian, see to Ari! Hesarium, if any of them even takes a breath too deeply, shoot them."

"Advanced Leader Bazium," Jolian protested. "You can't come onto my ship and attack my team!"

"Your team snuck onto our ship and stole a human!" Hesarium accused. "It was clever, but I found the switch-code where someone input false data to make it look like Ari got into an escape pod and launched it. I've never met Talins so deceitful. You have no ancestors waiting for you!"

There was a shocked murmur among Jolian's team probably both from the accusation and the curse.

"That can't be," Jolian said, turning to look at Dutamier who was unconscious on the floor.

"There's nothing obviously wrong with her," Sapurian said, drawing all their attention to the medic kneeling next to the bed. "Normally I'd suggest we go to the nearest Med Bay, but considering the current situation, I believe it would be more prudent to carry her back to our ship for further assessment."

"Agreed," Bazium rasped. He took a step, intending to pick Ari up, but his legs buckled. Only Norrium's hold kept him upright.

"I'll carry her," Sapurian said. "I'll be gentle and we'll all walk together back to the ship."

Bazium didn't like it, but it was more important they leave than he be the only one to touch Ari.

"Approved," he said to Sapurian. The medic was careful as he gathered Ari's limp body into his arms.

Bazium couldn't see him but heard Hesarium sound a warning rattle. "If any of you come near us as we leave, I won't hesitate to discharge my weapon into your useless hides."

Sapurian went first, followed by Bazium leaning heavily on Norrium and then Hesarium brought up the rear.

Jolian's team must have taken Hesarium's warning seriously because no one even made a sound as they passed. That was good because Hesarium had a darkness in him that meant he wouldn't hesitate to carry out his threat.

He'd never been so proud of his squad.

CHAPTER 21

Advanced Squad Delta 223—Mission Q73 Report (Excerpt)
The human response to pain can vary widely. Don't be fooled if your human doesn't cry or wail as some humans will be stoic and reluctant to admit to discomfort. The important thing is to learn your human's tone of voice and body language so you can better judge when they are in true distress.

When Ari opened her eyes and saw Bazium's face, relief flooded through her. It didn't lessen the horrific headache at all, but it did make her smile even as she slammed her eyes shut against the bright lights of the Med Bay.

"Hurts," she whispered as she swallowed convulsively trying desperately to keep hold of her nausea. Vomiting now would not make her feel better and might even cause her head to split open.

"I know," Bazium murmured. She felt his broad hand wrap around her own. "Sapurian is scanning you now."

"Oil," she rasped and lifted one hand to point to her head before letting it drop across her chest. "Oil in my hair."

"She's not making sense," Bazium said with a worried rumble.

"I can't find an obvious injury," Sapurian said. "Ari, can you tell me where the pain is?"

"Head," she answered.

"Did you take a blow to the head? There's no sign of a concussion or contusion," Sapurian said.

"*Headache*," Ari said, not surprised when that word didn't translate. "All the pain is in my head but not from an injury. Just give me something for pain."

Those words cost her and she was forced to focus on her breathing again. Sapurian and Bazium spoke over her, but pure misery distracted her from their conversation until Bazium spoke directly to her.

"Open your mouth, my little Brave. We're going to put a medication wafer on your tongue. Let it dissolve and you should start feeling better."

Ari opened her mouth without hesitation and felt the wafer laid on her tongue. Closing her mouth, she felt it melt. She counted her breaths and within five the pain in her head started to ease. The headache didn't go away entirely, but it was reduced to more tolerable levels.

Opening her eyes, she found Bazium's face only inches from her. Knowing Sapurian was in the room with them, she barely kept from kissing him, but she did smile.

"It's good to see you," she whispered. "Now get this gunk out of my hair!"

It took some explaining but she finally made them understand that Dutamier's bonding oil was the cause of her pain. What she didn't expect was how difficult it would be to get the oil out of her hair. It took four tries and as many different cleansers for them to find one that stripped the bonding oil completely off her.

"I've read that our ancestors didn't like the scent of anyone's bonding oil except for their partner's," Sapurian said as Ari sat up on the exam table, rubbing her clean hair. "But nothing about it caused physical pain."

"I guess I'm just lucky," Ari quipped.

Bazium sounded a rattle of distress. "This was not lucky," he argued.

Ari waved a hand in the air. "It's a human saying that means the opposite. But now we know how to get bonding oil out of hair, so that's good, I guess."

"It will never be an issue again," Bazium promised with an emphatic rattle. Then he started purring as he gathered her into his arms. "I'll make sure you're at my side at all times from now on."

"I get time in the cleansing unit by myself," she was quick to say. "Everyone needs privacy to pee."

He and Sapurian sounded rumbles of humor. "That is the one place you can go alone, but I'll be waiting at the door for you."

"Sure, whatever makes you happy," she said with a yawn. Now that her headache was completely gone, she felt strangely light, as if the pain had been a physical weight on her. With the lightness came a feeling of total relaxation. Snuggling into Bazium's arms, she closed her eyes.

"Can we sleep for a while?" she asked.

"Let me see to your injuries," Sapurian said as she drifted off to sleep.

"As long as I don't need to let go of Ari," Bazium answered. "You can check my health." Sapurian sounded a rumble of amusement as she heard him move around them.

Ari wanted to ask about Bazium's injuries, but sleep claimed her before she could form the words.

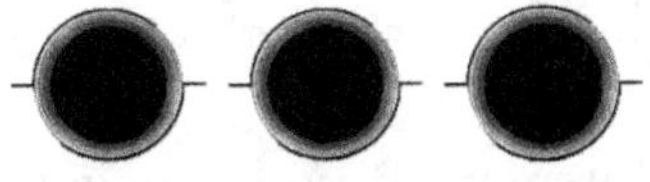

Ari woke to the sound of an argument between Bazium and Norrium.

"I have no interest in listening to his excuses or explanations," Bazium said with a low rattle of anger. "He should have had better control of his men."

"We need to maintain goodwill with this team," Norrium argued.

When she sat up, both Bazium and Norrium turned to look at her. "I'm sorry," Bazium was quick to say as he broke out in a loud purr. "We should have gone into the hall and shut the hatch for this discussion."

"It's fine," Ari assured him as she slid off the Med Bay bed. "I think I was ready to wake up anyway."

"We should ask Ari," Norrium said. "It concerns her."

"No!" Bazium refused at the same time Ari spoke up.

"Ask me what?"

"Jolian would like to speak to you," Norrium explained, ignoring Bazium's warning rattle. "He wishes to see that you are well and apologize."

"I want to talk to him too," Ari said as she reached Bazium's side. Wrapping both arms around one of his, she was careful to keep clear of his quills. Even a simple cuddle with a Talin could be risky business!

"Don't feel pressured," Bazium said. "There is no reason to speak to him."

"There is a very good reason," she argued. "He and his team want to go looking for humans. That means he and I need to have a talk. I don't want him to find some people and end up tossing them from Talin to Talin like a child's toy."

"She makes a good point," Norrium commented. "Words of caution coming from her will bear more weight than one of us."

"Fine," Bazium growled out. "But only Jolian is allowed aboard, no one else."

"He's waiting in the airlock," Norrium said. "Should I bring—"

Bazium cut Norrium off with a negative rattle. "We'll go to him."

He moved to pick her up, but she was quick to let go of his arm and step back. "I think I need to walk a little."

"You could still be weak," Bazium fussed.

"Baz, I'm fine," she murmured. "Walking and stretching my legs will be good for me."

"Baz?" both Norrium and Bazium said in unison. But Bazium asked, "What does that mean?"

"Uh, it's a nickname," she answered quizzically. "A shortened version of your full name, Bazium." Then it hit her.

Most species didn't have the concept of a nickname. "Humans like to give those closest to us nicknames as a sign of affection."

Bazium sounded a rumble of delight. "I'm pleased to be Baz. You must call me Baz at all times now." Then he looked to Norrium who was sounding a rumble of humor. "But not you. Only Ari can call me Baz."

"Of course, Advanced Leader," Norrium said with exaggerated formality. Ari was sure the male was being sarcastic, or at least as sarcastic as a Talin could be. She almost giggled.

"Let's go talk to Jolian," she said and tangled her fingers with Bazium's. Hand in hand they walked to the airlock. On the short walk she found out they'd be departing a day earlier than scheduled. Bazium didn't say it, but she was sure the reason for the change was because of her kidnapping. She couldn't blame him. She was eager to get away from Jolian's team too.

Jolian was standing in the center of the airlock holding an ornate box in both hands. He started up a happy rumble the moment he saw her.

"You look much improved," Jolian said as he held the box out to her. "I've brought you this as an apology."

Ari didn't move her eyes from Jolian, ignoring the box he held out. "I could have died."

A rumble of distress came from the Talin. "Tumial, Dutamier, and Opinal didn't mean you any harm."

"They might not have meant to hurt me, but they made me very ill," Ari responded. Her entire focus was on scaring Jolian enough for him to keep his team in check. She didn't care if she had to stretch the truth a little to keep any humans they met from being terrorized.

She didn't let Jolian's upset rumbles soften her resolve as she continued to talk. "Bazium already explained to you how fragile we are. The way those three attacked me was frightening. They bound my arms and legs. They wrapped me in a sheet. I didn't know what was going to happen. My heart could have beaten too fast and killed me."

Her words caused all the Talins around her to sound rumbles of distress, but she didn't take her eyes off Jolian.

"That happens to humans?" Bazium asked.

"I need to keep a very close eye on Aubrey's medications and body chemistry," Sapurian murmured at the same time. "If any of you are susceptible to this heart beating too fast issue, it will be her."

"I didn't know," Jolian said. "I'm sorry for the pain and fear you endured. Those three have been reprimanded and after this assignment, they will be returning to Talarian. They won't be going on any more missions with us."

"Can you tell me that the rest of your team members won't act badly? That they wouldn't try to steal someone or cause them to fear for their lives?"

"Of course they wouldn't," Jolian said with a defensive rattle. "My team is made up of intelligent and honorable Talins."

Ari wasn't intimidated in the least. "Before I was abducted, would you have thought any of those three capable of such an action?"

Her verbal volley struck home. A sharp rattle of shock came out of Jolian, and he flinched slightly as if she'd made to strike him. Everyone remained quiet as Jolian worked out his reply.

"I will go to my team," he finally said. "I will make them understand. No human we find will be terrorized. They'll be tamed gently with gifts of food, promises of shelter, and soft words."

"What if they continue to refuse?" Ari asked. "What if, even after you've given them everything, they hide or attack you?"

"I don't know," Jolian said.

Ari couldn't fault his honesty, but she had a counterproposal. "Make an offer," she told him. "Find some way to communicate and make an offer. Let them decide and then leave them to their fate."

Jolian sounded a rattle of disagreement. "But that could mean they die."

"Or they might survive," Ari countered. "Either way, it has to be their choice. If they agree to be pets, they will be like Aubrey and me, happy. But if you try to force them to be pets without talking, it could go badly. We humans put a lot of importance on choice. Forcing us to do something will cause anger and resentment. Even if we were going to do it anyway."

Jolian was quiet for a moment and then finally sounded a rumble of assent. "If I find some, I will make them an offer."

Ari tugged at the sleeve of her omnie. "If you have some of these, they'll be even more likely to agree," she said with a grin.

"I'll make sure we stock some," Jolian agreed with a rumble of amusement. "Are you done chastising me, little human?"

"For now," she agreed. Then, finally, she dropped her eyes to the box. "What's in there?"

Slipping one hand under the box to support it, Jolian turned it to face her and then opened it. Ari gasped at the sight of six large and perfectly formed Yurali crystals. As she stood there, transfixed by a sight she'd only ever seen in textbooks or educational vids, the crystals slowly changed color going from bright orange to a soft yellow.

"They're more beautiful than I could ever imagine," she whispered and leaned her face closer to the contents of the box. Each crystal was nestled in padding cut out to keep the delicate structure from being damaged. Even Aubrey, the highest paid of all of them, would never have been able to afford even one of these crystals in her lifetime.

Greed like she'd never experienced before made Ari's hands twitch. She was looking at enough wealth in one box to potentially buy a property and domiciles for everyone. There might even be enough funds left over for food and other necessities for months.

She wanted to snatch the box away, find some hidden place alone so she could hold and touch each crystal. She wanted to admire them and dream of a life where she could keep them all to herself. She longed to examine every facet of each Yurali and spend hours watching them slowly change hue.

"They're colorful," Bazium grunted next to her as he leaned over to get a better look. "What are they?"

"What are they?" Ari sputtered. "They're the most beautiful gemstone to ever exist, that's all!"

She was surprised when all the Talins around her rumbled with humor even as Jolian answered Bazium's question. "They're

Yurali stones used in telcorine engines. These are examples of large ones and could power a telcorine for several solars."

"Don't our battle cruisers use telcorine engines?" Bazium asked.

"Yes, any very large ship that won't be landing on the surface of a planet uses those engines," Jolian answered.

As the men talked about the various applications of Yurali crystals, Ari couldn't pull her eyes away from the splendor. Jolian spoke of practicality and expense to Bazium, but all she could see was the beauty as the crystals shimmered on the outside while their cores gently pulsed. To keep herself from reaching for one, she gripped her hands tightly together.

"My family trades in these," Jolian said, answering a question Ari had missed. "I picked these up at a good price and was going to send them back for my family to resell. But I'd rather Ari had them."

The stones she was looking at were worth so much that she should probably refuse. Or only take one.

Or maybe two.

Half. That's it. She would take half of them. No, that was too greedy. Two would be better. But he was offering her all six, so taking three was still less than what he was willing to give her. Her mind bounced between greed and restraint.

"Ari?" Bazium's voice pulled her attention from the crystals. Looking up, she found everyone was staring at her. How long had she been lost in thoughts?

"Sorry," she said and looked back at the gems. "They're just so pretty."

With a complete lack of reverence, Jolian plucked one from the case and handed it to her. She'd been clutching her fingers together so tightly it took her a moment to be able to bring her hands up and take the gift. Despite the glowing center and sparkling exterior, the crystal was cool to the touch.

Holding it up to the light, she gazed into its depths, wondering what it would look like exposed to different types of light sources.

"It appears you've picked an excellent gift," Bazium murmured, managing to draw her attention away from the gem.

Feeling a little embarrassed, she moved to put the crystal back in the box, but Jolian had already closed it and was handing it to Bazium.

"I'm happy with this one," she said, but without much force in her voice.

Jolian sounded an affectionate rumble. "You can share those with the other humans. If you're this fascinated, then they might be as well. I knew the crystals held appeal as decorations for some species, but I never expected you to be so entranced."

"But they're gorgeous," Ari protested, holding up the one she had in her hand. "Can't you see how stunning it is?"

She almost bit Bazium when he brought a broad hand up to pat her on the head and sounded a rumble of affection. "Yes, it's very nice. Almost as pretty as you."

Ari barely kept from rolling her eyes and tucked the gem close to her body. "If you could see it with my eyes, you'd realize they're gorgeous."

"It's only a stone," Bazium answered easily with a dismissive rumble.

This might be one of the most heartbreaking aspects of the Talins. They could see the practical aspect of the Yurali but not the splendor.

She almost laughed when she realized their views of humans were the complete opposite. They saw humans as alluring but not practical.

The universe was a strange place.

CHAPTER 22

Advanced Squad Delta 223—Mission Q73 Report (Excerpt)
As a group, our humans mostly get along but we see occasional squabbles. If the matter isn't resolved at the time of the quarrel, the humans who are arguing will stop communicating with each other and will even use third parties to relay messages. I've noticed that my Ari is often that third party. I've seen her not only act as messenger to help the parties resolve their issues. It seems that, unlike Talins who elect mediators and facilitators, human leaders also fill those roles. Their system places undue burden on their leadership. Perhaps this is one of the contributing factors to their civilization's demise.

"There's no reason you can't go back to sleep," Bazium said as he buckled his belt. Ari had awoken after an extended rest cycle and wanted to visit with the other humans. After bathing her and himself in the cleansing unit, he was doing his best to talk her into resting longer but she'd stubbornly refused. "Sapurian said you might be fatigued for several days."

"I'm all recovered," she argued. "And I want to talk to my people. You know how we humans are. We constantly need to reassure each other."

Bazium could swear she found that statement humorous. "There are many humans to comfort each other. You don't need to help with that."

"Ah, but I'm a special human," she answered. "You've said so yourself."

That was a point he couldn't refute. "You are the most special of all of them," he agreed, and then sank to his knees and gently eased her foot into the first slipper. Once he'd realized how easily human feet and hands became chilled, he was doubly thankful to have purchased the slippers as well as the omnies for all the humans.

"We'll be arriving at Unile Station tomorrow," he mentioned as he slid the second slipper on her dainty foot. Humans had such tiny phalanges on their feet. How did they keep from accidently breaking them on everything?

He was so distracted by that thought he almost missed her stiffening at his words. Sitting back on his heels he sounded a soothing rumble.

"You'll be safe," he promised. "Although all five of us have go onto the station, we won't be gone long and we'll secure the ship. If there are any issues, we'll be notified and we'll rush back. Unile might be a disreputable place, but we'll work quickly and return within several marks."

"I'm not worried," she said, but the tension in her body made Bazium think she was lying. Or at least not sharing her concerns.

Raising himself to his knees, he opened his arms, and she accepted his invitation without hesitation. Despite their time in the cleansing unit, he could still smell some of his bonding oil clinging to her hair and skin. It was faint but there. To soothe them both, he rubbed his active scent glands into her hair.

She took a deep breath and relaxed into his embrace. "You're important to me, Baz," she whispered.

"You're my everything, little Ari."

She was silent for a moment and seemed content to cling to him so he remained still. When she finally pulled away to hold him at arm's length, he didn't resist.

She framed his face with her hands, absently rubbing her thumbs over his scent glands. The soft pressure sent jolts of pleasure through him, but he forced himself to focus. His human had something significant she wanted to say to him.

"You've scent-bonded with me, and judging from the way I reacted to Dutamier's oil, I've scent-bonded to you. But we humans don't say that. We say I love you. Sometimes we forget to say it, and it can hurt the other person, so I want to make sure you hear me loud and clear."

She brought her face to his and brushed her lips across his.

"I love you, Baz. Bazium the Talin. Bazium, Advanced Leader of Advanced Squad Delta number 223. I've never loved another partner as I love you, and I doubt I ever will again. My body might not die if we're separated for too long, but I know my heart and spirit would shrivel and turn to dust. I don't like that you put a collar on me without my permission, but I've forgiven you. If it means I get to stay with you, I'd wear all the collars."

He was so overwhelmed by her naked emotions that he said the first thing that popped into his head. "Why would you need to wear more than one collar?"

"That was your takeaway from all that?" Ari huffed out. "I pour my heart out and that's what you focus on?"

"We Talins aren't schooled in conveying our emotions." He could tell she wasn't truly upset with him, but he still felt embarrassed over his poor response. "I feel a deep loyalty to you as well, my little Ari. I could go without speaking to any members of my family or clan again without sorrow. But if I was forced to spend more than a rotation without being in your presence, I'd suffer. Long before Collapsed Scent disease affected me, I'd want to end my own life if I couldn't be near you. You're the sun I orbit. I revel in your light and heat. I was raised to think of my people first, then my clan, then my family, and only lastly of myself. From the moment I met you, I could think only of you. If that is love, I love you."

She threw herself at him, wrapping her arms tightly around his neck. "That's borderline psychotic, but definitely love," Ari agreed with a soft laugh.

Rumbling with affection, he gently wrapped his arms around her, breathing in their combined scents. "Is that a good thing?"

"It depends on the situation. But right here and now it's a good thing," she explained. They stayed like that for some time before she pulled back. "I need to talk to a few people, but the moment I'm done, we're coming back here for cuddle time."

"Anything you want," he agreed, already looking forward to settling back down in the nest with Ari.

"That's what I like to hear," she murmured.

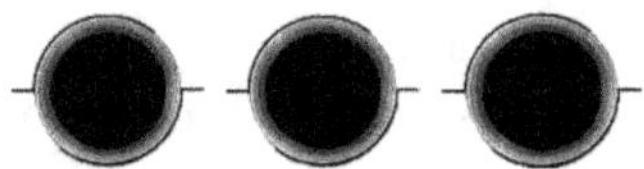

Everyone was ecstatic about the Yurali crystals Jolian had given her. Between the gems Aubrey received and the Yurali, they would be able to secure transport and lodging while they found a place with jobs for all of them.

She wasn't sure why, but she told everyone there were only five. She decided to leave the sixth one hidden in Bazium's room. She'd never been this greedy before, but she couldn't give that last stone to the group. She consoled herself with the fact that it was the smallest of the bunch, but there was no denying that she was acting selfishly.

Keeping one stone back along with the fact that she had no intention of leaving with everyone once she'd negotiated their passage somewhere safe, left her feeling greedy and self-centered.

Everyone was going to feel betrayed when she abandoned them, but leaving Baz to die was a line she wasn't willing to cross.

After the excitement over the extra wealth calmed, Ari managed to get Aubrey and Liz alone. Andres was off playing with Norrium and baby Lucia was with Daniella. She knew she didn't have much time so she quickly explained scent-bonding and the consequences of separation.

Both women reacted with shocked silence before tears welled in Aubrey's eyes. "I don't want Tarrian to die," she whispered.

"How can we be sure they've scent-bonded to us?" Liz asked, touching the top of her head.

"Unless you ask them, I guess you can't be," Ari admitted.

"Everyone will be so angry if I don't leave with them," Aubrey said. "But I don't want to go. I know I should want to escape. That I should be really angry about the collar. But I don't care. I don't care if everyone calls me a pet. I want to stay with Tarrian." She rubbed at her eyes with shaking hands. "I have a confession."

Liz spoke, "You can tell us. You know Ari and I won't judge. She's having sex with Bazium and I let Norrium hold my baby girl. It's okay, Aubrey."

Aubrey refused to meet their eyes. "I was going to stay behind when everyone left. I was going to tell Tarrian to leave me in our room and then I was going to hide in there and not answer the door if any of you tried to come get me."

"You were going to stay? Even though everyone voted to leave?" Ari clarified, breathing in a sigh of relief. She'd wanted Aubrey to stay but didn't want to potentially emotionally blackmail her with the threat of Tarrian dying. Knowing Aubrey was already planning to stay made her feel much better.

"I love him," Aubrey said simply. "Even after the collar, I loved him." She glanced around and then moved closer to her and Liz. "He made my collar special."

Before Ari could ask, Aubrey reached up and unlatched her collar. She didn't take it all the way off, simply opened it up widely enough to show she could remove it if she wanted to and then clicked it back in place.

Liz made an audible gasp and then slapped a hand over her mouth and looked around, but no one noticed.

Ari cursed under her breath. "Why didn't Baz think to do that with my collar," she muttered.

"Even though we can't talk to each other, he gets me," Aubrey continued. "I don't know how, but we manage to have full conversations without saying anything. I've never felt as close to anyone as I feel to Tarrian."

"That's beautiful," Liz murmured.

"I'm in love with Baz," Ari volunteered. "And he admitted he scent-bonded to me, so I'm not leaving." She turned her attention to Liz. "You need to decide if you're staying or going. No judgment from me no matter which you choose. But I need to know now."

Liz didn't even hesitate. "Staying."

Ari felt her shoulders relax. It was good to know she wouldn't be the only human staying with the Talins. She wouldn't have left Baz anyway, but this made her decision a little easier.

"You and I can stay in our Talin's rooms," Aubrey said. "But how will we keep Liz from getting dragged out with everyone when they leave?"

Ari shook her head. "I've been thinking about this a lot, and the easiest way would be to go with everyone onto the station."

"That doesn't sound easy," Liz argued.

"Hear me out," Ari said. "If Aubrey and I stay in our rooms, everyone will waste valuable time trying to get us out. And it leaves Liz trying to get herself, Andres, and Lucia away without help."

"Okay so we're all on the station, then what do we do?" Aubrey asked.

"I negotiate passage with some of the gems, get everyone loaded and then we step off just before the doors shut," Ari said. "If I have to, I can bribe the crew of the transport to not let anyone get back off to come after us."

Liz and Aubrey were quiet for a moment, and Ari worried they might be upset at the clumsiness of her plan. But then Liz chuckled and Aubrey grinned.

"I like it," Liz said. "The best part of that plan is we don't have to deal with Mari. We just step off and we're all done with her arguing about it."

"What?" Ari asked.

Aubrey made a confused sound. "Arguing?"

Liz regarded both women quizzically. "Mari was like a rabid dog while we were all deciding if we were going to leave or stay. She hounded people until they agreed with her."

Ari frowned. "No, she was in her room for most of the discussion. When she got back, we made sure she wasn't alone so she couldn't bully anyone."

"Uh, no," Liz said with a little shake of her head. "She came back almost right after she left. She didn't stay in her room, only went to get a picture of Tomas. She must have been talking to people for almost two hours before you noticed her. I thought you were deliberately ignoring her, but now I think she was keeping herself out of your line of sight. That room has all those support columns, so it would have been easy."

"*¡Puta!*" Aubrey cursed. "She knew she wasn't supposed to interfere like that."

Now Ari wished she could go back and do the whole discussion again. If Mari had been bullying people, no telling how many others might have wanted to stay with the Talins or were truly on the fence and got railroaded like Liz.

"I failed again," Ari mumbled, disgusted with herself.

"What do you mean?" Liz asked.

"I should have been better," Ari said. "I should have made it so Mari couldn't intimidate anyone."

"That would have been nice, but honestly it doesn't matter," Aubrey said bluntly. "I intended to stay and I bet Liz planned to slip away in the chaos of the station with the kids."

Ari met Liz's gaze. "Is that true?"

Liz nodded. "Aubrey guessed right, I never planned to really leave. Norrium is amazing, and Andres is happier than he's ever been. How can that compete with the hope that we all find mediocre jobs somewhere that will only tolerate us?"

Put like that, Ari couldn't argue. "Do you think anyone else has plans to slip away and come back here?"

"I don't think so," Liz answered. "The three of us are the most vested right now since no one else has a Talin paying extra special attention to them. And Mari did a good job of selling our escape as the only option, so I think everyone is convinced it's the right way to go. Nothing you could say was going to convince most of them otherwise. The only ones I think you need to talk to are Daniella, Christos, and Santos. I think they want to go where you go."

"You don't think that's a betrayal of the entire group if I take the most skilled people with me?" Ari asked, biting her lip.

"I think it's Darwin," Liz bit out with uncharacteristic viciousness. "For years I watched everyone look to Tomas and then you for all the answers, while rarely offering suggestions or alternatives. They were quick to criticize if something went wrong and slow to accept blame if they made a mistake. Do you know Janson said it was your fault that we ended up in collars? And Mari went around telling everyone that she asked to have the INT but that you were so power hungry you refused her."

Ari was speechless. How had all of this been going on without her realizing it? "Mari never asked to have the INT," she whispered. "I would have let her. I didn't want it."

Liz laughed humorlessly. "No one wanted it. We all knew it was a huge risk, and no one was shocked when you got so sick. Mari was manipulating the circumstances to fit what she wanted to believe. No one was ever going to be happy no matter what decision was reached. How could they when any choice we make leaves us vulnerable? But remember the glory days our great-grandparents lived? When you could go to those big stores filled with food and buy anything you wanted. What were those called?"

"Grocery stores?" Aubrey suggested.

"Yeah, that's them," Liz said with a nod. "Grocery stores barely existed when our grandparents were kids, and by the time they were adults those businesses were gone and we had the Essentials Ticket System. I hate to say it, but most of these people are still stuck on a past that our grandparents only got to experience as children. They want a golden era where we had a homeworld that was not only viable but fruitful. They think if we keep looking, we'll be able to recreate that life somewhere else, but that's pure idiocy."

"Do you think that's true?" Ari asked Aubrey.

"I agree with Liz," Aubrey said. "But I don't think Mari's sold on the idea of finding a paradise anywhere. She's too practical for that. I think she's convinced herself this is what Tomas would have wanted."

"Do you think this is what Tomas would have wanted?" Ari asked her two friends. "I keep going round and round in my head with it and I could see him going either way."

"I think he would have done the same thing you did, but he wouldn't have had to battle Mari," Liz answered.

"Should we come up with some kind of code," Aubrey asked. "So you can tell us when to start moving off the ship or hang back from the crowd?"

A sharp ding sounded through the ship. It was such a common sound everyone knew what it meant—an approach warning. They were near the station and would probably be docking soon.

"Looks like it's too late to come up with code words or a secret phrase," Ari murmured. "Just try to stick with me and if I point at a door or hatch, head for it."

"I guess that's better than nothing," Aubrey grumbled.

And wasn't that the key phrase for all of them at the moment? Whatever they had was better than nothing.

CHAPTER 23

Advanced Squad Delta 223—Mission Q73 Report (Excerpt)
****This passage was redacted from the submitted report***: *There was obvious evidence that the humans, especially acting as a collective, could be as intelligent and capable as a Talin. But I didn't expect the final proof to be a successful escape! How could they be smart enough to get away from us but lack the intelligence to comprehend how dangerous the universe is for them? Do these humans have no sense of self-preservation?**

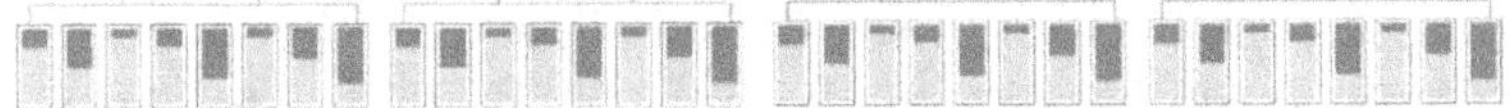

Bazium knew something was wrong the moment he and his men walked aboard their ship. The absolute quiet was unnerving. He'd grown accustomed to all the different sounds the humans produced. Their movements, talking, laughter, and of course the sounds of the cub playing. Although they weren't loud enough to constantly echo through the halls of the ship, the humans created a murmuring background sound that he associated with them.

Even when they slept, they were not quiet. Some breathed loudly through their mouths, others spoke as they slumbered, and many of them moved often even while asleep.

Soft noises should have filled his earholes the moment he stepped in the hall leading to the humans' section of the ship.

However, nothing but sterile silence, broken only by the sound of the biosystems self-check, clicked through each room and corridor.

"No!" Tarrian roared out. He'd realized something was wrong also, but he was quicker to react. He dropped the packages he was holding and sprinted down the corridor, the rest of them close behind. Bazium barely kept from plowing into Tarrian as he came to an abrupt halt at the open blast doors to the humans' section of the ship.

"I checked before we left. They were closed," Tarrian said, a rumble of worry drowned out by his rattle of aggression. "These were closed!" He turned to Bazium. "Someone has taken the humans!"

"No," Sapurian said, sounding a rattle of deep betrayal. "They left on their own. Look." He pointed to the display on the wall next to the blast doors. The cover was off, and it was clear the inside had been re-keyed to open the blast doors without the need for an Ident.

The display was on the inside. Only the humans could have done this.

When Hesarium sounded a wounded rumble, they looked to where he was kneeling next to a pile of items. It took Bazium a moment to realize it was the collars. Hesarium picked one up and held it reverently as he sounded a keening rumble.

"She left me?" Bazium whispered. "She said she loved me." He made no rumble or rattle because his brain was too busy screaming in pain at the thought that Ari had lied to him.

"They all left us," Norrium said as he brushed past them to pick up one of the cub's toys. "How could they do this? I promised Andres we'd play when I got back. And Liz is still nursing her other cub. What will they do on their own? I told her I would make sure she was never hungry and her cubs would never feel discomfort again." The rumble that came out of him was so woeful Bazium felt it deep in his chest.

In a rare show of temper, Tarrian punched the wall. He left a fist-sized dent in the metal. It must have provided some kind of relief because he roared and did it two more times. He was pulling his hand back for a fourth when Bazium caught his wrist.

"This isn't productive," he admonished the soldier.

"They ran from us," he roared at Bazium, breaking all kinds of protocol.

"And we will chase them down and bring them back," Bazium roared back. He sounded a war rattle, the noise echoing violently through the ship.

Sapurian sounded a sorrowful rumble. "What if they run away again?"

"We will talk to them. We will find out how to make them stay. We are Talins, but beyond that, we are Advanced Squad Delta 223—the most highly decorated Advanced Squad in all of the Talin fleet. We do not fail."

The men were silent for a moment, and then they responded in unison, *"Our bones are iron and pure determination flows through our veins!"*

The familiar words told Bazium his men were with him and ready for action. "What do we do with our bodies and will?" Bazium asked, sounding another war rattle.

His men answered his rattle with their own, the sound almost drowning out their voices. *"We triumph!"*

With his men focused, he issued orders. "Everyone put on your full battle gear. Hesarium, double-check the charges on everything. I don't want to risk our armor deactivating if we have to act as shields for our humans. Sapurian, pack a med kit specifically for the humans. Include a foldable travois in case too many are hurt for us to carry. Norrium, find me the head of this station. I don't care what you have to say. We talk to the station controller or we rip this station apart panel by panel. Tarrian, I want you carrying anything you need to get us in every spot on that station. If you can't open it with your kit, we'll blast it open."

Rumbles of agreement sounded along with rattles of aggression.

They were going to get their humans back and woe to anyone who stood in their way.

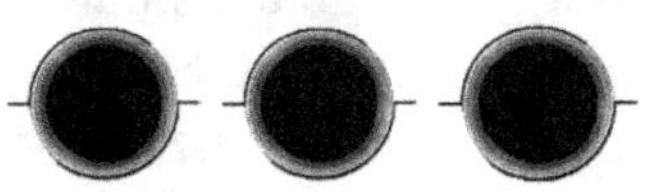

The Vicpor station controller looked suitably fearful as Bazium and his men towered over him. The much bigger Vicpors, surrounding the controller and wearing full armor, must all be female. Those females might look intimidating to most, but Bazium saw nothing but poorly maintained weapons and a lack of coordinated movements. It was obvious these women didn't train on a regular basis or care for their gear.

They posed no threat.

"There are no species here like the ones in your vids," the station controller repeated, his neck tentacles rubbing nervously over his mouth. "Now, I suggest you leave before we make you depart."

Bazium remained silent for a moment, allowing both the station controller and his guards to grow tense and fidget. One guard kept cycling her weapon on and off. It could prove to be a disastrous habit and was yet another example of the superiority of Talin training.

"We know they were on this station," Bazium said after enough time had passed to make all the Vicpor around him grow edgy. "If you tell us where they are, we will leave your station as we found it. If you don't, we'll go to war. It's that simple."

"You can't mean that," the Vicpor stuttered out. "You can't possibly be willing to potentially start a war for a group of weak and ugly creatures."

Tarrian sounded a loud war rattle behind him and tried to advance on the station controller. A glance from Bazium had him stop moving and quieted his rattle. He didn't silence it.

"They belong to us," Bazium growled out. "We want them returned."

"Fine, they were here," the station controller squeaked out, his eyes focused on Tarrian. "But they're already gone."

Bazium was out of patience. Fear and worry drove him to act with violent haste. Timing his movements precisely, he snatched the weapon out of the guard's hands after she'd cycled it off and before she could reactivate it. Swinging the weapon around, he delivered a mild blow to the station controller with the stock of the weapon before breaking it in two and throwing both pieces at two other guards.

The moment he'd started reaching for the weapon, his men were in motion. From one breath to the next all the guards had either been disarmed, knocked out, or both.

In the midst of the groaning guards, the station controller stood, shaking with fear and clutching the spot where Bazium had struck him.

Stepping close, Bazium wrapped one hand around the controller's scrawny neck, squeezing only enough to serve as a warning. The station controller's neck tentacles tried to bite at his hand and wrists, but they couldn't get through his thick, armored skin.

"Where. Are. My. Humans?"

The controller's skin turned a deep gray from fear. "No! No, don't kill me. Please, I have wealth! So much wealth. And it can all be yours."

Bazium tightened his fingers momentarily as a warning before he spoke. "I'm going to ask one more time, and then I'm going to break your neck and ravage this station if I don't get the answer I want. Tell me where the humans are."

Slime started oozing out of the controller's tentacles, the Vicpor version of crying. "We sold them. The ship has already left with them. You can have all the proceeds. All of them!"

Bazium bared his teeth at the Vicpor. "I want the locator credentials for the ship," he snarled out.

"Yes, I can do that," the station controller agreed quickly. He pointed to a display set in the wall. Bazium half carried half dragged the Vicpor to the display and then shoved him face first at it. The frantic Vicpor pull up the information and Hesarium was quick to lean over so he could copy and coordinate the data with their ship.

"I've got them, sir," Hesarium said as he interfaced with the ship through his Ident. "If we leave now, we can catch up to them within two marks."

Bazium didn't let go of the station controller yet. Giving the Vicpor a little shake, he sounded a rattle of rage. "If I find out you've lied to us, no place will be safe from my wrath. I will hunt you and every member of your family down. I will scour the universe until not a single living thing shares your DNA. Now, is there anything you want to tell me before we go?"

"They fought," the Vicpor whispered. "Some of them were injured and had to be carried. It wasn't my fault! They should have known better than to come onto this station without an escort. They brought it on themselves!"

Bazium tossed the Vicpor into a wall with a roar. The creature slid down the wall leaving a trail of slime before he landed in a heap on the floor. "You should pray to your ancestors that all of them are still alive or I'll return to take my revenge on your body!"

The sounds of the Vicpor wailing with fear followed him out of the room. With his men on his heels, he rushed back to the ship. They had to hurry. His little human, his Brave, his sweet Ari might be hurt or even dying. He had to get to her.

"The ship is registered to a Hamlershin company," Hesarium said as they boarded. He'd managed to follow and interface with his Ident without missing a step. "We don't have any trade or reciprocation treaties with them. They could refuse and threaten us with government action if we proceed against them."

"Then we go to war with the Hamlershin if we have to," Bazium announced, breaking all kinds of military rules and regulations.

None of his men argued with him. They didn't even rumble or rattle out sounds that would indicate they disagreed with his intent.

All of them were determined to get their humans back, even if it meant starting a war.

CHAPTER 24

Advanced Squad Delta 223—Mission Q73 Report (Excerpt)
Do not underestimate how clever humans can be with their tiny, clawless hands. They will surprise you every time. You should also know that if there is trouble to be had, the humans will find it.

Christos moaned softly as Daniella examined his leg. "It's broken," she announced grimly. She stared at the leg for a moment and then abruptly stood up. She stripped out of her omnie, pulled off her wrap, and then put the omnie back on. Using her teeth, she started ripping the wrap into pieces.

"Whoa, what are you doing?" Ari asked, concerned that Daniella was giving in to her grief. She shouldn't have worried.

"I'm going to try and set the leg; then I'm going to bind his legs together so the good one can act as a splint for the bad one," Daniella explained after ripping another strip off the wrap. "It's the best I can do since we have nothing to use as a splint.

"Right, okay, tell me what to do," Ari said. Christos kept himself mostly quiet as Daniella worked, and honestly, Ari was surprised he didn't pass out from the pain when she tugged at his leg. He even managed to joke about how hard it was going to be to take a piss with both his legs tied together.

After she'd finished, Ari tugged Daniella away from Christos. "How life-threatening is this?"

Daniella shook her head. "Honestly, I don't know. If nothing changes, the best I can hope for is that I put it back in place. But there's a good chance it'll heal crooked and he'll have a limp for life."

"That's the best outcome?" Ari asked with raised eyebrows.

"The worst is that he gets an infection and dies a slow, painful death. Or a blood clot forms and travels up to his heart. Or he gets compartment syndrome. For that I'd have to cut into his leg to relieve the pressure, but since we don't have any kind of tools to cut with, I'm not sure how I'd do that. Not to mention that comes with the risk of infection and a slow death too," Daniella stated bluntly. "Unless we can get access to at least some trauma med gear, there's nothing I can do."

"What about making a tourniquet out of a sleeve?" Mari asked, pushing into their conversation. Half of her face was rapidly turning black and blue with her left eye swollen shut. She'd rushed in to aid Christos when he'd been trying to fight off the Hamlershin. Mari had gotten tossed into a wall and knocked out and Christos' leg was broken. The Hamlershin seemed to barely notice their attempt at resistance.

"A tourniquet is for someone bleeding out, not a broken bone," Daniella spat out as she glared at Mari. "Leave the medical stuff to me and you can stick to what you're good at, getting us in trouble."

Ari wasn't surprised when Mari flinched as if Daniella had hit her. No one had heard the Physician Assistant speak so harshly ever before.

"Easy," Ari said, stepping between the two women. "We all knew there were risks with either decision. Tossing blame around isn't going to change our current situation. Only staying organized and focused is going to get us out of this."

Daniella turned her angry eyes on Ari. "We should have voted. You should have protested more. You're as much to blame as Mari!"

She didn't take offense at the woman's accusations only because she understood where Daniella's head was. Like the rest of them, Daniella felt helpless and scared. Unlike the rest of them, she had the skills to help Christos but was hampered by a lack of tools. That would be enough to cause anyone to have an emotional meltdown.

But understanding didn't mean acceptance.

"Walk away," Ari ordered calmly. "If there's nothing you can do for Christos except pick fights with other people, walk away."

Daniella's shoulders sagged at Ari's order, and she dropped her gaze to her feet. "No, I'm, uh, I'm done. Sorry."

"We're all pissed as hell," Ari assured her. "A single one of my Yurali should have gotten us tickets somewhere, not locked up in a cargo hold. None of you could have known those *hijos de putas* would double-cross us."

"I think they double-double-crossed us," Patrice interjected, trying for a little humor. "First they stole our stuff and then they sold us."

"Would a double-double-cross be like a double negative?" Christos asked weakly from the floor. "You know, like, two negatives make a positive. Right?"

Daniella dropped to her knees next to him, tears gathering in her eyes. "Sure, I'll agree with anything you say."

"Then this would be a good time to talk about us getting those matching tattoos," Christos said, reaching for Daniella's hand. Pain from trying to move made him hiss out a breath.

"Try to stay still," Daniella urged him.

"Yeah, going to do that," he said through gritted teeth. "You know, those Hamlershin might look round and doughy, but they're nothing but muscles under that rubbery skin."

Ari walked away from Daniella and Christos. She couldn't help there, but maybe Santos and Aubrey had good news for her. She'd told them to do a thorough sweep of the cargo hold and look for any weaknesses.

She found Angel standing on Santos's shoulders, testing a hatch high in the wall. Despite Angel's best effort, he'd only managed to get it slid open a little. I wasn't open enough for anyone to fit through. Even with putting all his muscle behind it, she could see Angel wouldn't be able to budge it another inch.

Giving up, he carefully climbed off Santos and the two of them leaned against the wall, panting.

"This air has to be low oxygen content," Angel muttered as he tried to get his breath back. "I'm not so out of shape that I should be breathing hard from that."

"I think you're right," Ari agreed, rubbing her hand over the INT. The first thing they'd done when they'd gotten on the station was have her INT programmed with as many languages as they had available. It had been quick and uncomfortable, and the tech who did it had warned her it would take a while for the INT to finish organizing all the information. Now she could understand Hamlershin, Vicpor, Marper, Ollie, and hundreds of other languages.

But speaking Vicpor hadn't done them any good when the next person they'd talked to had sold them "tickets" to this cargo hold.

The Vicpor station agent told them a Hamlershin ship was heading to a Veli station that was looking for skilled labor. It was too good an opportunity to pass up. Ari should have known better. No way could they have possibly gotten that lucky.

In truth, Daniella was right. If anyone was to blame for their current situation it was Ari. She'd been too eager to get everyone off the station before the Talins realized they were gone. She'd taken a deal that looked far too good to be true.

By the time they realized they were being herded into a cargo hold, half of them were already inside. They'd fought, but both the Hamlershin crew and Vicpors from the station had been ready for that. They mercilessly pushed, shoved, and hit until everyone was driven into the large cargo area. They helplessly watched the hatch close with a hiss, effectively trapping them.

Old blood stains and claw marks on all of the walls of the cargo hold told a clear story: this wasn't the first time live cargo had been locked in this place.

Their freedom had lasted little more than an hour, and she was positive this new captivity was going to be far worse than what they experienced with the Talins.

"If we keep working on it, we might be able to get that hatch open," Angel commented once he got his breath back. Stepping away from the wall, he rested his hands on his hips and looked up at it with a considering expression.

"Maybe," Santos said, but she could hear the doubt in his voice.

"Where's Aubrey?" Ari asked looking around.

"She found some wiring and she's trying to figure out if it goes to anything important," Angel said, pointing to the far end of the cavernous room.

"Have you guys found anything else?" Ari asked.

"Nothing," Santos said grimly. "It's not looking good."

Ari glanced up at the hatch and then back down to the guys. "Okay, get some help and see if you can get the hatch open. Worst case scenario is seeing if we can hide Liz and the kids up there and they can escape later when the Hamlershin have offloaded the rest of us."

"That's a fucking dim outlook," Angel grumped.

"I said worst case," Ari reminded him. "Maybe that hatch will lead to the ship's enviro room, and we can kill all the Hamlershin with some poisoned air, toss their bodies out an airlock and take over the ship. Then we'll go wherever the hell we want to. How's that for a cheery viewpoint?"

Angel grinned, looking more lighthearted at her bloodthirsty description. "Much better."

"I'm going to find Manni, Patrice, and Nina to help you guys," she told them.

"Yup," Santos said, looking relieved. Angel was a small guy, but if they were right and the oxygen levels were low, even supporting Angel was hard on Santos. Manni and Nina were two of their stronger individuals, and Patrice was by far the smallest adult in their group.

After that, if they needed more help, Ari would have every able-bodied person in the room dog pile in the same spot so someone could climb up and lever that hatch open.

She'd only taken a few steps away from Angel and Santos when Mari stopped her. The one eye that wasn't swollen shut was red-rimmed and streaming tears.

"Can I help? What can I do?"

That was the moment Andres started crying loudly, making Ari wince as the child's fear and frustration bounced off the walls around them.

"Maybe you could see if you can help Liz with Andres," Ari suggested.

"Andres doesn't like me. Liz told him I'm the reason he had to leave Norrium," Mari said, fresh tears streaming down her face. "Everyone's mad at me. How do I make this right, Ari? Please!"

Ari sighed. She didn't have time to play counselor to everyone as well as keep her own shit together. She really wished she had the luxury of indulging in a good panic!

Before she could say anything, the ship bucked violently around them. Anyone standing lost their footing, and Ari heard the sounds of bodies hitting walls and floor panels along with cries of pain and surprise. The lights flickered a few times as the ship shook and bucked again.

She couldn't do anything to steady herself as she got tossed around. Something hit her shoulder causing white hot pain to radiate from that joint. Gasping, she lay still for a moment even after the ship regained stability.

"Who's hurt?" Daniella called out.

"Here," a weak voice next to Ari whispered. Sitting up Ari winced from the pain in her shoulder. When she tried to move that arm it didn't want to work right. Hoping it wasn't broken, she let it hang limply at her side as she got to her knees next to Charlotta.

"What's going on, Lottie?" she asked as Daniella arrived to kneel next to her.

"Stomach," she croaked out.

Daniella was quick to get her on her back so she could feel around her belly, finding several spots that made Charlotta whimper.

"Definitely bruising," Daniella assessed. "Maybe even some internal injuries and bleeding. I can't tell." She looked up at Ari to say something and then noticed the limp arm. "And you have a dislocated shoulder."

"Better than broken, yeah?" Ari asked with as close to a grin as she could make. Every breath she took caused her more pain.

"Aspin!" Daniella called. "Can you help?"

Although Aspin didn't have any formal medical training, he was unshakable, so Daniella was quick to ask for his assistance when she had to do something unpleasant.

"This is going to suck," Ari muttered as Aspin made his way over.

"A lot," Daniella confirmed.

"Get it over with," Ari ordered. "And ignore anything I scream at you."

"I always do," Daniella assured her.

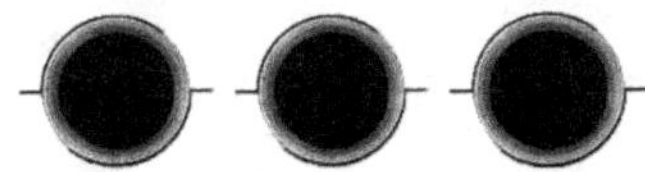

"What do you think is going on?" Santos asked. The ship had stopped jerking around, but the lights were still flickering unpredictably. Despite the circumstances, they'd managed to see to the injured. Thankfully Emery had managed to keep Christos from being tossed around during the more violent moments.

It had involved some screaming but Aspin and Daniella had gotten Ari's shoulder popped back into place. The pain was no longer brutal, but it was so tender and sore she'd tucked her arm into her omnie to limit movement.

"I don't know," she answered. "Maybe the ship's having some kind of stabilizer issue."

"Naw," Angel said. "I don't think it was a ship malfunction. I think they were being evasive."

They were all sitting with their backs against the wall. Everyone had suffered at least some bruising earlier, so now they were all leery of walking around if the ship was going to move erratically again.

"*¿Que?*" Santos said. "Evasive?"

"Yeah, like they were trying to evade someone," Angel elaborated. "As if a ship was coming at them."

"Shouldn't that be impossible," Ari argued. "Aren't there all kinds of safeties and stuff to keep that from happening?"

"Sure, on civilian ships," Angel answered. "But what if it was a warship coming at them?"

As if to prove Angel's theory correct, the sound of weapons fire echoing out in the halls beyond the cargo hold filtered in through the heavy hold hatch.

"They came for us!" Aubrey cried out, voicing what Ari was thinking.

Ari met Santos's gaze. "Frying pan or fire?" she whispered.

He gave her a half smile that was more fear than humor. "If the fire has a Med Bay to help Christos and Charlotta, all I can say is burn, baby, burn."

CHAPTER 25

Advanced Squad Delta 223—Mission Q73 Report (Excerpt)
Humans lack the ability to do proper risk assessment. If you are in charge of even one human, you must be vigilant. I haven't seen it yet, but I'm sure they could find trouble in an empty room!

The hardest part of rescuing the humans was catching up to the Hamlershin ship. He and his men had far too much time thinking about what could be happening to their humans as they pushed their ship's engines to the max capacity.

Once they found the medium-range cargo ship, they strafed it twice to disable the engines and sensors. Then it was only a matter of latching on and cutting a hole in the hull. These were all things they had both trained for and practiced in combat situations.

His crew acted with flawless precision.

The Hamlershin tried to fight, but they were no match for Advanced Squad Delta 223. They cleared the halls with rapid efficiency, delivering a swift death to any Hamlershin they found.

Not a single one of his men hesitated. All the Hamlershin onboard the ship had signed their death warrant when they'd refused to meet with the Talins to return the humans. Bazium had even offered them money, but the Hamlershin refused.

Bazium thought it was because the Hamlershin were thieves, so they believed the Talins were also. Their distrust earned them all death by Talin.

During the close-quarters combat, Norrium and Tarrian took several rounds when one lucky Hamlershin managed to catch them in a crossfire. But their armor took most of the damage and the wounds were minor. Norrium was bleeding down his arm, and Tarrian took a hit in his leg but both ignored it as the rest of them would have.

Wound care would come later; finding their humans came first.

"Here!" Hesarium shouted out and indicated a large hatch at the end of the hall. "They're in here! All of them!"

"Secure this intersection," Bazium ordered Tarrian and Sapurian. "Hesarium, get that hatch open."

His men did as he ordered. As Hesarium manipulated the hatch controls, he and the others returned fire. Soon there was no fire to return. Either the remaining Hamlershin had retreated or they were all dead.

"Access achieved, Advanced Leader," Hesarium called out.

Bazium turned his head in time to see the cargo bay door hissing open with jerky movements. It stopped halfway and refused to keep going, but that didn't matter. The opening was wide enough for two Talins to walk through side by side.

In an unprecedented lack of discipline, Tarrian broke rank and threw himself into the room.

"Aubrey!" he shouted at the top of his lungs. "Where are you, my Hurt? Where are you, my human?"

All the humans had been sitting and were now stumbling to their feet as he followed Tarrian into the room, Sapurian, and Hesarium on his heels.

"Tarrian!" Aubrey cried out as she stepped around someone lying on the floor. She said something else in her human language but was cut off as Tarrian dropped his weapon and snatched her into his arms, sounding a rumble of joy.

"My human, my Hurt, my Aubrey," he said as he rubbed his scent-glands into her hair with clumsy haste. "I thought I'd lost you."

Then Ari was at Bazium's side, smiling up at him. He dropped to his knees and tried to draw her into his arms, but her gasp of pain stopped him. Fearful that she was grievously injured, he tugged at the ties to the omni so he could strip her down and look for injuries.

She stopped his movements by putting her hand over his. "My shoulder's hurt, but it's fine." Then she pointed to one of the humans still lying on the floor. "Some of us are hurt badly. We need to get them help."

"We will, but I need to hold you first," Bazium said. The impulse to rub his aching scent glands into her hair wasn't something he could ignore.

Without another word, she moved into his space and put her good arm around his neck. "I need that too," she whispered.

"You left me," he said, his chest tight as he spoke.

"I didn't want to, but we took a vote and that's what the group wanted," she explained. He pulled back to see moisture dripping from her eyes. "I was going to come back. Several of us were going to come back. But then we ended up in here."

He sounded a worried rattle. "You're in pain."

"Yes, but the tears are for you," she said. "I never want to leave you again."

"What if your people vote to leave?" he challenged, his chest growing tight. Would his Ari ever pick him before the other humans?

"Even then," she whispered fiercely, pulling his face close to hers. "You have my love and loyalty now. If they want to go, they'll have to do it without me."

She ran her fingers over his scent gland, making him moan from the sensation. When her fingers were coated with his oil, she rubbed them over her lips and then drew him to her for a lip press.

The taste of himself combined with her was intense and caused a myriad of reactions in his body. His mating shaft hardened, but his chest muscles relaxed. His thinking felt muddled, but his emotions felt steady.

"You do strange things to me," he said after she'd broken the kiss and pulled away only enough so they could look each other in the eye.

"Good," she said and flashed her blunt teeth in a smile.

"Advanced Squad Leader," Sapurian called out. "Several humans need medical intervention."

"I'm going to carry you," he warned Ari as he gathered her up, careful to keep pressure off her hurt shoulder. Then he stood with her cradled against his chest. "Tell your humans to follow us back to our ship. Sapurian and Hesarium will move the wounded. Once everyone's settled and cared for, we'll all talk—all your people and my people. We won't force you to do anything, and you won't run. We'll talk until we've all decided what we'll do."

Ari gave him a relieved look. "I like that idea." Then she turned her head and shouted in her human language. Whatever she said made several people laugh, but everyone who was able stood up and moved to follow him as he carried Ari back to their ship.

Soon they'd all be able to understand each other, and then the truly arduous task would begin—convincing the humans that staying with the Talins was in their best interest.

Ari refused to rest until all the injured humans had been treated by Sapurian and settled in their rooms. Several of the humans needed to spend at least a rotation in Med Bay so Sapurian could monitor them. Using Ari to communicate, a few of the humans had requested to stay and help Sapurian while the rest dutifully shuffled off to their assigned rooms the moment they were done.

After everyone had been cared for and either settled in their room or the Med Bay, Ari visited each to make sure they were comfortable. Bazium was impressed by her dedication and patience, especially when she visited Aubrey in Tarrian's cabin. The moment she saw Ari, she started crying. She grabbed Ari's hand and wouldn't let go as she spoke rapidly through her sobbing and tears.

"She says Tarrian is hurt and won't let Sapurian look at the wound," Ari explained as she glanced over to the Talin looming over her and Aubrey.

"I'm fine," Tarrian responded. "Tell her that for me."

"I saw you take a round in your leg," Bazium said with an impatient rattle. "Why haven't you let Sapurian treat it?"

Tarrian sounded a dismissive rattle. "It was nothing but a minor wound. It's more important Aubrey is cared for."

Frowning, Ari spoke up. "But that's the issue. Aubrey's not going calm down until she knows you're healthy."

Bazium listened as Tarrian's rumble went through several fast changes. First confusion and then understanding—a brief submark of sounding a frustrated rattle—then finally back to a strong rumble of soothing and adoration.

"Will it stop the moisture from your eyes if I let Sapurian assess my leg?" he asked.

Ari was quick to translate and Aubrey answered with an emphatic nod. Then she spoke a few words that Ari repeated to Tarrian.

"She says you're important to her and your pain is her pain," Ari explained.

Tarrian rubbed his cheek into Aubrey's hair. "You humans are too soft," he whispered. "Too soft to be on your own."

Ari didn't comment on Tarrian's assessment, only said a few more words to Aubrey who'd closed her eyes and snuggled into Tarrian's embrace. Aubrey answered and Ari turned to Bazium.

"It's settled," Ari said with a relieved sigh. "Aubrey was only upset because Tarrian wasn't being taken care of."

"You've visited with everyone now. Does that mean I take you back to our quarters?" he asked.

"I want to check on Liz and the kids one more time," she answered.

They found Liz and the baby asleep on a bunk with Andres snoozing on Norrium's lap. As he slept, Andres clutched the fierce Talin's hand to his chest like a beloved toy.

After that Ari let Bazium see to her comfort. He was quick to carry her to his cabin, eager to get her alone.

First, he stripped her down so he could examine every inch to assure himself she had no other damage besides her shoulder. The only evidence of her injury was a slight discoloration of the skin and the way she held that arm. Sapurian had assured him the discomfort in her shoulder would resolve quickly with the medication he'd given her.

His next step had been leading her into the cleansing room. Kneeling in front of her naked form, he ran a cleaning cloth over her soft, tan skin. He could faintly smell the Hamlershin's ship on her. All traces of nearly losing her had to be erased.

"I can wash myself," she murmured as she slid her hand over his head and down the back of his neck. He didn't need to remind her to be careful of his sharp backplates. Her touch was already cautious.

"Let me bathe you," he answered as he focused on running the cleansing cloth over the slight swell of her belly. With regular meals, all the humans had gained weight and looking more like the images from the Orlok database. He adored the way Ari's body was filling out. He looked forward to her growing rounder and softer the longer she lived with him.

She was the only perfect thing in his world. She brought color where there had only been gray. She introduced joy to his awareness.

Until her, he'd only been surviving, not living.

Although Ari didn't tend to linger over her bathing routine, she didn't protest as he spent almost two marks washing her from head to toe. It took several rinses to get the last of the Hamlershin smell off her.

Once she was clean, he was quick to wrap her in a large, soft blanket and carry her to their nest. He could no longer stomach the idea of resting in his bunk. If he wanted to slumber, he needed to be curled around Ari in their fluffy nest. Otherwise, sleep would never come.

With her in his arms, he settled down. Leaning against the edge of the nest supported by a wall, he arranged her in his lap and gave in to the need to scent mark her.

She made an appreciative humming sound and snuggled in closer. When both his scent glands were empty, she did something new. She sat up and ran her fingers through her hair, distributing the bonding oil more evenly into her mane.

"That's perfect," she murmured with her eyes closed. He hadn't realized it before, but as she worked his bonding oil in, the smell changed slightly. He drew their new combined scent into his lungs and felt all the tensions he'd been carrying release. The smell he'd associated with sexual activity was actually his bonding oil reacting to her mane and skin.

It all made sense now. Humans might not have scent glands of their own, but this chemical reaction was acting as a bonding scent for his body to latch on to. He would have never guessed humans would be so compatible with Talins. But then again, he was coming to realize his species was so arrogant that they probably overlooked or refused to acknowledge many things.

His good fortune had led him to Ari and the rest of the humans. Now negotiation and compromise would get them to stay.

CHAPTER 26

Advanced Squad Delta 223—Mission Q73 Report (Excerpt)
Humans can be reasoned with, but you have to be prepared to speak with them about a topic for marks, if not rotations. They are inquisitive, so don't be surprised if they ask questions you never considered. Never answer in haste as it's better to take your time than to give them an incomplete or inaccurate response. If at some later date they find your answer is flawed, they will hold that against you, and it can be hard to regain their trust.

Fifteen rotations had passed since he and the crew had retrieved the humans from the Hamlershin ship. One of the reasons they'd stopped at Unile Station was to pick up INTs and the necessary medication for all the humans. When they'd found out about the INTs, every single human had demanded one. Sapurian was kept busy for several rotations implanting and monitoring all the humans.

None of the humans protested taking the medication that kept the tendrils from growing too fast. He suspected none of them wanted to go through what Ari had dealt with.

Along with the INTs and medication, Bazium had also bought the device used to input languages into the INT. It hadn't come programmed with any human languages, but he'd been able to pull them out of Ari's INT. After that, it had only taken a handful of submarks each for him and his men to get their INTs programmed.

He'd never forget the first words Aubrey spoke to Tarrian as soon as he could understand her.

"You're my Talin, so don't get yourself hurt again. Okay?"

He'd sounded a soothing rumble so loud it had echoed off the walls in the Med Bay

With everyone able to communicate, Ari relaxed a great deal. He hadn't realized what a burden it had been until he watched her being pulled in three different directions at once as various humans tried to interact with his crew.

Now they were all gathered in the largest room on the ship. They used the room for storage, and it was bare of any comforts, so the humans had brought pillows, blankets, and pads with them so everyone could sit in a large circle as they discussed their future. Because the Talin furniture wasn't designed with backs and was also built large, most of the humans didn't use it, preferring a well-padded spot on the floor to a backless chair or high bench.

With Ari in his lap, he sat on the floor with them. Tarrian sat to his right with Aubrey in his lap and to his left was Norrium. Andres was sitting on one of his stretched-out legs, playing with his clawed toes while Liz sat between his legs, nursing Lucia.

Sapurian had taken the spot next to Norrium and was busy rifling through his medical reports on his Ident to make sure he'd filled out all the documentation for the humans correctly. This had to be the hundredth time he'd checked himself, but he was worried that any little mistake would mean rejection of the humans by the Talin government.

They all sat in silence staring at each other, no one sure how to start the conversation.

At the far end of the circle opposite him and Ari was Mari. Her face had fully healed, but Bazium had noticed she wasn't the same human as before the Hamlershin rescue. She was much more subdued and tended to spend most of her time isolating herself in her room. He'd brought it up with Ari, but she'd dismissed his concerns.

"Mari will talk when she's ready," Ari had said. "Until then I'm not going to force her."

Apparently, this meeting was where she decided to start talking.

"I'm never calling any of you master," Mari stated in a clear, bold voice. All eyes turned to her, and she lifted her chin. He thought it was meant to be a gesture of defiance, but it struck him as an attempt to appear strong.

"I would never ask you to," Bazium answered honestly.

"What about the collars?" Santos called out. "Are you going to make us wear them?"

Bazium could see that now was the time to be brutally honest with the humans. He reminded himself that no matter what was said or decided today, Ari promised to stay with him. He had to trust her, or he would never get through this without losing his temper.

"I'm not going to force you to do anything," he stated and then made a rattle of impatience when several humans started talking at once. "Let me speak and then all of you can ask me questions."

They all fell silent, their expressions ranging from curiosity to hostility and fear.

"I will start by outlining your circumstances, so we are clear. Humans have no homeworld. No political or military power. No trade treaties or special alliances. You are orphans in this universe. You are vulnerable."

There was some grumbling but no one argued with him. Mari kept her mouth closed but she looked close to tears.

"The Talin Empire is large and exceptionally powerful," he continued. "But we are also a closed society, and many of our own people aren't allowed to live or even visit our homeworld, Talarian."

That revelation caused a few gasps of surprise and more than one sympathetic look. It was one thing to know you couldn't go home because the world wasn't viable, but to have a homeworld and not be allowed to go there must have struck some of the humans as cruel. In truth he agreed with them, but he was one soldier against the monarch and Apogee Assemble. It wasn't as if he had the power to change anything.

"There is only one way to assure that humans will not only be accepted on Talarian but all of Talin-controlled space," he explained. "That is if you are pets. Registered and collared pets. You would need to be owned by me and my crew, and we would act as your protectors. Think of it as a guardianship, the title of pet would be for legal reasons only."

That started up a fierce debate, and he was forced to stop talking. Ari got their attention for him by putting two fingers in her mouth and blowing out. A sharp, piercing sound came from her, startling everyone into silence.

"He's not finished yet," she said in what he now understood to be her "authoritative" voice. "If you don't want to be pets, he's got another option. But let him finish before everyone starts arguing."

That settled them down and all eyes focused back on him.

"If you don't wish to stay with us, I have an alternative place. I've been in contact with a Veli business that does mineral surveys and is expanding to several more ships. They will offer you a similar deal as the Orlok, work for room and board. I tried very hard but I couldn't get a better deal than that. For anyone who wishes, I can drop you off at the Veli station where the company is based. From there they'll assign you to a ship and your future will consist of work and nothing else. But you will not bear the title of pet or wear a collar."

He fell silent, thinking he'd finished giving them their options, but Ari had more to add.

"This is not something we decide as a group," Ari said. She wasn't using her authoritative tone anymore. Now she was speaking to them as a friend. "Every person needs to decide if they stay or go. As I'm sure you've all already guessed, I don't need to decide. I'm staying."

Curling her small fingers around his wrist, she held up his hand to everyone. "This is Bazium and he is my Talin. I love him and he loves me."

"How can you know that?" Mari asked. To Bazium's surprise she sounded truly interested, not hostile.

"They call it scent-bonding," Ari explained. "If I leave him, he dies. It's that simple."

There were some gasps and Angel spoke up. "Aubrey, are you scent-bonded too?"

"You humans aren't as affected as we are," Tarrian said, answering for Aubrey. "But I'm scent-bonded to Hur—Aubrey. She is my life now. If we're parted for too long, my body will no longer function, and I will join my ancestors."

His little speech made many of the humans make sounds of surprise. A few even had their mouths hanging open in shock.

"These guys are serious about commitment," Santos muttered loudly, making several people chuckle and breaking the tension.

"But why do we need to be pets? Why can't we be spouses or family?" Mari asked.

It took some time, but Bazium and his crew explained to everyone the strict laws and taboos revolving around marriages, bonding, children, and non-Talins on Talarian. By the time he was done explaining, many of the humans were nodding with understanding.

"So the choices are being pets or being indentured servants," Charlotta summed up. She was cuddled with her two partners, all of them looking grim. "If we stayed with you, would you need to separate us?"

"Never," Bazium assured her, happy to tell her about this part of their plan. "I and my crew are all from the same clan but different families. Norrium has agreed to be adopted into another family in our clan. They are very wealthy and have several sizable compounds on Talarian. They will give him the largest. We're going to build enclosures so it looks like you are kept as exotic pets, but in truth you'll be housed in the manor we are having built right now. There will be plenty of room for all of you and more if any of you decide to have children."

The humans shared looks of astonishment. Had they thought he didn't have a plan to care for all of them? That explained a lot about their reluctance.

"Norrium seems a little old for adoption," Nina commented dryly.

"The couple adopting Norrium have lost both their children. They can have more produced and raised by the cresh, but by the time the children are mature, the couple will be too old to mentor and train them. Norrium has agreed to train the children as if they were his own, so the couple's name and lineage can continue. That means he gives up the right to have children."

Liz made a little gasping sound. "You didn't tell me that."

"It doesn't matter," he said in a soft, gruff voice. "Lineage and honors mean little to me. I want you and the cubs safe."

Liz leaned close to Norrium and whispered something that made him sound a rumble of amusement and then start up a soothing rumble.

"You'd let us live as couples?" Charlotta asked, drawing his attention back to the rest of the room. "Or thruples? You wouldn't force us apart or send us off to other families?"

"I'm aware of your relationship with Nina and Sofia," Bazium said with a soft rumble of affection. "We would never separate you. Even now I'm crafting a report that would make the authorities on Talarian aware that humans need to be allowed to love as they see fit or they will suffer. We are carefully setting the stage so your every need will be fulfilled. If we are clever enough, Talins will line up to give you things."

"But why?" Manni asked, voicing the question probably hovering in everyone's mind. "Why would you want to give us anything? Why even go through all the effort of making us pets? If we're pets, we can't work for you. We can't increase your wealth, we can only drain it. The Veli and Orloks I understood, but this I don't."

"You do give us something. Something we are no longer allowed to seek from each other," Bazium said, wishing he didn't have to explain this part. He hated the way it made him feel vulnerable. But Ari had warned him this was coming and he was braced for it.

"I've learned from Ari that humans long ago set aside emotional and sexual taboos. You have a freedom Talins don't. We are not allowed any kind of softer feelings. Parent to child. Spouse to spouse. Sibling to sibling. We are raised in a world of obligation and honor. We have become a powerful empire because of it, but we are also missing something fundamentally wondrous—affection."

He paused for a moment, but no one spoke, so he continued.

"None of you hesitate to hug each other. You sit close and hold hands. You press your lips to each other's cheeks, chins, and foreheads without a second thought. You act as if touch is as necessary as breathing. We Talins don't have that, but with you we could. If the Talarian authorities perceive humans as weak and emotionally needy, then of course your owners would need to comfort you with touch. If you find our bonding oil soothing, then we should rub it on your heads. If you need to cling to us, we would of course let you."

"This is making me understand the miners' reaction in a whole new light," Aubrey commented. "I thought they were being ridiculous, but now I get it. They wanted hugs. You guys are all touch starved."

Bazium wasn't prepared for the humans in the circle to give him pitying looks. He was a member of one of the mightiest empires the universe had ever seen, and these humans felt sorry for him?

He managed to stop himself before he said anything that would ruin the positive momentum. He was sure most of the humans were swaying toward coming to Talarian. Without a doubt, if the majority decided to stay with the Talins the rest would follow. He could deal with their pity to achieve that goal.

After a few more questions, everyone went quiet. Mari broke the silence.

"We should discuss all of this, just us, the humans," she said. "Maybe you and your crew could leave so we could talk freely?"

Bazium stood effortlessly with Ari still in his arms. "I'll leave you to converse."

"Ari, Aubrey, and Liz should stay," Mari protested when it was obvious the women and Liz's children were leaving with the Talins. Her tone was both demanding and pleading at the same time.

"No," Ari said firmly when Bazium had turned around. He'd been about to set her down, but her strong denial had him freezing in place. "I can't contribute anything to your discussion. I'm staying with Bazium. If anyone wants to leave, I wish you luck and hope we can stay in contact. The only thing I ask you to remember is that none of the choices are perfect, but then again, neither is the universe."

Aubrey and Liz echoed her words about staying as they cuddled close to their Talins.

"But what if we want to stay with you," Mari asked quietly, her eyes dropping to the floor. "What if we still want you to be in charge? To make sure the Talins take care of everything like they said they would. Could we all of us stay with you then?"

It was clear Mari wasn't asking for the group. She was asking for herself.

Ari patted Baz's shoulder, her wordless request to be set down. He put her gently on her feet but made an unhappy rumble when she walked to Mari.

"I'd be happy if you wanted to go to Talarian with me," Ari told her. "But only if you can leave Tomas and your ego behind. We all loved him, but you can't live your life by what you think he would do. You have to decide what you want to do, not a ghost."

A tear tracked down Mari's face. "You're right," she whispered. "I just want him back so badly."

"That's not happening. So what do you want, Mari?" Ari asked.

"I don't want to live in fear anymore," Mari admitted. "I don't want to dread being cold or hungry. I don't want to worry that a section of radiation shielding will collapse or the atmo generator will fail and kill me. I want to have children and know they will grow up and be able to have children of their own."

"Then you know what the answer is," Ari said gently. Mari nodded, and when Ari opened her arms, the woman collapsed into her with a sob.

"I'm so sorry!" she cried. "I acted horribly, and I was wrong. I could have gotten us all killed."

"Easy, my friend," Ari murmured.

Bazium marveled at his human's forgiving soul. After he'd gotten the full story of what had happened and the role Mari had played, he'd almost demanded she be sent to the Veli and not be allowed to remain. But Ari had advocated for Mari, and Bazium had relented.

There was probably little his human could ask for that he wouldn't give.

"No one died," Ari said as Mari's sobs eased. "You thought you were doing what was right. I've forgiven you, so let's go enjoy a cup of that sweet drink these guys have while everyone talks."

Mari nodded and clung to Ari as she moved the two of them back to Bazium. He was quick to lend his support on Mari's other side. Not only did she accept his touch, but she leaned into him, wrapping an arm around his waist as if he were another human.

No one spoke as they exited the room, trailing behind his crew and their humans. It was out of his hands now. The rest of the humans had to decide what they wanted to do. He hoped they would stay, but even if they didn't, he had his Ari and he would dedicate his life to making sure she didn't regret her choice.

CHAPTER 27

Advanced Squad Delta 223—Mission Q73 Report (Excerpt)
A human can become scent bonded to one of us and suffer horribly if they're separated. Be aware, if you let a human become addicted to your scent, you will need to take special care. Remember, they're delicate and needy, so if they bond to you as they would another human, they'll expect to get to stay close to your side as much as possible.

The next day Ari was sitting with Bazium in the galley. Tarrian, Aubrey, Liz, and the kids were there with her. Sapurian and Norrium were in the control room going over star charts and checking on the ship's fuel status.

The single table in the galley was covered in food choices, all of them approved by Sapurian. Now it was up to Ari, Aubrey, Liz, and Andres to figure out what wouldn't agree with the human palate. Bazium was determined to make a detailed list of acceptable foods to submit to the Talin authorities so on the off chance they wanted to feed one of the humans, they wouldn't accidentally give them food that didn't taste good.

It was yet another example of him going above and beyond to assure their comfort.

"Not ick," Andres declared as he grabbed another handful of purple mush in a bowl. Liz laughed and moved the bowl closer to Andres.

"I guess that one passes the Andres taste test," she said.

Ari was sitting in Bazium's lap, so when she reached for a platter piled high with pancake-looking items made of seeds, he was quick to snatch up the plate and set it down in front of her. She broke off a piece of one and nibbled. It turned out the seeds were only on the outside and the inside was soft and savory.

"Mmm, reminds me a little of *tostones*," she told everyone.

"Oh, I want to try that," Aubrey said, and reached for one as the door to the galley slid open. Standing there were Christos and Daniella holding hands. Norrium was right behind the couple.

"I was walking back from the control room when these two were leaving the human area," he explained and ushered them in.

Christos was walking with a slight limp. Sapurian was able to set the bone to healing and managed to create a brace for Christos's leg so he could walk around without too much discomfort.

Christos spoke first. "We were looking for you guys. Everybody's made their choices."

Ari felt Bazium tense. She was ninety percent sure she knew what Christos and Daniella were going to say, but the ten percent of uncertainty had her holding her breath and clutching Bazium's hand.

"Only seven people want to leave," Daniella said in a rush. "The rest of us are staying."

Relief swept through Ari. She wished everyone had decided to stay, but she wasn't surprised there were holdouts. She could probably even name the ones who insisted on going to the Veli. In the end, the important thing was that everyone got to make their choice.

She scrambled off Bazium's lap and rushed to the couple. She hugged both of them and then noticed something.

Stepping back she eyed Daniella's stomach then looked up at the woman. "Yeah?"

Daniella blushed. "Pretty sure," she agreed.

"What?" Christos said, eyeing both of them with confusion.

"Um, I'm pregnant?" Daniella explained.

Norrium reacted the loudest as his rattle of excitement bounced off the walls of the room.

"Cubs!" he cried out. "We're going to have more cubs! I'll get Sapurian so he can check on the pregnancy. I can't believe it didn't show up in any of the scans before!" He pointed to one of the empty chairs with an urgent rattle. "You should sit. I'll fetch pillows after I've informed Sapurian. Don't go anywhere!"

Then he was dashing out of the room making all the humans laugh. "He's going to be worse than any human father," Daniella murmured with a grin.

"I'm not so sure about that," Christos argued. "I was only a second away from suggesting the same thing."

"Looks like you're going to be getting way more attention than you expected," Ari teased her, and then sobered as another thought occurred to her. "I need to go talk to everyone. They need to prepare. Living on Talarian isn't a given. We have one more hurdle to clear before we have a new home."

"What?" Liz asked from behind her.

Bazium answered for her. "An official from the External Affairs Council wants to meet some of you and make sure humans are fit and well-behaved enough to be allowed on Talarian. Both the External Affairs Council and the Apogee Assembly will abide by this person's decision."

"No pressure, though," Christos commented.

Ari slid her gaze to Aubrey, and they shared a grin remembering when they interacted with Jolian and his team.

"We've got this," she assured them. "We can be charming as fuck. You just watch."

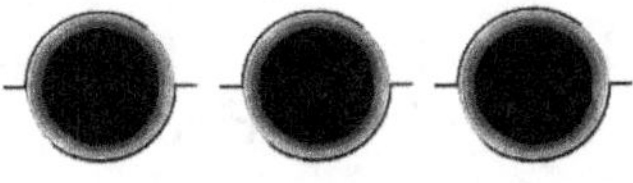

It had taken several marks of discussion and planning but now they were scheduled to meet with the External Affairs Council official at a Talin space station the following rotation. Bazium and Norrium would take Ari, Aubrey, Liz, and her kids to meet the official in his office. Sapurian and Tarrian would stay behind with everyone else.

Tarrian hadn't been pleased to be parted from Aubrey but had finally agreed. Out of all of them, he had the least control over himself when it came to his scent-bond, and they couldn't risk him acting out if he perceived a threat.

Finally, he was able to carry Ari back to their room. The moment Bazium had gotten Ari alone, he hadn't been able to control himself.

He'd stripped her down and started licking his tongue over every part of her. Her moans and pleas had made him so hard and needy that by the time he sank his throbbing mating shaft into her sweet heat, he'd only lasted a few thrusts. The moment she'd fallen apart in his arms, crying out with pleasure, he'd succumbed and followed her.

Now he was on his back, and she was half sprawled across him. He could hear her breathing slowly returning to normal and her heartbeats calming.

Although he'd promised himself he wouldn't ask, he found the question he'd been thinking about since Daniella's announcement sprang out of his mouth unbidden.

"Do you want children?"

He wasn't sure what he'd expected for an answer, but Ari's casual, "Nope," wasn't it.

"No?"

Levering herself up on her forearms across his chest, she met his gaze. She looked so beautiful with her dark hair in a messy halo around her head and draping over her shoulders. He started rumbling with affection at the sight.

"I like kids, but I don't have any burning need to have my own," she explained, her expression relaxed as she talked. She even propped up her chin with her hand.

"You don't?" he asked cautiously.

"Nope," she repeated. "For the past year I've been in charge, and I've kinda felt like I've been everyone's mother. That's probably not going to change any time soon. Even with you guys, everyone looks at me to answer their questions and make decisions. The thought of having kids to care for on top of that doesn't interest me. Besides, even if I wanted to have kids I couldn't. I had myself sterilized before we even left Earth."

Bazium felt a surprised rattle escape him. "You did?"

"Yeah, it was right before I had to quit school and move back to New Rico," she said. "Lots of people were already leaving, and there was talk about shutting down the school, which they did a few months later. I was sitting in my one-bedroom apartment I shared with six other people and thinking, *If I have to move back to New Rico I won't have access to any health care.* I didn't know Daniella was going to be there too. So, I went to the student health office and had everything done I could think of. The doctor wasn't happy with sterilizing someone so young, but she couldn't argue with me when I pointed out that the world was going downhill fast. So she did it."

Her smile suddenly faded and her expression turned worried. "Wait, did you want to have kids, Baz?"

"Yes, but not Talin children," he said, admitting his deep longing for the first time. "I wouldn't be allowed to raise my children myself, and now that I've been able to interact with Liz and her cubs, I want human cubs to raise."

Ari didn't look thrilled by that. "Oh. Um, then I guess we have a problem because I can't give you kids."

The sudden shine to her eyes made Bazium realize she was holding back tears. His rumble turned soothing and he tugged her arm out from under her chin so she was lying flat against him.

"You misunderstand me, sweet human," he murmured to her. "I want to help Liz with Lucia and Andres. I want to help Daniella and Christos raise their child."

"Nina, Charlotta, or Sofia will probably start popping out babies soon too," Ari said with a soft chuckle. "Those three have been wanting kids forever but life on the mining compound was too scary for them to be willing to risk bringing a vulnerable life on board. Liz's husband was an asshole, so even after we didn't have any more birth control, he insisted she have sex with him. That's one of the many reasons no one was overly sad when he died. But that's how she ended up with Lucia. Not that we don't love Lucia, but Liz's pregnancy and birth were scary for all of us."

"Considering your lack of medical supplies and equipment, I don't doubt it," Bazium agreed.

"So you want to be everyone's uncle, huh?" she said, her tone teasing. It was a relief for him to hear the change.

"Yes, uncle. Or secondary father, or whatever they might need," he said.

"Being an auntie or uncle is the best way to go," she murmured. He could feel her body relaxing into his. "You can have fun with them and then hand them back when they're cranky."

"I look forward to having a giant human family," he whispered as her breathing deepened and her body went lax. His human had fallen asleep.

CHAPTER 28

Advanced Squad Delta 223—Mission Q73 Report (Excerpt)
Be aware that human cubs have only two settings; awake and asleep. While asleep they are mostly safe, but while awake, they can be as destructive as a volner in a ship's vents. They don't mean to cause harm, but they have even less ability to discern dangerous from safe than a full-grown human (see earlier in my report where I explain how badly humans assess risk).

It's interesting to note that the cubs are even more interested in clinging than adult humans. They will clutch at your arm, leg, shoulder, waist crests, or neck with great joy. For as troublesome as the cubs can be, they are also adorable and highly affectionate.

Ari tried to tell herself that she wasn't nervous. For the dozenth time she ran her fingers over her collar. All the humans had voluntarily put them back on but with one major change; the collars' locks had been modified so the humans could slip them on and off at will.

Unprompted by Ari or Bazium, everyone agreed they should wear them most of the time so they'd always be prepared if a strange Talin or government official turned up unexpectedly. For

Ari, though, it was the perfect example of being part of a plan instead of having a plan forced on you. The humans all ended up with collars, but this time willingly because they had the power to take them off if they wished. That bit of sovereignty was important, which the Talins were starting to understand.

Bazium had gone a step further and modified Ari's collar so it was ringed with bright blue stones. The setting had been hastily added, and he'd promised her he would have a nicer one made once they were on Talarian. Ari wasn't sure she wanted a different one. This one, with its slightly nonuniform settings and different-size stones, felt more perfect because Bazium had made it with his own hands.

In the short time she'd been wearing it, she'd gotten used to the feel of the irregular gems under her fingers. They felt comforting and helped calm her nerves, especially now that she was about to meet the External Affairs Council official who held so much power over their future.

Bazium was walking in front of her, leading their little group. Behind her was Liz carrying the baby, then Aubrey, and finally Norrium carrying Andres. Andres was chattering with interest, pointing and asking questions faster than Norrium could answer them.

Nikaniel Station was a brand-new station with all the most modern systems and layout. It was on the furthest edge of Talin-controlled space and was meant to stand as an example of the might and wealth of the Talin Empire.

Normally Ari would be staring at everything, but she didn't notice any of the shiny new technology or sleek design. Her entire focus was on keeping herself calm and ready to improvise. She might have acted confident when they were talking earlier about this meeting, but it was mostly a façade. They had no way of telling if this official would be as easily charmed as the miners. One wrong move and this Talin had the power to refuse them and shatter all their carefully laid plans.

The door to the office was open, but Bazium stopped at the threshold and sounded a questioning rumble. Peeking around his big body, Ari was able to see the three Talins inside the office—two males and a female.

The female in the office matched the image of the External Affairs Council official that Bazium had shown her. This was the Talin they needed to focus on charming—Outer Region Coordinator Olimian.

Ignoring the other two Talins in the room, Bazium greeted her as soon as the three of them turned to face him.

"May the ancestors grace you with wisdom and loyalty," he intoned formally, slapping his hand hard against his chest plate in a traditional greeting. "I'm Advanced Squad Leader Bazium looking for Outer Region Coordinator Olimian."

All three Talins were quick to straighten up from the desk display they'd been looking at to return the gesture.

"I'm Outer Region Coordinator Olimian," she said and then gestured to the male closest to her. "This is Station Controller Sitorian and next to him is Captain Porium. They both wished to meet your human pets."

"I'm honored to have such esteemed Talins interested in my pets," Bazium said smoothly. If Ari couldn't see the tension in his back, she would think he was relaxed and even eager for this meeting. "I've never met you before, Captain Porium, but your battleship added my team to the Vervian advancement list. You have my thanks for that."

Captain Porium sounded a pleased rumble. "Which Advanced Squad is yours?"

"223," Bazium answered.

"You and 105 were the two Advanced Squads at the top of the advancement list and the first to deploy," Porium said with an impressed rattle. "The odds were against us, yet 223 and 105 didn't show any hesitation. You and your men are a shining example of Talin virtue."

"It was our honor to fight for the empire," Bazium answered. Ari schooled her expression. Bazium had told her that was the mission he'd lost Lalorian, his second in command before Norrium. It had been the last straw for him as an Advanced Leader and probably the trigger for the Fading. But here were these Talins pretending it had all been a glorious battle without hardship. Idiots.

"Did I hear correctly that you plan to retire once you're back on Talarian?" Porium asked.

"Yes," Bazium said with a rumble of affirmation. "I and my men all belong to the same clan and we plan to retire together. After I'm settled, I'll be looking into employment as an Apogee Assembly committee member. Possibly the Committee for Progress or the Arsenal Committee."

Ari bit her lip, she knew that was a lie. Bazium had admitted he hated politics but it sure sounded good.

Olimian sounded a rumble of approval. "Becoming a committee member is an excellent goal, but may I suggest looking into working for your Clan Assemblies? I find the chance for advancement there far superior to within any of the committees."

"That is good advice," Bazium agreed, playing along. "I will look into it."

"Enough of this," Station Controller Sitorian said with an impatient rattle. "I want to meet the humans."

Ari was a little surprised at his rude behavior. It seemed very un-Talin like considering they were so fond of protocol. Judging by the sound of Olimian and Porium's rattles of surprise, she wasn't the only one.

"Bring them in!" Sitorian demanded as he tugged Olimian and Porium away from the entryway.

Olimian whispered something to Sitorian that he ignored as his complete attention was on them while they all filed into the spacious room. They ended up standing in a line with Bazium and Norrium bracketing her, Liz, and Aubrey. Andres had climbed up Norrium and was lying doubled over his shoulder. He was kicking his little legs and pretending to reach for the Ident hanging on Norrium's belt.

"Is that a cub?" Sitorian asked, stepping within an arm's length of Norrium. The warrior was helping Andres stay balanced with one arm around his small waist. Andres was so distracted he didn't notice Sitorian.

"Yes," Norrium answered. "This is Andres and he's four Earth standard solars old." At Sitorian's questioning rumble Norrium translated that into a Talin timeframe.

Sitorian sounded a soft rattle of surprise. "He's very old to still be so small and immature."

"Human young are slower to grow and mentally advance," Norrium explained. "He's well within the healthy and normal range for a human cub."

Levering his upper body up by pushing against Norrium's chest, Andres looked up far enough to see Sitorian's belt. The station controller's Ident lit up and he was immediately attracted to the bright yellow Ident.

"Oh!" he exclaimed and reached his arms out in the air. "Pretty!"

Because he was a child, they were being more cautious with his INT than the adults. His tendrils were still growing and wouldn't be done for another few months, so the word he shouted out with excitement wasn't in Talin.

Sitorian didn't ask for a translation. Instead, he unclipped his Ident and held it up. "Do you like it?" he asked.

He didn't need anyone to tell him Andres was interested when the boy clapped his hands with glee and struggled to slide down Norrium's back. In a practiced move, Norrium knelt down and eased the boy to the ground.

Andres rushed around Norrium and held his hands open to Sitorian. Liz made a soft, distressed sound, but Ari wrapped an arm around her and put her mouth to the worried woman's ear.

"Bazium and Norrium won't let anything happen," she whispered.

Liz gave a slight nod and remained silent as Sitorian stared down at Andres's open arms while sounding a puzzled rumble.

"He wants you to lift him up and hold him," Ari explained. She turned to Bazium and held her arms out like Andres was doing. Bazium bent his knees and lifted her into his arms. Ari wrapped her legs around Bazium's waist and nestled her head on his shoulder.

"They like to cling to us," Bazium explained as he held her tightly. She thought he'd set her down once the demonstration was over, but it looked like he wasn't interested in letting go.

"How interesting," Olimian commented as Sitorian went down on one knee and carefully lifted Andres. Because he hadn't had a bad experience yet with a Talin, Andres didn't hesitate to settle into Sitorian's embrace. The moment Sitorian had him resting on the crest Talins had at their hips, Andres reached for the Ident dangling from Sitorian's fingers.

"Pretty!" he declared as he held it to his face with one hand, while the other was resting on Sitorian's arm.

"Station Controller!" Porium protested. "Your Ident will have sensitive information on it."

Sitorian's head whipped around to Porium. "It's locked and on glow display mode. Do you think I'm incompetent or that this cub is a spy meant to infiltrate the station?" he asked with enough venom to make Ari wince.

"I didn't mean any offense," Porium began but Sitorian cut him off with an impatient rattle. He stopped the rattle quickly when Andres jerked from the harsh sound.

"Yet I still found your words offensive," Sitorian bit out even as he started up a soothing rumble for Andres. "I've read Bazium's import application thoroughly. I knew before he even entered this room that the cub would find my Ident fascinating. Why do you think I set the glow so high?"

Sensing the tension, Andres reacted as he normally did. He tried to share his new toy.

Tapping Sitorian on the chest he held up the Ident and said, "Wanna play?"

Ari was quick to interpret for Sitorian. "Andres is asking if you'd like to play with the Ident also. He's worried you're upset and wants to make you happy."

A rumble of affection sounded from Sitorian as he regarded the child. "You're a good little cub," he murmured. Looking up he addressed Norrium. "Is his dam here?"

"That's me," Liz said. She took a small step forward. Her expression was tense as she held the sleeping baby in her arms.

"Ah, you have another cub," Sitorian noted. "This cub looks freshly birthed. Where is their mane?"

"Her hair—er, mane will grow out when she's a little older," Liz explained, growing a little more confident with Sitorian's calm tone. "She's only a month old."

Bazium was quick to give him the equivalent age in a Talin time frame.

"How long until she's more like your other cub?" Sitorian asked. "And how long until they leave the nest to find mates of their own and breed?"

Liz's jaw dropped at the question and then a grin formed on her lips. Ari was thankful Liz remembered to keep her lips closed as the humor of the situation struck her.

"He won't be an adult for many more years. Or solars, I guess. And as far as finding a mate and breeding, who's to say? We humans don't always want a, uh, mate. Or sometimes we find several mates and all live together. He'll figure that all out when he's ready."

"I read in Bazium's importation application that human pairings have many permutations," Sitorian commented as he took the Cube from Andres and spoke into it. The bright yellow light slowly started deepening to gold, making Andres laugh with delight and snatch it back.

"As far as Lucia goes, she'll start crawling soon and then walking, but it'll be a few solars before she's as active as Andres."

"Pity," Sitorian said with a regretful rumble, and then he looked to Bazium. "I wish to buy the dam and her two cubs from you."

Liz gasped and shook her head. She looked back at Bazium, her eyes pleading. Ari tapped Bazium to let her down and then rushed to Liz's side.

"Easy," she whispered. "Bazium will take care of it. Have some faith in my guy."

Bazium didn't rattle, but she could see him clutching his fists and he took a step forward to stand in front of her and Liz.

"None of the humans are for sale," he said, his tone mild. "They don't react well to being separated."

"Surely the loss of a few won't bother the rest of the pack too much," Sitorian protested. "Is there a sire? I'm willing to purchase him also so they can stay together."

"The sire died before we reached the mining compound," Bazium explained. "But this pack of humans has been through so much trauma that they often sleep in large nests together and the loss of Liz and her cubs will be felt by all of them. They will mourn, and they're such delicate creatures they can become physically ill from their emotions."

Sitorian sounded a displeased rattle but was quick to stop when Andres went still and looked up at him. Sounding a soothing rumble, he tapped the Ident to make it change colors again before speaking.

"That isn't the reaction I was hoping for," he admitted. "I expected to pay a high price for several of them, but I never expected you to refuse me outright."

"I apologize, Station Controller Sitorian," Bazium said. "But even if I could separate a few without doing damage, you live on a space station. Their bodies don't function well in such artificial surroundings."

Ari almost rolled her eyes at that but did her best to back Bazium up. "We struggled on the mining compound. As you can see, in the years we were there, only Liz managed to get pregnant. We do much better on-planet with open sky over our heads and dirt beneath our feet."

Oh, she should start writing fiction, she decided. That sounded almost poetic.

Sitorian sounded a pleased rumble. "I'm almost finished with my current commission," he said. "If I remember your application correctly, you'll be settling everyone in Urok. I can buy any parcel there. If you would sell me the dam and her cubs, I could make sure she was close enough that she could visit the rest of the pack every day. And I wouldn't take possession of them until my enclosures met with your satisfaction."

Ari could tell Bazium was struggling to figure out how to say no. To her surprise, Aubrey came up with an answer.

"Sir, if I may, you need to understand something about us humans," she said with quiet confidence, stepping up to stand next to Ari and Liz.

Bazium stepped away so he wasn't standing between them and Sitorian, but he stayed close in case he needed to intervene.

"What do I need to understand, little human?" Sitorian asked with an indulgent rumble.

"Owning us doesn't mean you'll have our trust or affection," she said and pointed to Andres. "He is very open because he's young, but if his dam is unhappy with her situation, he'll grow despondent. If you have the patience and time, perhaps you could start visiting us and see who among our pack might be interested in making a home on your compound. I promise you, earning our trust is far more rewarding than simply buying us."

"And these soldiers did that?" Sitorian asked. "They earned your trust?"

"Yes, very much so," Aubrey said with confidence. "I was ill with emotions when they got to the mining compound. Tarrian was so kind and gentle that even though we couldn't communicate, I learned to trust him implicitly. If I was separated from him, I would be so sad I don't think I'd be able to live."

"Easy," Ari whispered in Aubrey's ear. "You don't want to sell it too hard."

Aubrey turned to her, tears gathering in her eyes. "I think it might be true," she whispered back before rubbing a hand over her face and facing Sitorian again.

Sitorian was quiet for a moment as he digested Aubrey's words. "How fascinating," he finally said. "A pet you have to gentle to your will. What a delightfully novel concept."

By now Andres had made himself comfortable in Sitorian's arms. He was nestled against the Talin's chest, tapping the Ident Cube as it gradually changed shades of gold, amber, and yellow.

"You have other pairs, yes?" he said without looking up. "Breeding pairs that might become pregnant as the pack settles into their new home on Talarian?"

"Many," Bazium answered. "But all of them will be reluctant to leave the pack."

"I will visit," Sitorian declared. "I will be there every day, and I'll charm them into wanting to live on my compound and have many cubs."

Suddenly Ari's heart broke for Sitorian and all the Talins like him. He wanted children. He probably felt a deep longing that he wasn't even allowed to consciously acknowledge.

Liz must have realized it too because she boldly stepped out of Ari's embrace and stood in front of Sitorian.

"Mama?" Andres said, his voice slightly sleepy.

"Give the toy back," Liz instructed.

"But shiny!" Andres protested. He quieted the moment he got a look at his mom's face. Andres wasn't foolish. He knew exactly when and how much he could push his mom.

"This is a good toy," Andres said as he held out Sitorian's Ident. "Good color. We can play again, okay?"

Liz looked to Sitorian. "He's inviting you to come play with him again and to bring the Ident," she explained.

Sitorian took the Ident and clipped it back on his belt, but when Norrium stepped forward to take Andres, he hesitated to hand him over. They all saw it, the moment he thought about refusing to let go of the little boy. Ari tensed, and she saw Norrium's quills ruffling and his claws emerging.

Then Liz turned slightly so Sitorian could see Lucia's face resting against her mother's shoulder. "You can't hold Andres and Lucia at the same time. You don't have enough hands," she teased gently.

Without another word, Sitorian handed Andres over to Norrium and dropped to both knees in front of Liz. "Show me how to hold her," he demanded.

Liz's smile as she handed over Lucia reminded Ari of the Madonna statue in the old Catholic church back on New Rico. They had the same beatific smile that spoke of infinite patience and caring.

When Liz handed him the baby, his rumble was one of adoration. Sitting back on his heels, he held the little one with exaggerated care.

"She's so delicate," he whispered.

Liz laid a hand on his shoulder and again, Ari was struck by the iconic overtones the three of them created. The formidable Talin on his knees next to a small, powerless human. It felt like Liz was the mother Sitorian never had and Lucia was the child he wasn't allowed to raise.

"She's tougher than you think," Liz murmured.

"She doesn't need to be," Sitorian said, his voice quiet but fierce. "None of the humans need to be tough ever again."

He looked up at Bazium and Ari was taken aback by the intensity of his gaze. "I will resign my commission immediately and follow you back to Talarian. You will help me construct suitable housing on my property, and I will visit the humans every day. You will give me a list of all the things they need. And I will provide things that make them happy."

"I can't—" Bazium started but Sitorian didn't let him finish.

"No, Bazium, I don't expect any of your pack to agree to leave, but other humans must be out there. When they're found, I'll be ready," he explained. "I will have a place they will be happy and other humans they can interact with. We will make Talarian a paradise for human pets."

Olimian sounded a rattle of protest. "Station Controller, I haven't made my final decision on whether these humans will be allowed on Talarian or not."

With great care Sitorian handed Lucia back to Liz. Then he got to his feet and faced Olimian. He stared silently at Olimian until she sounded an impatient rattle.

"You have something to add, Station Controller Sitorian?" Her tone wasn't civil.

"I'd hoped not to do this, but you've forced my claws. You will approve everything," he said in a low voice that was more resigned than menacing. Leaning in close he whispered into her earhole. Whatever he said was effective because she stiffened and then sounded a rumble of assent.

"I see your point," she said quickly. She stepped away from Sitorian as if she was suddenly wary of him and addressed Bazium. "I'll submit my final report by the end of my work cycle today. It will be favorable, but I need you to finish your mission report so I can file them together."

"I will have it done within the next rotation," Bazium promised her.

"Then we are done here. All of you can leave my office," she said and pointedly looked past them to the still-open door.

"I'll walk you all back to the ship," Sitorian was quick to offer. "And perhaps I could meet the rest of the pack."

"Of course, former Station Controller Sitorian," Bazium said with a humorous rumble. "Follow us."

CHAPTER 29

Advanced Squad Delta 223—Mission Q73 Report (Excerpt)
Because humans are prey animals, the most important thing to remember is that you have to let them come to you. If you've read my full report you will have noted that patience is key, but not the only thing you'll need to tame the humans. You need to let the human's capricious desires take precedence. One human will approach you while the one you were trying to attract was not interested. It's impossible to understand human motivations and why they pick one Talin or another to favor. It's best to be open to all the humans and see who is most interested in spending time with you.

If a dam or sire allows you to hold one of their cubs, it's the highest mark of trust, especially when the cub is newly born. You need to treat the cub as the delicate object they are and the moment the dam or sire wants them back, be ready to return them. If you build trust with the dam and sire, they might even be willing to leave their cub alone in your care for marks at a time. That's when you'll know the humans have truly bonded to you.

Ari was half sprawled across his chest, sleeping peacefully when his Ident chimed. Picking it up, he saw a message from Norrium.

A ship is following us. Civilian transport registered to the Anize Clan.

Curious but not overly concerned, Bazium untangled himself from Ari and gently tucked her in. As usual she grumbled a little but settled down when he put a pillow in her arms. Because humans required longer sleep cycles than Talins, he often found himself awake while she slept.

He adored it because her rest requirements meant he had many excuses and opportunities to cuddle.

But now he needed to have an extensive conversation with Norrium and didn't want to disturb her sleep. Leaving their cabin, he headed for the control room.

"Bazzie!" Andres cried out at the same time he felt a small body impact the back of his leg. He heard several humans chuckle as he cried out and pretended to trip forward.

"You've gotten so strong!" he declared as Andres wrapped little arms and legs around Bazium's lower leg. "Arg, you're so heavy! I don't think I can walk like this!" Despite the retardants they gave the cub, his INT had integrated efficiently, with no discomfort, and faster than any of the adults.

Andres chortled as Bazium took an exaggerated step and grunted loudly with the effort. "Can't go!" Andres said. "Has to play with me!"

"I have tasks, cub," Bazium explained with a fond rumble. "But I promise to play later."

Looking up, Bazium saw Liz and Santos standing in the hall. At his look, they both stepped forward.

"Come on, big guy," Santos said, holding out a hand. "You said you wanted to see the engine, and Hesarium is waiting for us. You don't want to make him sad. Do you?"

"Oh, engine!" Andres said and then made a sound that Bazium thought might be his impression of an engine. It sounded more like something wet sliding off a table. "Want to see now. Now! Now!"

"Then let's go go," Santos agreed and carried him off with Liz right next to him. The smell of Norrium's bonding oil wafted through the air as Liz passed, making Bazium happy for his second in command. This was the first time he'd smelled the oil on Liz. She must have accepted Norrium as her Talin last night.

The humans had the run of the ship now that they'd dropped off the seven humans who'd wanted to leave. Those seven had decided they would rather risk living with the Veli than stay as pets under the Talins. There had been a lot of tearful goodbyes and Bazium had given them all the wealth he could spare, but it hadn't been much.

He and the crew had pooled their resources because it had been so expensive for Norrium to set up the land for so many people to live on. Even with seven fewer people, it was going to be a struggle to keep everything going in the years to come with him and all his men retiring from the military.

Ari had helped by producing one of the Yurali crystals she'd hidden away in their room before the great escape and subsequent kidnapping. He told her she could keep it, but she'd insisted they sell it to help with finances. They'd already found a buyer on Talarian and would complete the sale soon after getting home.

The crystal helped, but it didn't solve all their financial issues. Still, he was confident they'd figure everything out. Especially with all the interest in humans they were already getting.

Before she'd fallen asleep earlier, Ari had suggested a fostering program where a couple of people could go live with a Talin household for a set period of time. That would both ease the financial burden and free up room. Bazium didn't like the idea but was willing to do it if some of the humans were interested.

He was still thinking about that when Mari stopped him in the hall.

"Advanced Leader Bazium," she said softly without meeting his eyes. "I've finished going over your report and I've added some suggestions."

"That's work well done," he answered, keeping his tone mild. "I didn't expect it before next rotation."

The Mari standing before him was not the same woman as before. After rescuing everyone from the Hamlershin ship, she'd become subdued. She rarely spoke and mostly kept to herself. He was still surprised she wasn't one of the seven who'd decided to leave.

Ari hadn't shown any surprise when Mari had remained behind. She'd tried to explain to him the complex emotional and psychological process Mari was going through, but he'd stopped her. It was enough that Mari had stayed and Ari wasn't upset about it.

Bazium considered asking Ari to explain Mari to him again because the woman was still acting uncharacteristically cowed. Ari had said Mari simply needed time to straighten out her thoughts. How thoughts could become crooked mystified Bazium, but he assumed it was a human thing.

"I wanted to get it done quickly so you would have plenty of time to request changes," she explained. "I thought I'd be done even sooner, but it took me a while to untangle your governing hierarchy so I could tailor it to reflect well on you. I think my suggestions are a good balance between making humans sound intelligent but still unsophisticated."

"I've been struggling with that aspect," Bazium admitted. "It's a relief to have help."

Mari risked a glance up before dropping her eyes back to the floor. "You should have Ari read it too. Her input is important. She'll probably think of things that didn't occur to me. I should go. Bye."

Before Bazium could say anything else, Mari turned and ran back toward the human section of the ship. He hated how skittish she'd become, but at least the other humans were talking to her now. For a while only Ari and Santos would interact with her. For days everyone else acted as if she didn't exist or spoke harshly until she went away. No one had resorted to physical violence, but a few times he'd thought they were close.

It seemed everyone blamed Mari for the debacle with the Hamlershin. He thought that was unfair, but Ari told him to stay out of it and let the humans work it out among themselves.

Before now it'd never occurred to Bazium that humans could be cruel to each other, but Ari was quick to correct him. It turned out humans could be atrocious to other humans. He'd decided to keep that out of his report but did add a section about humans being quick to form groups and that groups should be introduced carefully to each other. He remembered writing something about humans seeing strangers as dangerous, whether those strangers were human or nonhuman.

He looked forward to reading Mari's comments and suggestions because he'd trained as a soldier all his life, not a diplomat. Before now writing reports had been a quick duty. This report had turned into nothing but a complication that had him second- and triple-guessing himself. It'd be a relief when it was done and submitted.

Setting thoughts of Mari and the report aside, he finished his journey to the command room. Norrium and Tarrian were there, both looking at the same display. His Ident chimed as he took a spot at Norrium's shoulder so he could also study the display.

Three ships were following their flight path.

One ship belonged to former Station Controller Sitorian. It turned out Sitorian's family had a controlling share of Nikaniel Station. With that kind of wealth no one was going to raise a fuss if he abandoned his post with no warning. It also meant he had an entire ship at his disposal and was able to hire a crew at a moment's notice.

Having such a powerful ally was going to be very beneficial once they got back to Talarian.

The display tagged Sitorian's ship in orange, but now not one but two other unfamiliar ships were following them. The Anize Clan ship was marked in yellow with nothing but a name and clan affiliation. The third ship was lit up red with no information tags at all.

Space was too vast for these unknown ships to have ended up following them by accident, especially not so closely. The Anize Clan ship was far more powerful than theirs and could easily overtake them. The other ship wasn't as formidable but also had no reason to be on the same route and at the same speed as his squad's slower ship.

"Do we know why these ships are following?" Bazium asked, trying to remember his protocol. Because these were Talin ships in Talin-controlled space there was a limit to the types of questions he could ask without causing insult.

He wasn't afraid of being attacked. That would be ridiculous. But he was still uneasy about the whole situation. No soldier believed in coincidence.

"We just found out the captain of the Anize Clan ship, Captain Yorgimon, is a distant cousin of Sitorian," Norrium explained with an impatient rumble. "She and Sitorian grew up in the same cresh and are good friends. She was traveling back to Talarian and deviated when she got a message from Sitorian about the humans."

"She changed her entire schedule to follow us?" Bazium asked with an incredulous rattle. "That's ridiculous."

"There's more," Tarrian commented.

Norrium sounded a rumble of amusement. "Captain Yorgimon wants to meet Liz and the cubs."

Bazium ignored that. He'd deal with Captain Yorgimon later. "And the third ship?"

"I was waiting to hail them until you responded to me," Norrium said. That must have been the chime he'd heard moments ago.

Bazium hesitated. He already had an eager Anize Clan captain who wanted to meet Liz and the cubs. What additional disruptions was this other ship about to cause?

"Advanced Leader?" Norrium asked.

Bazium focused his gaze on his second in command. "Let's forgo titles from now on, Norrium. The moment we hit Talarian's atmosphere we're no longer military, and I for one am eager to leave it behind."

Norrium sounded a brief rumble of affection. "Very well, Bazium. Are you ready to talk to this third ship?"

With a rumble of assent, Bazium turned to face the large wall display. He started speaking the moment Norrium gave him the signal.

"This is Advanced Squad Ship 223," Bazium intoned in his most formal voice. "You're pacing our ship at a close distance. Are you in need of assistance?"

There, that sounded reasonable and even solicitous. Much better than sounding a challenging rattle and demanding to know why this ship was following them.

"May the ancestors grace you with wisdom and loyalty," a familiar voice said.

"And lead you to honorable actions." Shock spiked through Bazium as he voiced the rote response. "Queen Artium, I was unaware that you were off-world."

She sounded a rumble of amusement. "No one was aware. I was visiting Omeanin Colony and my royal guard asked to keep the trip a secret to make guarding me easier."

"Of course, Queen Artium," Bazium said quickly as he mentally cataloged all the armaments onboard. "Do you require an additional military escort? Our ship has limited combat capability, but there's a large military cruiser not far. They could have ships here within three marks."

Another rumble of amusement. "We aren't in need of assistance," she assured him. "But I did hear a rumor about these humans you've found. I want to meet them."

This wasn't possible. The monarch's wife, Queen Artium, could not be asking to come on board his ship for the express purpose of meeting the humans? Monarch Nylian was brand new to the throne. He'd only been ruling for a few solars. As newly seated leaders, Nylian and Artium were still an unknown, and Bazium couldn't tell if he should be honored by her attention or terrified.

Of course there was a third option where he experienced a combination of both dread and elation.

Judging by the way he wanted to rumble with worry and at the same time his back plates ached to rattle with excitement, he was definitely experiencing the third option.

"Let me speak with the head of your royal guard," he said. "If they believe it safe, we can bring several of the humans over for you to see."

"I want to meet the same cubs and dam Sitorian met," she insisted with an enthusiastic rattle. "Captain Yorgimon was telling me that Sitorian sang their praises as charming and affectionate creatures."

"Captain Yorgimon?" Bazium echoed.

"Oh, yes, she's a friend. Before my husband became monarch, we hired her for all our transport needs," she clarified. "We still talk when time allows."

That explained how knowledge of the humans had gotten all the way to the queen. For as rapidly as technology in the Talin Empire was advancing, information that spread via word of mouth was still shockingly swift.

"As long as the dam is willing, I'll bring them," Bazium allowed. "Please allow me to speak to your royal guard now."

It took almost a mark to finish making arrangements with Hamulian, the head of the royal guard for Queen Artium. After it was done, he slumped down into his command chair and let loose an exhausted rumble.

"That sounded important," Ari said.

Sitting up, he looked over to find her leaning against a wall, barefoot with sleep-tousled hair. Both Norrium and Tarrian sounded soft rattles of mild surprise as they turned to regard the little human.

"You're a quiet one," Tarrian observed.

"It's easy to go unheard when you guys are so loud all the time with your rattles and rumbles," she teased. The men rumbled out sounds of amusement before turning back to their displays to continue working.

Bazium opened his arms to invite Ari onto his lap. "How long have you been there? And why aren't you wearing your slippers?"

"I was standing there long enough to figure out that someone from the royal family wants to meet us," she said and padded over to climb into his lap. "And I forgot to put them on before I came looking for you."

"When I'm done here, I'll carry you back," he said as he tucked her against his body. "Are you intimidated to meet more Talins already?"

"Not intimidated," she said. "Only a little sad. I understand why we have to pretend that what's between us isn't love, or scent-bonding, or whatever, but I wish we didn't have to."

"I know, my sweet Brave," he whispered to her. "Someone with as much courage as you would never want to hide. But perhaps now that we have the interest of several prominent clans and the royal family, we might be able to change Talin culture and law for the positive."

Sitting up, she regarded him with intense interest. "That sounds like you've been plotting."

"Perhaps," he allowed. "It's unlikely we'll see much change in our lifetime, but maybe we can start new trends that will eventually allow humans more agency and Talins more vulnerabilities."

"I like the sound of that," Ari said with an emphatic nod. "I'm here for it, Baz. I'll meet however many Talins you want and be adorable and charming. They won't know what hit them."

"Please don't strike anyone," Bazium was quick to say. For some reason that made her chuckle.

"It's a human expression," she explained. "It means I'll dazzle them with my personality."

Bazium sounded a rumble of approval. "Oh, in that case you may hit them as hard as you like."

CHAPTER 30

After everything Queen Artium has told me about the humans, I'd be interested in viewing them. I've already read your Q73 mission report and understand that rapid change is difficult for them, so I'm willing to wait until they've properly settled in before visiting.

If I find them as pleasing as my wife indicates, I might see about finding some of my own. The royal menagerie hasn't been in use since my grandfather, but as everyone knows, having a meaningful hobby is important for the full development and maintenance of a healthy Talin lifestyle. If these humans are on the brink of extinction, starting a breeding program here at the royal residence would be a worthwhile endeavor and fulfill that requirement for me as the Monarch and example of Talin virtue across the empire.

"This is not fun!" Daniella repeated through gritted teeth for the fifth time in the last minute.

"You're doing good," Ari said. "And you're so close to holding your baby girl in your arms.

Looking up at Christos, Daniella scowled. "Your dick is never coming near me again!"

"Never," Christos agreed, looking pale and scared. "I've got two hands. I can take care of you with one and myself with another. We're all good, promise!"

Daniella's chuckle was interrupted with a groan. "Don't make me laugh!"

"I won't do that ever again either," Christos said as he leaned down to kiss the hand he was holding with both of his. Ari had Daniella's other hand as the sweat-soaked woman panted on the specially made bed the Talin healer had built specifically for her.

"Oh crap, here comes another one!" Daniella wailed, squeezing Ari's hand for all she was worth.

"The cub's head has emerged," the lead healer assured all of them with a soothing rumble. She was crouched at Daniella's feet, ready to catch the baby. "Just another contraction and she will slide right out."

The bed reminded Ari of a short chaise lounge more than anything else. Daniella was half seated, half crouched in a position the healer had assured them was the most natural for giving birth. Daniella had approved the design of the bed, saying it looked a lot like the birthing chairs women had used in the past. The healer had been delighted to hear that as she and Daniella had discussed human physiology at length.

The hilarious contrast had been the way the healer had patted Daniella on the head at the end and given her a piece of candy with the admonishment to "be a good human and tell your owner the moment you feel uncomfortable."

These Talins were damn good at cognitive dissonance. Humans were smart enough to have an in-depth discussion on anatomy but not to self-govern.

Daniella had grinned and accepted the candy while biting her lip. The moment they were out of the office with Bazium and Sapurian escorting them home, both women dissolved into laughter.

The rapid popularity of humans among Talins meant a soft landing for any human who found themselves in the Talin Empire.

It had only been six months and already it seemed like having human pets had caught on among the Talins, partially due to the royal interest.

After meeting Ari, Liz, and the kids, the queen demanded humans of her own. According to a recent letter they'd received, the monarch was just as interested as his wife. Ari had talked to everyone, and one couple and the thruple had agreed to try living with the monarch and queen.

For the first fifty days, Ari had gone to visit them every day, but it soon became apparent that the five humans were being spoiled beyond belief. Wraps and omnies in all different fabrics and colors, information squares for everyone with access to the Talarian UniBase, and jeweled collars that didn't even lock!

Each day had brought more requests to buy humans from Bazium at outrageous prices. But except for the five who lived with the royal family and Daniella and Christos living with Sitorian, no one had agreed to leave the group.

Jolian and his crew had found a few humans still alive on a Miox Minerals processing station. Ari had seen vid capture of those poor people and realized some groups had been worse off than hers. Out of over a hundred souls first employed by Miox Minerals at that compound, Jolian had only found five alive. They would spend the trip to Talarian recovering from near starvation. Ari didn't want to even think of their mental state.

Because so few had been found so far, Talins encouraged Bazium to urge his humans to reproduce by sending them wealth. There were enough funds to send Sapurian, Hesarium, and Santos on a mission to see if a good-sized colony of humans would be interested in life among the Talins. It was the only colony Ari knew about, and she hoped they didn't get there to find everyone already dead.

Daniella's death grip on her hand brought Ari back to the present. "Evolution is a dumb bitch!" Daniella announced.

The healer sounded a rumble of concern. "There is no one named Evolution. Is she hallucinating?"

"We sometimes say strange things when we are in a lot of pain," Ari assured the healer. "I'll tell you when she says something to be concerned about."

Daniella glared up at her. "But she is a dumb bitch."

"I agree," Ari said quickly. "And organic chem is a mean bitch, and gas giants are pretty bitches." That made Daniella chuckle and then groan.

Beyond the primary healer crouched in front of Daniella, two other healers and four healers in training had joined them. Daniella had agreed to let all of them attend the birth for educational purposes, but she made the primary healer swear none of them would touch her without permission.

Behind all the healers were Bazium and Sitorian. Bazium looked interested but not worried. However, Sitorian was pacing and agitated enough to cause a ruckus.

"Why is this taking so long?" he demanded. "Is the cub hurt? Is Daniella injured? You need to do something!"

Daniella reprimanded Sitorian before anyone else could speak. "You're not helping. Stay calm or leave."

Sitorian sounded a loud, soothing rumble. "Yes, little dam, I'll be quiet now. Please don't become injured or die. I have the nicest things for all three of you."

Good to his promise back on Nikaniel Station, Sitorian had bought land not far from Norrium's compound. It had been empty but he was quick to have a house built and an enclosure that looked like a miniature version of the house. The house and enclosure were set in the middle of at least a hectare of land with an artificial stream and small pond.

As Daniella's pregnancy had advanced, Sitorian had spent more and more time with her and Christos. Every time he visited, he brought gifts for them and the baby. He asked endless questions about birthing and raising humans.

Finally, he'd talked Bazium into letting Christos and Daniella tour his home and property. After that Daniella and Christos had agreed to move to Sitorian's place. The Talin had been beyond ecstatic and had engaged a private healer to visit every few days for a checkup. Daniella had told him it was unnecessary but gave in to his overly cautious actions with grace. Probably because Christos agreed with Sitorian.

And now they were all gathered at the healer's facility while Daniella gave birth to the first human born on Talin.

No sooner had that thought entered Ari's head than Daniella groaned and strained one last time, and then the cry of a newborn filled the room. The healer was quick to cut the cord, check over the baby, and then hand her to Daniella.

"She's a perfect and healthy female cub," the healer announced with so much pride you'd think she had given birth.

Ari leaned over and smiled down at the squalling infant. "Hello, Aline," she whispered even as Sitorian hurried to Daniella's side so he could gaze down at the baby. "Welcome to our new home."

Much later Ari was sitting in Bazium's lap in the privacy of their room as he rubbed his cheeks against her hair and purred loudly.

"As adorable as human cubs are, I'm very glad you don't want one," he murmured.

"It's a little messy and painful," she agreed. "What was it like for Talin women when they used to give birth?"

"Nothing like that," Bazium assured her. "I read that there was discomfort but nothing on the scale of pain Daniella displayed."

"Daniella wasn't wrong when she called evolution a bitch," Ari commented with a sleepy grin.

It had been a good day, but a long one too. And tomorrow five Talins from the Apogee Assembly were visiting so there'd be no indulging in an afternoon nap for her. Everyone had demanded that she be there any time strange Talins visited. When she'd predicted that she'd still be acting as a leader even after they go to Talarian, she'd been more accurate than she realized. She wasn't only a leader but also acted as an ambassador for both Talins and humans as they learned each other's customs.

"I have news from Sapurian," Bazium told her. "In the excitement with Daniella and the cub I'd forgotten it until now."

"Have they arrived already?" Ari asked with surprise. "I didn't think they'd get there for another ten rotations."

"They are splitting up," Bazium explained. "They came across a request for assistance notice on the public display at Ki-Jol. The phrasing of the notice caught Hesarium's attention. He's sure humans wrote it, so he insisted on answering the notice.

Sapurian and Santos left him at the station while they continued with the original mission."

"What's he going to get there without a ship?" Ari asked.

Bazium sounded an unconcerned rumble. "Hire passage on a commercial ship or book a spot on a merchant transport. It's doubtful he'll find anyone, but he has good instincts so it's worth investigating. Besides, we have plenty of funds with all the donations that have been pouring in."

"You Talins sure get obsessed easily," Ari teased.

"Not usually," Bazium responded, interrupting his soothing purr with a thoughtful rumble. "I don't think I've seen something become so popular so quickly among us. It proves that with all our advancement we've been ignoring something."

"What do you mean?"

Bazium's scent glands were empty, so he straightened. Ari brought her hands up to run her finger through her long hair. He loved seeing her hair saturated with his bonding oil.

"We focus on goals and efficiency," he explained. "We are preoccupied with expansion and might. All of that means we've left behind the softer things, and I think we're all suffering in silence because of it."

"Softer things?" Ari said with a grin as she ran a hand over his hard chest. "I don't think any of you were ever soft."

"Perhaps not physically, but at one time we did bond with our partners and raise our own children. In our past we were allowed to feel the gentler emotions of adoration and attachment. Now those are considered unnecessary weaknesses."

"I know, and it's all so sad," Ari murmured. "Is life worth living if you don't get to have love?"

"And that's why I think you humans have garnered so much attention so rapidly," Bazium concluded. "Many other Talins are reacting to your kind the same way my crew and I did within submarks of meeting you. I didn't realize it until later, but we can be soft with you. We can be all the things we aren't allowed to be with each other. Humans are the perfect excuse for vulnerability and gentleness."

"Is that why everything I've been reading makes us sound completely helpless and a little stupid?" she asked. "At first I thought it was because you had to make us sound that way to be allowed on Talarian, but all the 'research' being published about us has taken those themes and run with them."

"Yes, exactly my point," Bazium agreed.

"It's not a bad thing," Ari said after a moment of silence. "You guys need us as much as we need you. None of us humans like the power imbalance, but we'd be dealing with it no matter where we went. At least here you're not exploiting our labors and working us to death."

She felt Bazium stiffen for a brief moment. "I'm sorry you feel trapped."

Ari was quick to face him and bracket his face with her hands. "I don't feel trapped. I feel loved," she assured him. "But the humans coming into this for the first time might take a while to get used to the idea of being a pet. I'll be there to help them."

She gave him a quick kiss on the lips. "You're stuck with me," she told him with exaggerated fierceness. "Just try to get rid of me and see how that goes for you!"

He rattled out a negative sound. "Never."

"Together we'll carve out a place for humans among the Talins," she murmured, snuggling back into his embrace. He started purring again as he leaned over and rubbed his scent glands into her hair. It was soothing to both of them.

He sounded a rumble of agreement and then went back to purring. She closed her eyes and pulled in a lungful of hazelnut.

There would probably be bumps along the road of Talins and humans learning to live together, but she could tell plenty of powerful Talins were already on their side. She and Bazium would work to make this place as close to a paradise as they could.

For the first time in a long time, the future of humanity didn't look bleak. It was filled with promise and hope.

APOGEE ASSEMBLY ANNOUNCEMENT

Apogee Assembly Announcement of Law Finalization
General Governing Statute 67885.32: Human Pets

The Apogee Assembly has created social and legal guidelines regarding human pets. No law can be passed that counteracts this General Covering Statute unless it is to replace the statute entirely.

The guidelines are as follows:

1) There will be no free humans on Talarian or any Talin-controlled space station or Colony. Human ownership must be clearly stated. However, a family or clan can communally own them.

2) This statute allows for the creation of the Committee for Pet Welfare. This committee's main duty will be to safeguard the treatment of human pets. Manuals and guidelines for the appropriate care of humans will be created and maintained by this committee and made available to all Talins.

3) Wild caught humans must go through a health check and decontamination process before they are allowed to mix with resident populations.

4) A qualified healer must verify all human deaths as either accidental or natural. Unverified human deaths will result in the removal and reallocation of all pets remaining with that family or clan as well as possible fines.

5) Humans cannot be sold to non-Talins.

6) The Committee for Pet Welfare reserves the right to talk to any human pet at any time. Access cannot be refused.

Although more laws will be developed in the future, one thing we would like to stress to all Talins is that being allowed to own a human is a privilege, not a right. If you abuse that privilege, your human will be taken away and given to another family or clan that will care for them properly. So far only a few hundred humans have been retrieved, but there's hope to bring many more back to Talarian as we take over more Orlok mining stations and processing plants. With the cooperation of willing Talins, we can create a sustainable, thriving population of humans among us.

We will be their dedicated keepers and they will be our loyal pets.

Dear Readers,

Thank you for reading *Creating Captivity: Human Pets of Talin—Origins, Book 1*. If you want more Human Pets of Talin—Origins Series the next book is available: *Gossamer Chains* (*Human Pets of Talin—Origins, Book 2*).

You can also read the original series that started this world: Human Pets of Talin. This series takes place five hundred years after the Origins Series. In this series humans are a well-established pets among the Talins.

I hope you enjoyed reading *Creating Captivity* enough to leave a review! As an indie writer without a publishing company, I depend on your support. Your good reviews keep me writing.

If you have any questions, comments, or suggestions feel free to contact me via email: author@rk-munin.com

If you're interested in following me on social media, receive some free books, or check out my other series you can find links to everyone on my website:

www.rk-munin. com

Have a fruitful rotation,
Rye,

OTHER BOOKS BY RK MUNIN

-Science Fiction-

Hissa Warrior Series
Rescuing Halin (Mian and Halin)
Buying Tiran (Mara and Tiran)
Tempting Selon (Lara and Selon)
Defying Kilan (Deena and Kilan)
Healing Mavito (Raleen and Mavito)
Claiming Yopin (Mouse and Yopin)
Teasing Woken (Safena and Woken)
Defending Revin (Kamaril and Revin)
Trusting Warik – Coming soon

Human Pets of Talin Series
Loving Captivity (Sora and Searin)
Escaping Captivity (Lakin and Dalt)
Negotiating Captivity (Nalia and Derani)
Fighting Captivity (Zia and Palforma)
Tender Captivity (Jinna and Holian - This is a novella you can get for free by signing up for my newsletter)
Craving Captivity (Lasha and Tamerin)
The Twelve Nights of Halloheen: A holiday mashup novella (Isla and Tisuran)
Stealing Captivity (Kasi and Ignatias)
Reading Captivity – Coming soon

Origins (A Human Pets of Talin Series)
Creating Captivity (Ari and Bazium)
Gossamer Chains (Rain and Hesarium)
Purring, Presents, and Parties – Coming soon

Golden Cages – Coming soon

-Paranormal /Urban Fantasy-

Ours Evermore Series
Two Wolves for Soren (Soren, Kalli, and Quinn)
A Hacker, Vampire, and Chimera Walk into a Bar….(Tobias,
Briar, and Memphis)
When Darkness Meets Dawn (Imani, Lex, and Mac)
Tag, You're It (Short Story)
Kidnapping Their Third (Cora, Pike, and Kimble) – Coming soon
Pastries on a Plate and Blood in a Mug (Novella) – Coming soon

Alpha Series
Alpha Mage (Emma and Kade)
His Alpha Mage (Avery and Jason – Novella)
Alpha King (Cathleen and Lazlo)

New Clan Series
Stray Wolf (Steph and Eli)
Lost Lion (Maeve and Cyrus)
Reluctant Cervid (Tavi and Donovan)
Broken Thorn (Sabina and Theodosius)

www.ingramcontent.com/pod-product-compliance
Lightning Source LLC
Chambersburg PA
CBHW060437310726
48977CB00001B/221